Cash stood in •
everything sh

Shannon
massive
through
Cash mo
covered

She wa

She felt his gaze on her. He leaned against the doorjamb, watching her, his arms crossed over his chest, his biceps stretching his white dress shirt.

"Need help with anything?" he asked, as though he knew what she'd been thinking as she stared at his bed.

"I want to go to bed with you."

"No."

No? He turned her down? "Why not?"

"We want two different things in life."

"Like what?"

"I want a relationship. I want kids and a family now."

He was turning things upside down, making a hash of her assumptions of what men were, and she didn't know what to make of it.

Dear Reader,

No Ordinary Sheriff is the last in my Ordinary, Montana, series. I've enjoyed writing about this fictional town. As with most towns, it had its share of good and bad characters, and happy and sad experiences. As with all romances, stories closed with happy endings.

The town "grew" as I wrote about it. It started as one story about Hank and Amy on the Sheltering Arms Ranch. As I added characters to each story, they asked for their own novels and Ordinary became a series. This is the sixth and final installment.

Cash Kavenagh showed up a number of times as Ordinary's sheriff. He begged for his own story, his own happily-ever-after. Finishing almost where I started, the heroine, Shannon, is Janey Wilson's sister. Janey was little Cheryl's mother. Cheryl starred in the first novel, *No Ordinary Cowboy*.

Here is Cash and Shannon's story! Hope you enjoy it. I love to hear from readers, so please contact me through my website, www.marysullivanbooks.com.

Best,

Mary Sullivan

No Ordinary Sheriff
Mary Sullivan

Withdrawn Print

TORONTO NEW YORK LONDON
AMSTERDAM PARIS SYDNEY HAMBURG
STOCKHOLM ATHENS TOKYO MILAN MADRID
PRAGUE WARSAW BUDAPEST AUCKLAND

Recycling programs
for this product may
not exist in your area.

ISBN-13: 978-0-373-60704-4

NO ORDINARY SHERIFF

Copyright © 2012 by Mary Sullivan

This edition published by arrangement with Harlequin Books S.A.

For questions and comments about the quality of this book
please contact us at Customer_eCare@Harlequin.ca.

® and TM are trademarks of the publisher. Trademarks indicated with
® are registered in the United States Patent and Trademark Office, the
Canadian Trade Marks Office and in other countries.

www.Harlequin.com

Printed in U.S.A.

ABOUT THE AUTHOR

Mary Sullivan likes to turn people's assumptions on their heads. She believes that all things are possible for those who believe in themselves. Watch for role reversals in *No Ordinary Sheriff.* Can a man enjoy cooking and creating the comforts of home? You bet. Can a woman be an effective cop and love her job? You bet. Contact Mary through her website, www.marysullivanbooks.com.

Books by Mary Sullivan

HARLEQUIN SUPERROMANCE

To my fabulous siblings—
Pat, Margaret, Dianne, Paddy, Dorothy and John—
thank you for supporting my writing.

CHAPTER ONE

ON MONDAY MORNING, Shannon Wilson stood in front of her brother Tom's apartment door with dread running cat's claws across her nerves. She'd already given him a good ten minutes to answer.

Her sister's voice came through her cell phone. "I'm concerned about him," Janey said. "He looked terrible when he was here."

Two weeks ago, Tom had come to see Shannon, and he had looked awful, emotionally spent.

Go to rehab, she'd said.

Sure, he'd replied with his sweet lopsided smile.

She'd known he wouldn't.

Instead, last week Tom had visited Janey in Ordinary, Montana.

"Before he left," Janey said, "he wouldn't stop hugging me and telling me he loved me."

Shannon needed her to stay calm. "I'm sure he's fine."

"Promise you'll check up on him?"

"I'll head over to his apartment as soon as I

hang up." *Liar. You're already here.* "I'll call if there's a problem."

Had those visits been Tom's way of saying goodbye? Had he planned to hurt himself? Shannon knocked again, rapping so hard her knuckles hurt, covering the phone with her other hand so Janey wouldn't hear.

Come on, Tom, answer.

"I'm so worried." Janey was the older, wiser sister, but Shannon had an urge to reassure her.

"I know." *Me, too. Terrified.* "You go to Disneyland. You worked your butt off for this trip, sis, and planned it for a year. It's your family's dream vacation. Go. I'll take care of things here."

"I don't know—"

"If you don't leave, I'll come to Ordinary and drag you to California myself."

Janey chuckled. "Okay, okay. I'll bring you back a souvenir."

Shannon tried to laugh, but it sounded phony. "Something really tacky?"

"You got it." Janey's answering laugh was genuine. Good. Shannon had managed to assuage her fears.

"Call me if you need me."

Not likely. Her sister really had earned this trip.

Shannon ended the call. She glared at Tom's apartment door. What about her own unease?

Who would reassure her, when she was the one always taking care of others?

When she'd called Tom half an hour ago, he'd sounded out of it, but not drunk. Which drug was it these days? She knocked again, loudly enough to rouse everyone in the building.

He'd said he was home and didn't plan to go out—why wouldn't he answer?

Swearing, she hurried down to the first floor through a dirty stairwell that reeked of boiled cabbage. The smell nauseated her, reminded her of the poverty she'd clawed her way out of.

She knocked at the first apartment. The superintendent answered.

"There's something wrong with my brother in 308. You have to get me into his apartment."

"I can't—"

"Yes. Now." Her panic made an impression and he followed her upstairs with his set of master keys.

On the third floor, he unlocked Tom's door.

The stench hit her first—garbage and stale cigarette smoke. He'd started smoking again. Despite everything the family had done, *was* doing for Tom, it wasn't enough if he wouldn't take care of himself.

Why couldn't men handle the problems in their lives?

She stepped over a pizza box.

With the toe of her shoe, she nudged aside a grubby shirt. There was something on it—God, old vomit. Oh Tom.

Afraid of what she would find, she stepped into the living room. Laundry and dishes littered every surface. Dust coated the room.

When she walked across the stained carpet, something crunched under her foot. An unfinished pizza crust.

At first, she looked right past Tom.

He lay on the sofa so folded in on himself she'd mistaken him for a pile of laundry. She approached. His clothing was soaked with sweat, his once hale body ravaged, his stomach concave as though it were eating itself. He'd grown even thinner in just the past week. The deep clefts bracketing his mouth looked deeply ingrained, as though he'd carried them for a lot longer than his thirty years.

Shannon sank to her knees beside him and touched his arm. Too hot. He stank.

"Tom," she whispered. "What have you done to yourself?"

He raised a hand as if to touch her cheek. Too weak to complete the action, it fell back to his stomach.

"Cathy," he whispered and smiled.

Cathy? He thought she was his dead wife? What was he on?

His pulse raced beneath her fingers. How could a man's heart beat so fast without hurting itself?

She turned to the super. "Call 9-1-1. It's an overdose."

Of what, though? He'd done so many different drugs, taken anything to deaden memories of the crash.

She wiped his forehead with her sleeve. "Tom, talk to me. What did you take?"

"Shannon?"

"Yes. What did you take? I need to know."

"Meth."

"How much, sweetie?"

He didn't respond. "Tom, how much!"

Still no answer. She was going to kill the bastard who sold her brother the meth.

"Where's Cathy?" he whispered.

Shannon grabbed the photo of Cathy and the two boys from the coffee table. His fingerprints coated the silver frame and glass. She wrapped his hand around it.

"Here, honey, they're right here." He thought they were still alive. That would last only until the drug cleared his system.

Tom, you're breaking my heart.

"Where did you get it?" she asked.

"Huh?" He was falling asleep.

"The meth," she yelled and shook his shoulder, her fear making her harsh. "Where did you get it?"

"Ordinary."

"Ordinary? You're kidding. Who in Ordinary would sell you meth?"

He whispered something and she leaned close. "Cooking. Main Street." His voice was thin.

He looked past her. "Where's Cathy?" Panic started to set in. His pupils dilated until they were huge, and Shannon took his hand. He nearly cut off her circulation.

The terror in his eyes begged her to do something, anything, to save him.

How? What?

"Tell me what you need, honey." His eyelids drifted closed.

"Stay with me, Tom." He opened his eyes at her words. If he fell asleep he might not wake up again. She *refused* to let him die, damn it.

She sprinted for the kitchen. In the freezer she found ice cubes furry with frost and an old freezer pack. She carried them back to the sofa.

Where should she put them? On his chest? His forehead? For God's sake, why hadn't she ever studied first aid? Her hands shook, but she managed to tuck the cubes into his T-shirt, because she didn't have a clue what else to do.

Cathy smiled at her from the photo, watching every move with her lively brown eyes as though asking her sister-in-law to take care of her man while she was gone. Shannon swore she could detect Chanel No. 5, Cathy's favorite, and smell the kid-sweat of Casey's and Stevie's hair. She almost turned, half-convinced they were about to barrel into the room with mischievous grins to throw themselves into their aunt's arms.

But Shannon's arms were empty. She slid Tom's hand over the picture so she couldn't see their faces.

He was burning up. Most of the ice had already melted

The photo skittered sideways. The rhythm of his breathing changed. His chest rose and fell too rapidly.

"Come on, come on," she whispered to the ambulance, as though the mantra would get the paramedics there any sooner.

The Montana ambulance system was usually pretty quick. Shannon knew a bunch of paramedics in Billings. They were good at their jobs. So why was it taking so long?

"Tom, are you still with me?"

He didn't respond, no longer seemed to recognize her.

"Hey!" she yelled to the super. "Where's the ambulance?"

"I called." He hovered at the apartment door

but didn't enter, as though an overdose were contagious. "They said just a couple of minutes."

She heard the pounding on the stairs then, almost mistaking it for her own heartbeat, or maybe Tom's where her fingers sat on his wrist.

When a pair of paramedics entered the room with a stretcher, she said, "He took meth. I don't know how much. I don't know when. Do something. Hurry." Her voice broke. She still gripped Tom's hand even though it had fallen slack.

"Okay, we got him." The paramedic spoke quietly. He eased her away from Tom. "We'll take care of him. We know what we're doing."

She nodded and stepped back, bunching a fist against her mouth.

Calm down. Tom needs you.

The paramedic quickly took her place, kneeling beside Tom. "His blood pressure's through the roof," he told his colleague who stood beside the stretcher and took notes.

Tom looked from one man to the other, confused. When the paramedic tried to take his temperature, he weakly flailed at the man.

"Tom," Shannon said. "Take it easy. These people are here to help."

His throat gurgled.

"What's happening?" Her voice rose an octave.

"He's choking on his saliva." The paramedic turned Tom onto his side.

Shannon pressed a hand against her roiling stomach.

"Shannon, are you okay?"

At the sound of the deep voice behind her, Shannon turned slowly, giving herself time to put on her game face. Officer Dave Dunlop had entered the apartment.

They had history. She wanted to forget it. He wanted to make up for it.

"Dave," she said, keeping her voice cool enough to discourage familiarity. She was tired of putting him off. He had to get the message one of these days. "It's Tom. My brother."

"Looks like he isn't going to make it."

Shannon gasped. Dave had a habit of being socially inept. Wrong response, wrong time. Not the best trait in a cop.

"For God's sake, Dunlop," one of the paramedics said. "Show some humanity."

Dave grimaced. "Sorry, Shannon."

Within seconds the paramedics had Tom on the gurney and wheeled out the door.

Dave stared at Tom as he passed. "Poor bugger. I wouldn't have recognized him."

Shannon tried to follow but Dave wrapped his fingers around her arm.

"Let me go. I need to get to the hospital."

"Shannon, I can help you with this. I can take

care of you." Trust Dave to use a time like this to try to ease his own conscience.

In her experience, women handled things, not men. Men had their uses—brute strength, fun in bed, pillow talk—but she was better off on her own.

"Give it a rest. It's too late to make things up to me."

She pulled out of his grasp and he let go easily enough. He wasn't cruel. Just clueless.

"If you really want to help," she said, "call the cops in Ordinary. Someone there is cooking meth. That's where Tom got it."

"They've got cops. They'll deal with it."

"I need you to notify them. They'll take a call from you more seriously than if I just show up to ask."

"Okay. I'll call today."

She glanced around. What should she bring to the hospital? Tom owned nothing of value. His days were populated by despair, cravings and addictions.

Nothing else in his life meant anything to him anymore.

A glint of silver on the filthy carpet caught her attention. Tom had dropped the photo of his family. This mattered. Only this. When he awoke in the hospital, he would want it.

She picked it up and left the apartment. Dave

followed her down the stairs, his presence like a weight on her back.

"What are you doing in the old neighborhood?" he asked. "You said nothing could drag you back here."

She didn't answer. Of course she would come back for her brother.

Shannon ran to her car. She didn't expect Dave to have much luck with the cops in Ordinary. She relied more on herself than on the local cops. They'd never found Janey's rapist, had they? She'd had to do that herself once she was old enough.

She sped to the hospital. By the time she got there, Tom had slipped into a coma.

There was nothing they could do for him but keep him on life support and wait for a change, the doctors said. What did that mean? Were they waiting for his death?

She stood by his bedside. The terrifying image of him with tubes running everywhere was burned onto her retinas.

Slipping the photo under his limp hand, she gave instructions for it to stay near him, either on his body or on the bedside table.

She brushed too-long hair from his sweaty forehead and willed her tears away. Better to be angry. Furious.

"I'll get whoever did this to you," she whispered with an intensity she hadn't felt since Janey's rape. "I'll crush them."

"Shannon?"

She turned around. Dad. Who had called him? Dave? Good. He'd done something right.

"Tom's bad." Her voice cracked and she moved into her father's arms. As usual, though, she ended up comforting him more than receiving comfort. Dad had fallen apart after Mom's death, too, but that time it had been Janey who'd held the family together. These days, with Janey living in Ordinary raising her own family, the job had fallen to Shannon.

She called the twins to tell them what had happened and then held her father while he cried. She'd deal with her own grief later.

"FRANK?" SHERIFF CASH KAVENAGH stood behind his desk in the Sheriff's office in Ordinary, Montana, and stared at the man who was technically his father. "What the hell are you doing here?"

Francis Kavenagh might have shared his DNA with Cash, but he hadn't given much else of himself to his son.

Autumn sunlight streaming through the office's open door limned Frank's once-broad shoulders. He was shorter than Cash remembered.

Behind him, cars drove by on Main Street.

A junker Cash didn't recognize sat at the curb. Frank's?

One of Main Street's shop owners walked along the sidewalk, but didn't glance at the stranger. Thank God. A brisk November wind blew in. Another ordinary day in Ordinary. Or not. Cash's father was here.

Cash's eyes weren't deceiving him, though. Nor was his nose. It was Frank, all right. He still wore the same old lady-killer cologne—Kanøn—applied with a heavy hand. It had been popular thirty or more years ago.

"Why are you here?" Cash asked again, the belligerence in his tone unintentional. He came by his attitude toward Frank honestly. Life had taught him to distrust the man.

"I wanted to see you." Frank's voice had weakened, didn't have the authority it used to.

Pushing sixty, he looked closer to seventy. He'd been vain about his thick head of hair, but most of it was gone, the remaining yellow-gray like an old bedsheet. Sort of matched the tone of his skin.

"I told you to never come to Ordinary," Cash said.

"I know."

"Get in here and close the door before someone sees you."

Frank did.

Broken veins dotted his cheeks and the creases of his nostrils.

"You look like hell. I guess the hard living finally caught up."

Frank winced. "Yeah." He stepped toward the desk. "Can I sit?"

Cash nodded. He didn't want the man here, should boot him out, but— He seemed unwell. Cash didn't care, but couldn't turn him away.

"I tried to talk to your mother." Frank fell into the chair with a sigh that started in the soles of his shoes. "She wouldn't see me."

"She's happy now." Cash sat down on the business side of the desk. "She got herself a good husband the second time around. Leave her alone."

"I figured that out." In a gesture so familiar it hurt to watch, Frank ran his hand over his head as if fixing his non-existent hair. "I need to tie up certain things. Make them right."

"'Tie up things?' What is this, some kind of deathbed confession scenario?" Despite the joke, unease circled in Cash's gut.

A cynical smile spread across Dad's face, colored with sadness. "Yes."

Cash froze. "Seriously?"

"Yeah. Cirrhosis of the liver. End-stage. I wanted to see you before I...go. To apologize for the way I treated you and your mom."

"It's been twenty years."

"I know."

"You couldn't have apologized before now?"

"I should have."

"I thought you didn't care."

Frank stared at him. "For a long time I thought I didn't, about either you or your mother."

"Yeah, I got that."

Frank met Cash's bitter smile with a grim one of his own.

"I know I don't deserve a thing from you—"

"You got that right."

"—but I want you to know that you and your mom were the best thing that ever happened to me."

"It sure didn't feel that way."

Frank glanced away and nodded. "It took losing you two for me to realize it."

"So, what do you want from me? Money?" Man, that bitterness was giving everything Cash said a real hard edge.

"No, son. Nothing. I came for you, not for me."

"What do you mean?"

"I was a rotten role model. You never got married and had kids."

"That has nothing to do with you." So what if Frank's concerns echoed his own? He'd tried to find someone to settle down with—honest to God he had—but that was nobody's business but Cash's. *Particularly* not Frank's.

Frank had never appreciated Cash and his mom, yet Frank thought he had to right to criticize Cash for not having married yet?

You've been worried about that yourself a lot lately.

So what? That's my right. Not Frank's.

Besides, Cash was only thirty-six. Who knew what could happen in the next few years?

Frank raised a placating hand. "Okay. I'm sorry. For everything."

Frank's dry-eyed apology moved Cash more than tears would have. What he wouldn't have given for this sincere, humbled man to have been his father twenty years ago. Cash resisted the apology.

"You're a dollar short and a day late. I don't need anything from you."

"I can see that, Cash. You've done well for yourself. I asked around."

"Who did you talk to?" Someone here in town? Cash felt a moment's panic.

"Don't worry. I did it long distance. You have a good reputation in the area." Frank stood. "You're a better man than I was. I'm proud of you."

"Am I supposed to go all gooey and soft now?

After you neglected me and mom during the marriage and since the divorce?"

"I know. It's not much, is it? But it's true."

He didn't know what to say. The man looked bad enough to elicit sympathy, but all of those years of anger backed up in Cash's throat. Choked him. Strangled every decent word he might have said.

Frank gripped the door handle and Cash's heart rate kicked up despite his anger, the child in him preparing to watch his father walk out of his life again.

"I just hope you find a good woman to love," Frank said. "And don't waste the opportunity like I did with your mother."

"Don't you worry about me," Cash countered. "There are plenty of women in town who'd be happy to take up that position."

Cash wasn't boasting. He knew it from experience.

"Good." Frank opened the door to leave.

Cash held his tongue. They'd said enough.

"I know you won't believe me, Cash, but I love you."

With that Frank was gone.

In the weighty silence left behind, Cash breathed heavily, trying not to succumb to regret and maudlin sympathy. Frank had forged his own way.

Cash's hands formed into fists and he leaned on them on the desk, hard, so he wouldn't run after Frank.

Even so, when the doorknob turned, his heart lifted.

But it wasn't Frank.

His deputy, Wade Hanlon, stepped in, ready to relieve Cash as he did every night.

Hating himself for it, Cash rushed past Wade out the door, looking both ways up and down Main Street. Just past the edge of town a car veered off the road and rumbled onto the unpaved shoulder. A ball of dust enveloped it before it righted itself into the lane. The rusted old junker.

Dad.

When the dust cleared, Cash could just barely tell that the car he was driving was the old junker that had been parked in front of the station.

Dad didn't have money.

Cash started to run. To catch it.

Dad. Stop.

He'd made it a block before someone honked, startling him to a halt. Timm Franck eased his old pickup closer and rolled down the window. "Hey, Cash, are you okay? What are you doing in the middle of the road?"

Had he actually run out into the street to chase Dad?

He'd just made a fool of himself on Main Street.

Had anyone else seen Frank? Had they realized he was related to Cash? These were Cash's people, Timm a good buddy, but they knew nothing about his past. He intended to keep it that way. Cash settled on a lie. "I was trying to catch someone speeding through town."

"On foot?" Timm laughed. "That's a new one."

"I saw a car rushing past, tried to get the plate number."

Timm smiled. He'd bought the lie. "Wonder who it was?"

"I didn't recognize the car. Someone driving through, I guess."

He'd always promised himself he'd be a better man than Dad, but here he was, lying to a friend.

How could he stand here and behave so calmly when his stomach was turning somersaults? *Because you learned a long time ago to bury emotion.* Mom had done enough crying for the both of them and Cash had learned to be the strong one.

"See you later," he told Timm and strode back to the office.

Everything was fine. He was fine.

SHANNON CALLED HER superior at the Domestic Field Division of the DEA in Denver.

"Have you found anyone to help me out?" she asked Sam Morgans.

"Nothing's changed since you called yesterday. We're working at max. I've got no one to send to Ordinary right now."

"You've got me."

"You're on vacation—one I practically begged you to take. Remember?"

"I remember, but—"

"Stop. There've been plenty of studies. Police officers working in stressful positions need regular time away from the job."

"I know. I'm on vacation, okay?"

"Good. Now rest. As soon as I have a team available, I'll send them up to Montana."

"But still not likely for another month?"

"That's right. You enjoy your vacation. Got it?"

"I've got it. Thanks, Sam."

Shannon cursed.

This sucked. Someone had sold her brother bad meth and they were still out there, selling that crap to others. Tom had said it was being cooked in Ordinary, Montana.

Despite the overdose, on that point, he had seemed lucid.

Whoever Dave Dunlop had spoken to in Ordinary had said there was no way the meth had come from there. "Look somewhere else" was about all Dave could get from them.

When she'd protested, Dave had said the cops knew their town. He couldn't butt in.

So the local cops were a dead end.

Maybe Dave couldn't do anything, and maybe the DEA had no one right now, but she was available. She could snoop around. And would. Vacation or not, Tom's overdose trumped everything.

She got out of her car and entered the hospital. It was Thursday. Tom had been here since Monday. So had she, sitting with him every day.

She entered his room. No change. *Tom, wake up. Please.*

She stayed with him for a while but the whole situation ate at her. She was sitting here in a hospital room with her sick, and probably dying, brother while a meth manufacturer and drug dealer walked free in Ordinary.

No way.

Shannon stormed out of Tom's room and did what she always did in times of stress. She took control.

A couple of hours later, she arrived at Janey's house just outside of Ordinary. She had a quick meal then jumped into the shower to wash the city's grime from her skin, along with her anger and grief, wishing like crazy this was a normal Thursday night and that this had been a normal week.

But it hadn't been, and this was a bad time for wishful thinking.

Tom still floated in his coma—and she still hadn't told her sister.

She dialed Janey's cell number. "Janey? It's me."

"How's Tom?" Some kind of animated music played in the background.

"Not good. That's why I'm calling."

"Just a minute. The kids are watching a Disney movie. I can't hear."

A second later, it went quiet on the other end and Janey said, "What were you saying?"

"Where are you?"

"In the bathroom of the hotel room with the door locked." She laughed. "It's the only way I can have peace and quiet. About Tom?"

"He overdosed. He's in the hospital. In a coma."

She heard Janey gasp. "Oh my God. We'll come home right now."

"Oh, no, you won't. I almost didn't call because I knew you'd say that, but I had to tell you."

"But—"

"No buts. Honestly, there's nothing you can do."

"Poor Tom. Life has been too hard on him."

"It sure has." Shannon changed the phone to her other ear and took a sweater out of a drawer Janey kept packed for her. "I'm staying at your place, okay?"

"Of course, but why are you there?"

"Tom got the drugs in Ordinary. I'm taking a look around."

"Ordinary?" Janey's voice held disbelief.

"Apparently the town isn't the source. It isn't being made here, but he definitely got it here."

Shannon's next bet was on the biker bar Janey used to complain about.

"I'm going to check out the biker bar in Ordinary first."

"Biker bar? That's gone. The Sheriff chased them out of town. They're all over in Monroe now at a place called Sassy's."

"Okay, I'll scope it out."

"Shannon, be careful," Janey warned in her big-sister voice.

"I will. I'm good at my job."

"I know. I worry anyway."

"I'll see you when you get home Sunday."

No matter what her sister said about being careful, Shannon was going to check out that bar. The distance between bikers and drugs was no big leap for imagination.

She hung up and spread her favorite lotion over her skin, then dressed in panties, a bra and a pair of jeans. She had just picked up the sweater when she heard something downstairs.

She stopped and held her breath.

Another noise. A creak on the stairs. Damn.

There was definitely someone in the house.

She finished pulling on her sweater and took her gun out of her purse. Hiding behind the bedroom door, she waited.

CHAPTER TWO

Navigating a minefield of children's toys, Cash crept across the veranda to the front door of the Wright house. With the toe of his cowboy boot, he nudged aside the cop car he'd bought for Ben's third birthday.

Cash's buddy, C.J., was married to Janey and crazy about his wife. They had a bunch of great kids C.J. adored. Cash was still single—children a daydream—and nothing but an honorary uncle to his friend's children.

Now Dad was dying and Cash might be the end of the Kavenagh line. He wanted what C.J. had with Janey, a family life instead of the horror show his childhood had been.

'I was a rotten role model. You never got married and had kids.' Was it Dad's fault?

Yeah. Maybe. He didn't know.

The crisp wind that had arisen with nightfall spoke of autumn running into winter. He inhaled the scent of leaves breaking down on damp earth then exhaled on a sigh. If he had a bunch of kids, he might be in California visiting Disneyland, too, like the Wrights.

Instead he was here, investigating a light on in the upstairs window of what was supposed to be an empty house.

Hailey Hall babysat Janey's kids sometimes. She would have a key to the house. Cash had caught her and her boyfriend, Jeff, in the weirdest nooks and crannies around town, making out like, well, teenagers.

He wouldn't put it past those kids to use the place while it was empty.

He opened the front door and stepped inside. Time to teach them a lesson by scaring the wits out of them.

He looked for anything out of the ordinary, treading carefully in the darkness in case the intruders weren't Hailey and Jeff. His gun sat like a metal backbone, tucked into the waistband of his pants.

This was only Ordinary, but crime touched even small towns. No sense taking chances.

Moonlight poured in through the kitchen window, illuminating groceries on the counter—including a white box from a bakery over in Haven. He lifted the lid and checked inside. Doughnuts.

Damn kids. They had some nerve bringing snacks. A plate, silverware and a mug sat in the drying rack along with one small pot. An empty tin of canned pasta and sauce had been thrown in the recycle box. They'd made themselves at home. He was going to give them a good piece of his mind.

Only one of them had eaten, though. Probably Jeff. Kid was growing like a weed.

Cash heard a sound from the top floor—a drawer opening and closing, maybe.

He climbed the stairs. In the dark, his hand touched a stuffed animal that one of the children had left on the railing. He rubbed the soft fur between his fingers. Yeah, a bundle of kids and a great wife to wake up to every day would go a long way toward dispelling this feeling he'd had lately of…of…holding his breath, of needing… *something* to happen, even before Frank showed up this evening.

Another noise, softer this time, pulled him out of his reflections. *Snap out of it.* Self-pity wasn't usually Cash's thing, but at the rate Hailey and Jeff were going, they'd have children long before he ever did.

Crazy teenagers. They were going to curse him from here to Memphis because, really, where were a couple of horny teenagers supposed to go when they still lived with their parents?

He strode down the hall and banged his fist on the wall to give them a chance to cover up before he walked in.

Hailey must be wearing that great-smelling perfume.

"You two had better be using condoms." He stepped to the doorway.

The bed was empty but he had the sense of someone being in the room. The skin on the back of his neck tingled, but before he could react, the door slammed against the side of his face and pain exploded in his forehead. "Son of a bitch!"

He reached for his weapon.

A woman jumped from behind the door with a gun in her hand.

They stared each other down, weapons drawn and aimed, tension as thick as honey in the room.

Cash didn't glance down to see what kind of gun she held, semi-automatic or pistol. He watched her eyes. If she planned to pull the trigger, she would show it a fraction of a second before with a subtle flinch.

"Who are you?" she asked.

"Who am *I?* You've got a lot of nerve, lady, breaking into my buddy's house. What did you think you could steal?"

"I'm not stealing anything. My sister lives here."

Then why hadn't he met her? "What's your sister's name?"

"Janey Wilson. At least, that's who she used to be. Now, she's Wilson-Wright."

Okay, so she knew Janey. That didn't mean she was Janey's sister.

"What's your name?" he asked.

"Who wants to know?"

He had to give her credit. She was cool as a brick of ice. All business. Even with a gun in his hand, he didn't intimidate her.

"I'm Cash Kavenagh, Sheriff of Ordinary."

Her eyelids flickered. She knew his name.

"Let me see ID. Slowly," she said.

He drew his wallet out with careful movements, his aim never wavering and his eyes still focused on hers. Amateurs got trigger happy and people died.

He handed the wallet to her and she double-checked that it was he in the photo.

"Okay, you're the Sheriff." She handed it back.

"Now that we've got that settled, who are you?"

"Shannon Wilson. Janey's sister."

"You don't look anything like Janey." Janey was short and voluptuous, a dark-haired Goth with immaculate white angel's skin. This woman, a cool drink of lemonade on a hot day, had long golden hair, flawless tanned skin and pink lips. Her toned athlete's body made his libido race double time.

Some of Janey's attitude shone through. Man, she was gorgeous. And tough. He liked that.

"Your turn," Cash said. "Let's see ID."

Still aiming her gun, she took her driver's license out of a purse she picked up from the bedside table and handed it over.

Okay, she was Shannon Wilson, but...

"Let me see the permit for the gun."

She looked like she might refuse, then sighed and passed it to him.

It was legit. What was a woman doing with a Glock 23.40?

"Why do you carry it?"

"Protection. I'm an investigative journalist. Sometimes I get into sticky situations."

Why carry a semi-automatic revolver instead of a small pistol?

Growing up in the house of Kavenagh, Cash had developed a finely tuned bullshit detector, courtesy of his father. At the moment, it clanged like a fire alarm.

"What are you doing in Ordinary?" he asked.

"Vacationing."

A lie.

"No way. Janey or C.J. would have warned me if you were going to stay here."

She shrugged. "I only called Janey to tell her a minute before you showed up."

"How'd you get in?"

"I have my own key."

"Why haven't we met before?"

"We have." She dropped her permit back into

her purse. "At Janey's wedding. It was a long time ago."

He had a vague memory of a pretty blonde, precocious and flirtatious. She'd come on to him, but had been eight or nine years younger than he. He'd run the other way.

"Because of my job," she continued, "I haven't visited a lot, but Janey and I talk on the phone all the time."

"You haven't visited once in ten years?"

"Yes, but you and I seemed to miss each other. You were visiting your mom a couple of times. Once you were on a training course in Bozeman."

"How do you know that?"

"Janey told me." She smiled. "I asked where her good-looking friend from the wedding had got to."

She'd been interested in him. She'd been too young, though. She wasn't too young now. She was beautiful, with a woman's body and knowing gaze.

He was interested, all right.

He tucked his gun back into his waistband and she put hers away in her purse.

Cash leaned against the doorjamb and crossed his arms. "You wanna tell me why you're really here?"

She raised one blond eyebrow.

He waited her out.

"Fine. I'll tell you the truth, but first I need a coffee."

She brushed past him and that great-smelling perfume followed her out of the room. So did Cash, like a bird dog on the trail.

Vanilla. She smelled like sugar cookies.

Cash's hand touched that stuffed animal on the stair rail again and his gaze fell on the sway of Shannon's hips. She had great hips.

Downstairs, she turned on lights as she went.

She took her time making a pot of coffee, not once looking at him.

He sat at the table in silence, enjoying the elegance and efficiency of her movements. A couple of minutes later she put coffee mugs on the table, along with the box of donuts, and sat across from him. She pulled something out of her back pocket—a black leather badge holder like his—and slid it over to him. He opened it. DEA. Special Agent Wilson.

Stunned, his gaze flew to hers.

"Janey never said you were a cop." It put her off-limits. Damn.

Unlike his father, he didn't fool around with co-workers, even if she didn't work in Ordinary. He didn't want to have anything to do with female cops. His dad had screwed everything with breasts, no matter her age or her occupation, from female cops to hookers.

He'd cost one cop her job. It had been the end of his career, too.

"Why didn't you just tell me you were DEA?"

"Because I didn't want anyone here to know."

She bit into a donut and a dot of jelly ended up on her lower lip. He tried not to imagine himself licking it off.

"What's the case? You've got to be here for a reason."

"I'm on vacation."

He ignored that. "Is it centered in Ordinary?"

She sighed and nodded. "I think it might originate with the bikers in the next county, though. I'm here to see what I can learn."

"About what?"

"Someone in the area is cooking crystal meth."

"How do you know? I haven't heard a thing about it."

"It's happening."

"Why are you so sure it's here?"

"My brother visited last weekend and stayed with Janey."

"Tom? The one who lost his family to a drunk driver?"

She nodded.

"I met him. Nice guy, but messed up. No wonder. What about him?"

"He brought meth home with him. Said he got it in Ordinary."

Cash's mind raced. Where in Ordinary? From whom?

"So the DEA sent you here to investigate? Why didn't they contact me?"

"A cop in Billings called your office and was told there were definitely no drugs here and that you wouldn't investigate."

"I didn't talk to anyone. Must have been my deputy." Wade should have brought that info to him, but his deputy was still fairly new. There were a lot of things Cash still had to explain to him. "I'll call the DEA and let them know I'll cooperate."

She raised a staying hand. "I'm not here officially."

"What?"

"I really am supposed to be on vacation, but I can't let this go."

"Why not? You have no jurisdiction here."

She put her donut down on a paper napkin, carefully, and he had the sense that she was trying to hold herself together. "It's important to me. Tom overdosed." She looked like she might break down but then sucked it up. As he'd thought upstairs, she was tough. Strong.

"He's in a coma," she said.

"Is he going to live?"

"I don't know." She wrapped her hands around her mug.

"You need to take a giant step away from this."

She shook her head. Those full lips thinned to a determined line, her chin took on a mulish jut and those pretty green eyes suddenly became cop eyes—hard-edged and suspicious.

"I spoke to the domestic field division in Denver and they have their hands full right now. There are meth labs everywhere these days."

"Then wait."

"I can't."

"I'll call your bosses."

"I've done nothing wrong. I'm on vacation. My sister will be home soon and I'll visit with her."

"Who are you kidding? My guess is you won't sit still while you think there are drugs in the county." It wouldn't be the first time a cop went rogue for a family member in trouble.

She shrugged, admitting nothing. Distrust radiated from her. She didn't have faith in the local law enforcement—and that included him.

She likely thought he didn't have the goods to do the job, that he was a country hick who couldn't deal with anything more serious than speeding tickets.

He'd been raised in San Francisco. By a cop. He understood exactly what human beings were capable of, and he knew how to deal with it. All of it.

He walked to the sink and rinsed his mug.

"I'm taking care of C.J.'s horses while he's away. Mornings and evenings I'll be around. I'll also be investigating drugs in the area." He pointed a finger at her. "You stay out of it. Got it?"

She nodded, but she was lying again.

"I mean it." Cash left the house.

He walked to the corral to gather in C.J.'s horses and his own, Victor, who Cash boarded here on the Wright land.

Wind whistled through the tops of the poplars lining the driveway. Their few remaining leaves chattered like a bunch of old women, sending him confusing messages about his dad and families and model-beautiful tall blonde women.

She was a grown-up now, no longer a kid who was off-limits.

He was angry with her because she'd come into his jurisdiction to investigate a crime she had no right to look into. She was too close to the victim, and needed to keep out of it.

His body, though, and some part of his mind or his heart, wondered: What if he gave it a shot? What if he asked her out?

She was gorgeous, and she'd thought about him over the years. She'd asked Janey about him whenever she visited Ordinary, hadn't she?

He'd seen the look in her eyes. She still found

him attractive. *He* certainly found *her* attractive. How could he not?

Cash put away the horses for the night and got into his truck to drive home, his thoughts drifting to Shannon.

His house sat between Ordinary and Haven and it wasn't a long trip. He turned down a driveway nearly hidden from the road that ran half a mile through a tunnel of trees.

The house was pretty in the moonlight with its purple gingerbread trim—too pretty for a man. He'd bought the two-bedroom from Timm Franck's sister, Sara. It sat on a piece of land that would allow for a sizable addition later, when he started his family.

As he stepped out of the truck and stared at his house, his stubborn mind returned to thoughts of Shannon. Again.

Forget it, buddy.

Why?

Because she's a cop.

Yeah. She is. So what?

How important was that, really? They worked for different jurisdictions. Hell, different levels of government even.

He knew she was off-limits. At least, his rational mind did, but she'd kick-started both his libido and his crazy need to move forward on that family.

Maybe her being a cop could work in his favor. She would have the same values and morals as he. She would understand that the job got crazy, that sometimes the hours were long and dangerous.

And she was hot. She drew him in like no one had in a long, long time. How insanely perfect was that?

Hope sent that feeling of holding his breath, of waiting for something to happen in his life, to change and move forward, scurrying off into the night.

A sigh gusted out of him and he stared at his dark house, unable to resist a couple of "What ifs?" What if Shannon were waiting inside for him? What if she were his and they could start on that family he wanted so badly. How good would that feel?

What was that old saying? If wishes were horses, beggars would ride? Hope did that to a person—made a beggar believe he could be a wealthy man.

The only ones waiting inside for him were Paddy and Danny.

Cash opened the front door. The dogs bounded out and circled the bushes that would one day be replaced by a stable. He left them to their business.

He stepped inside and turned on the living room light. Empty. What if it weren't?

Cash went straight to his computer. He had a buddy he'd studied with, Denny O'Doyle, who'd ended up working in Washington. Cash emailed for info about Special Agent Shannon Wilson of the DEA.

What kind of woman was she?

An hour later, he got his response. Shannon Wilson was on the fast track to the top. She was smart, independent and…ambitious. The DEA had big hopes for her. Huge hopes. She was going places.

Cash's heart sank. Great. An ambitious cop. Wasn't that just the kiss of death? After Dad, Cash had had a bellyful of cops with ambition.

She was DEA, she likely investigated drug problems in every part of the country. Probably thought Ordinary was a hick town compared to the places she'd been.

He wandered to the living room and stared at the empty furniture. Shit. For a few minutes there, he'd had this incredible dream.

He went to the front door to call in the dogs but his voice caught in his throat. Disillusionment and disappointment weighed on him. That feeling of being stuck in life slunk back in from the shadows of the yard and settled in his chest.

No way would Shannon settle in a place like Ordinary, Montana, and no way would Cash leave, not when he had a great job, amazing friends and this house.

He knew what life in the big city was like, chock full of temptations to distract a man from what was really important—family—and Cash wanted no part of those distractions.

EARLY THE FOLLOWING morning Cash returned to the Wright ranch, his nerves humming.

He thought of the woman in the house.

She's on her way to the top, Denny had written.

He walked to the stable and pulled open the heavy doors. He didn't mind taking over this task while C.J. was gone.

C.J.'s neighbor to the east was taking care of the cattle. Cash need only worry about the horses.

He fed them, then turned them loose in the corral.

Still no movement in the house that he could discern. Too early for her to be up, maybe. He returned to the stable to muck out the stalls, enjoying how his muscles burned at the effort, how this activity differed from sitting behind a desk writing reports.

When he finished his chores he washed up at the sink in the barn then grabbed a pressed, beige uniform shirt from his truck and changed out of his flannel shirt in the meager warmth of the stable. He'd head straight into Ordinary for work from here.

He slipped into his sheepskin ranch coat and pinned his Sheriff's badge to the outside. He traded his old work boots for his polished cowboy boots.

There'd been no flicker of light in the house. Odd. He hadn't taken her for a lazy woman.

He pulled onto the highway for the drive to town and had gone no farther than C.J.'s neighbor's land when he saw Shannon jogging along the shoulder toward him.

Facing traffic. Smart girl.

The rising sun highlighted one side of her body.

She wore a snug long-sleeved t-shirt under a quilted vest, and tight jogging pants that hugged mile-long legs. Her calves and thighs looked strong.

She'd pulled that pretty blond hair into a ponytail that swung with each step. She looked young and stunningly beautiful.

The breath lodged in his throat.

He pulled over and rolled down his passenger window. She approached, panting steam into the cool air.

"You always run this early?" he asked.

She nodded, her cheeks pink from exertion. "It's the most beautiful part of the day."

She looked across the fields and the early-morning light turned her hair and skin to gold. Her face was relaxed, unlike he'd seen it last night.

Cash imagined how tempting she must look waking up in bed before crawling out for her run. He would have trouble letting her go.

"It's gorgeous out here, isn't it?" She smiled at the scenery and he wished he'd put that smile on her face this morning.

She's on a fast track to the top.

Cash cleared his throat. "How long was your run?"

"I just finished five miles."

Fit, all right. And ambitious. A real go-getter. He wouldn't be dating her.

Just Cash's luck. He finally meets the perfect woman and she's off-limits—and not only for her ambition. His first instinct about her being a cop was the right one. Cash didn't sleep with co-workers. Ever. His father had done enough of that and look what happened to him. Disgrace. Public humiliation.

Dad had worked tirelessly, had investigated every angle, had spent weeks on end ignoring his family while he worked cases, on his way up to Commissioner of the San Francisco police force. Always the big shot. Dad hadn't walked. He'd run. And strutted.

Cash valued his job and his relationships in

this town. He would fight for them tooth and nail, against any enemy, even a green-eyed girl who was already turning him inside out. Cash set his jaw hard to ignore his frustration.

He had to keep his distance.

She reacted to his frown and backed away from the car.

"See you around," she said.

In his rear-view mirror, he watched her run away from him. A sudden groin-stirringimage of her naked legs wrapped around his waist jumped to mind.

"Hell."

This attraction was wrong.

He didn't need his dying Dad coming around telling Cash he was late getting a wife and family, nor did he need a stunning DEA agent visiting town to wreck his stable life. He needed to reconnect with his priorities, his goals. He wanted a family. He wanted it here in Ordinary, where people appreciated and respected him. Where life was sane.

He whipped out his cell phone and called Timm Franck.

"Ordinary Citizen." Timm published the town's newspaper.

Without preamble, Cash said, "You know Angel's been trying to hook me up with Danielle Beacon?"

"Good morning to you, too," Timm answered with laughter in his voice. "Sure, I remember. You ready to take the plunge?"

"Yep. How soon?"

"You're serious! Okay. How about tonight?"

"Can't. It's Austin's movie night."

"I forgot. Let's double date tomorrow night then, at Chester's."

"Have Angel call Danielle then tell me what time to pick her up."

Cash hung up and chuffed out a frosted breath in the cold truck. He closed the passenger window and pulled out onto the highway.

He needed to rub the image of the prettiest woman this side of the Rockies out of his mind, even if she did have slim, strong legs that went on forever. Another woman could help him do that.

So you say.

Yeah, so I say.

All the way into town he told himself that a little determination could go a long way.

CHAPTER THREE

WHEN CASH ARRIVED in Ordinary, he glimpsed Austin Trumball, his Little Brother, sidling into the laneway at the edge of town, his manner secretive.

Twelve-year-old Austin was a good kid, but lost these days. Cash was always on the lookout for him. He had a bad feeling about Austin, that without a little guidance, he could end up in trouble.

The only place that laneway led was the alley running the length of Main Street behind the businesses.

Why was Austin going back there? Over a year ago Cash had caught him dumpster-diving, starving and scrambling for food thrown away by the restaurant. Cash had applied to become his Big Brother the next day. He tried to feed him a couple of real meals a week.

If Austin was looking for food, Cash needed to know. He'd give him twenty bucks to go to the diner for a burger.

He parked the truck in front of the cop shop and walked back to the alley.

He found Austin behind Chester's Bar and Grill. Smoking. Damn.

Why couldn't Cash protect the boy from all of the bad temptations in life?

When he saw Cash, Austin dropped the butt and stomped on it.

"Don't move." Cash grabbed him by the collar and eased him against the brick wall. He bracketed the boy with an arm on either side. The pungent scent of marijuana hung in the air.

Crap. It hadn't been just a plain cigarette.

Puffs of air crystallized into vapor as the boy panted. He looked at everything but the sheriff towering over him. Cash could see that sharp little brain working—calculating the odds of getting away.

Cash thought they'd developed a real strong bond in the past year, but apparently not. Austin had been on a great upswing after Cash had taken him under his wing. Something had changed though. For the past month something had been wrong. Cash shook his head, so damn discouraged that he hadn't gotten through to the boy.

"Where'd you get it?" Cash asked, angry that he couldn't protect Austin better.

Austin, caged between Cash's arms, looked up at him with all the defiance such a skinny boy could muster. He shook his head, the mulish jut of his jaw evidence that he wasn't about to give Cash an answer.

Cash worked hard to keep himself from shaking the answer out of the boy.

With the unpredictability and speed of youth, Austin slipped under Cash's arm to run. Cash snagged the tail of his filthy jacket and pulled him back. He heard Austin's breath whoosh out of him. He didn't want to hurt the kid, but needed Austin to understand how serious this was. Austin was headed down a road that would one day lead to a jail cell.

Cash leaned close and lowered his voice. "I know all the moves a kid like you can make." His fear for the boy made his tone hard, unsympathetic.

He saw Austin's dilated pupils, the dark bags under his eyes, and the sunken cheeks of his thin face. For a while under Cash's care, Austin had begun to look good, but man, this was regression.

Austin had classic golden boy good looks and the smile of an angel the rare time one could be coaxed out of him.

"Where'd you get the marijuana?" Cash asked again, his tone more demanding.

A flash of fear lurked beneath Austin's defiance. "I—I found it."

"C'mon, Austin, you've never lied to me before. The truth this time."

"Screw you, man." Austin looked like he wanted to either fight or cry. Why was adolescence so hard for some kids? "Why don't you leave me alone?"

Because the haunted look in your eyes tells me you want to be rescued.

Cash placed his hand on Austin's shoulder, but Austin shrugged it off. The boy squeezed his lips shut and shook his head. Cash knew he'd gotten as much out of him as he was going to. For stubbornness, Austin was hard to beat. Except maybe by Cash himself.

An image of Austin's mother flashed into Cash's mind—a sweet but helpless woman who reminded Cash of his own mom—and Cash didn't need a psychiatrist to tell him why he'd chosen this boy to care for.

Cash hadn't given up on himself. Even during the toughest days, after Dad had lost his job as Commissioner of the San Francisco police force, his house and his car to bankruptcy, and his wife and son to separation followed rapidly by divorce, sixteen-year-old Cash had pulled himself *and* his mom through.

Later, after he'd studied to become a police officer, he'd left California. He couldn't work where his father had hammered his sterling career into lead.

Austin deserved a chance at a good life, too. Cash wouldn't give up on him.

He grasped the front of Austin's thin ski jacket and shook him gently.

"Austin, get your shit together or you'll end up a drug addict. Or unable to take care of yourself. Like your mother."

Austin trembled, probably as much from fear as the cold.

"Is that what you want?" Cash asked, knowing Austin was terrified of exactly that fatc.

"You've gotta stop pushing your luck." Cash let go of Austin's jacket, more frustrated than he could say. Maybe he should give Austin a taste of what jail time felt like, give him a really good scare. Yeah, putting him in jail was a great idea.

Decision made, he ordered, "Follow me."

Austin's gaze shot to Cash's face. *What* was going on with him these days? Who was Austin hanging out with who were getting him into this kind of trouble?

"Where to?" Austin asked.

"To the Sheriff's office."

"Wh-why?"

"I just caught you in possession of marijuana, didn't I?"

Austin nodded.

"I'm a cop, aren't I?"

"Yeah, but you're my Big Brother."

"That doesn't give you a free pass to commit crime. Is that why you wanted me in that role?"

Austin mumbled, "No."

Cash hadn't really thought so. At the beginning, they'd had too much fun together. Not lately, though.

Austin should be in school, but at the moment it was more important to teach him this lesson than to drive him there.

Cash herded him out of the alley and onto the sidewalk of Main Street.

Austin tried to wrench his arm free of Cash's grip.

Cash's fingers dug into Austin's bony elbow. With a quiet yelp the boy came along.

On the way to the Sheriff's office, Cash nodded to the people of Ordinary who passed them by. Austin hung his head and shuffled beside Cash.

Cash's office sat between the small grocery store and Scotty's Hardware. Seeing it filled Cash with pride.

In a backhanded way, Frank had inspired him to become a cop, if only to prove that it could be done in a better way.

That a man could be a good and honorable cop and make a difference to the people around him. That a man didn't have to drive his way through every obstacle with the force of a Mack truck to get to the top. That a man didn't have to want to get to the top. That a man could be happy in his job, just the way it was, just where it was.

Cash opened the office door and stepped inside, taking Austin with him. He nudged him into a chair in front of the desk.

Wade Hanlon came out of the washroom.

"Anything interesting happen last night?" Cash asked.

"Not a thing."

Cash turned to Austin. "Stay put there for a minute. I need to talk to the deputy."

Austin put his hands in his pockets and hunched his shoulders.

Cash gestured Wade toward the back of the room and asked quietly, "Did someone call from Billings asking about methamphetamines in Ordinary?"

"Yeah, that afternoon I took over while you went to the dentist. I told them we didn't have that problem here."

"Apparently, we do."

"We do?" Wade looked surprised but also a tad sheepish. He probably didn't like disappointing his new boss. "How do you know?"

"There's a man in hospital in Billings who overdosed on meth he says he picked up here."

"Do you think he's telling the truth?"

"Yeah, I do. I know the guy. He's a friend's brother."

Wade looked even more embarrassed. "Sorry, Sheriff. I had no idea."

"In the future, let me know about those kinds of calls. I need to know everything that goes on around here. *Everything*. Got it?"

"Sure. Of course."

"Keep your eyes and ears open around town. That meth is here somewhere."

"Okay, boss."

Wade stepped to the desk and opened a Styrofoam container from the diner. It held a couple of cinnamon buns. "Those're for you. There's fresh coffee. See you tonight. Seven, right?"

Cash and Wade worked opposite shifts.

Cash took Austin to the movies on Friday nights, so Hanlon came in an hour early.

After Wade left, Cash walked around the desk.

He noticed Austin's gaze flicker to the cinnamon buns. Yeah, he'd have the munchies right now, from the marijuana. Looking at Austin's thin face, he amended that.

"When was the last time your mom bought groceries?"

Austin shrugged and remained close-lipped. Cash had to admire his loyalty to his mom. In his own way, the kid had a lot of class. Connie Trumball wasn't doing much of a job mothering her boy, but Cash had yet to hear Austin bad-mouth her.

Connie wasn't a great mother, but she was Austin's.

Cash took a can of ginger ale from a small refrigerator and handed it to him.

Austin looked up, surprised.

Sometimes Austin was so closed off he seemed encased in concrete. At other times, like right now, the boy had cellophane for skin. Cash got such a clear glimpse of Austin and his quiet suffering, of his settling for less in life that Cash wanted to hold him and whisper, *wish for more, dream for more. Don't settle. You deserve it.*

"Take it," Cash urged.

He slid a bun across the desk.

"Eat," he ordered.

Austin hesitated, then picked up the sticky bun and took a huge bite. He licked icing from his fingers, then slurped loudly when he washed it down with ginger ale.

Cash pushed the second bun across the table. "I can't eat this one, either. Want it?"

Austin shrugged, then took the box and dug into the second bun. When Austin finished he wiped his mouth with the dirty sleeve of his jacket. Cash cringed. That coat belonged in the garbage.

"Okay," Cash said as he stood. "Let's go." Cash

pointed toward the jail cell. "You commit the crime, you pay the price."

Austin shot him an owl-eyed look of terror. He stood and swallowed, his little Adam's apple bobbing in his thin throat.

"I have to go to school."

"Not today." He pointed toward the cell. "Go."

Austin shuffled in and Cash locked the door behind him. He had more to say to Austin, but not until the boy had spent some time behind bars.

"Might as well sit," Cash said. "You're going to be here awhile."

Austin sat on the narrow cot and stared at Cash with huge eyes.

"I have to go out," Cash said. "Nap if you want. There's a blanket on the chair."

Austin shook out the folded blanket, then lay down and pulled it over himself, covering his old jacket, cheap running shoes and all. In a matter of minutes, he was out like a light.

Austin was a sweet kid in so many ways. Since his father's death half a dozen years ago, though, the only attention he craved was a father's.

Cash thought of his own dad. Staring at Austin brought home how much Cash had missed in his relationship with his own dad.

It didn't seem right to never see Frank again.

What if yesterday was the last time Cash ever saw his dad? Panic drove fear through Cash's blood. He'd always known that Dad was on this earth somewhere and it had felt right, even if only for Cash to feel righteous in ignoring his father.

But if Dad were gone? Truly gone? Dead? Not a trace of him left on this earth?

Cash couldn't avoid the truth. It would hurt like hell.

A pressure had been building inside of Cash since that moment he had run after his father's car yesterday. That pressure was the need to find his father, to talk to him again. Soon. How much time did Dad have left? Did Dad have enough money for proper medical care? To eat? To live out his dying days in dignity?

Austin stirred in his sleep and Cash thought of how much Austin would want to see *his* dad if he could, but fate had taken that option away from the kid.

Austin had no choice.

Cash did.

Cash didn't want to waste whatever time was left with his dad. He needed to find his father before Frank died.

Decision made, Cash put on his cowboy hat and headed out the door, locking it behind him.

He forced himself to calm down. Right now, Austin needed him. There were things Cash had to do to take care of the boy.

His breath fogged in the cold Montana air. He

knew full well it was a no-no for Big Brothers to buy their Littles gifts, but Austin needed so much. Cash would be damned if he'd let the boy freeze in that flimsy fall jacket.

If anyone didn't like that he was providing essentials for Austin, they could sue him.

The irony of a cop breaking Big Brother "laws" didn't escape Cash.

Before he bought anything, he had to go talk to Austin's mom, to tell her where Austin was and why. He didn't want to, though. She pushed his buttons, made him remember too much of those years when he'd had to take care of his own emotionally fragile mom.

He phoned her instead. He'd memorized her number in case something happened to Austin when he was out with Cash and Cash needed medical history.

When Connie answered the phone, Cash told her what he was doing with Austin today.

"Whatever you think is best, Sheriff."

He disliked the tremor in her voice. He wanted *her* to make the important decisions about Austin's life. They shouldn't be left to a relative stranger. Cash wanted her to be the adult, the parent she should be, to give Austin the strength and guidance a kid like him deserved.

Cash visited the school next.

On the drive over he passed Mary Lou

McCloskey driving in the opposite direction, speeding like a demon. Mary Lou, one of the sweetest women in town, knew better. He'd have a word with her at some point. At the moment, worried about drugs in the area getting into the hands of preteens, he needed to talk to the principal.

Ordinary Middle School sat on the edge of town. Once there, Cash spoke to Paul Hunt, the principal, explaining why Austin would be away today.

Twelve, thirteen and fourteen-year-old kids laughed and talked in the halls between classes.

"Any idea where Austin could have picked up the marijuana?" Cash asked.

"None. The kids here are pretty good, but you know weed's a temptation for them. It's easy enough to find."

"There's more. I've heard a rumor there are methamphetamines in the area. Have you seen any?"

"No, but that's worrisome." Paul had been leaning back in his chair but sat straighter now. "Meth is dangerous stuff."

A boy ran down the hallway past the principal's open door. "Taylor, slow down," Paul called. "No running in the halls. Sorry, Cash, what were you saying?"

"There's a man in the hospital from taking meth he picked up in Ordinary. In a coma."

Paul stood and closed the door. "That turns my blood cold. Are you sure he got it here?"

"Pretty sure. There's a problem throughout Montana. I just hadn't suspected it was this close to home."

"Me, either. I don't have anyone at the school who looks like they're taking it."

"Yeah, it ravages people quickly. You can usually tell."

"Listen, Cash, we have an assembly in a couple of weeks—students and parents. On Thursday. Will you come talk about the dangers of drugs? Both the kids and their parents need to be informed about this issue."

"Good idea. What time?"

"After lunch. One o'clock."

These kids were too young to do meth, but you just never knew... Cash stood to leave. "Call me if you hear even a whisper about meth in the school."

"You got it. I'll keep an eye on Austin when I can."

"Appreciate it."

The stores were open by the time Cash left school and he bought a thick, durable ski jacket. New, not used and worn like the stuff Austin's mom bought him. Cash also picked up a wool hat and Thinsulate gloves.

After a stop at the New American diner for breakfast, he returned to the cop shop.

Austin slept soundly in the cell with his mouth open and drool dripping toward his ear. He had one arm flung above his head and the other dangling over the side of the cot.

Cash sat at his desk and booted up the computer. He searched data in San Francisco for Frank's whereabouts first, but Dad had hidden his tracks. Why? Why come all the way to Ordinary to tell Cash he was dying and then drive away without leaving contact information?

Maybe because of your reaction to him? You weren't exactly welcoming.

Yeah, and I refuse to feel guilty about that.

He dialed his mom's number in San Francisco. Jamie answered instead, sounding peeved.

"Hey, buddy, it's Cash. What's wrong?"

"It's Mom and Dad." Yeah, Jamie definitely sounded sullen. "They won't let me do stuff I want to do. They treat me like I'm a kid."

Technically, Jamie *was* still a kid at fifteen.

Every time Cash had this conversation with his half-brother, he lost his patience. He couldn't relate. He'd lived such a different adolescence. What he wouldn't have given for the stable family life that Jamie had.

Cash spun the desk chair around to look at Austin in the cell.

"Jamie, at the moment I'm sitting in my office. I just put a twelve-year-old kid in the jail cell. His father's dead and his mom's useless."

Austin stirred, mumbled something, then settled.

"Count yourself lucky you've got two loving parents who care enough to set limits."

"You're kidding, right?"

Cash sighed. "I'm not. This kid is raising himself. I'm pretty sure he'd trade places with you without blinking."

Cash squeezed the bridge of his nose. "Put Mom on the phone."

A minute later, Cash's mom came on.

"Cash, how are you, honey?" She sounded great, so much better than the woman she used to be. She'd found love and it fit her in all the right places.

"Hi, Mom, I'm good. I hate to ask, but do you know where Dad lives these days?"

"Last I heard he was still in the same old apartment."

"He isn't anymore."

"He tried to contact me, but I wouldn't take his calls."

"He's dying, Mom. Cirrhosis of the liver."

She was silent for a long time then said, "That's too bad. It isn't a surprise, but it's…unfortunate."

"I didn't tell you to bring you down, I just need to find him."

"Why?"

"I don't know. I guess because he's my father and he's dying." Austin stirred again and Cash turned around to stare through the open horizontal blinds onto Main Street. "He looked bad."

"He's family, that has to count for something."

"Will you attend his funeral?"

"I'll have to think about it, Cash, but probably not."

"Okay." Even if she didn't have enough respect for Frank to attend, Cash hoped she would be there to support *him*.

He hung up.

On his own again.

Cash swiveled in his old desk chair to face the office again, ignoring his numb behind.

Austin sat on the edge of the cot, his hair flattened on one side of his head.

"What do you think?" Cash asked. "You learned your lesson?"

"Yeah."

"You sure?"

"Yeah," Austin croaked, his voice sounding groggy.

"Tell me what you learned."

Austin shrugged. "I shouldn't smoke weed?" He really didn't get it.

"Listen, I've been where you are. I spent a lot of years taking care of my mom when she couldn't take care of herself, when my dad wasn't around."

Austin wouldn't look Cash in the eye.

"What would happen to your mom if you got into serious trouble, serious enough to end up in jail? You think she has any idea how to take care of herself?"

"No," Austin mumbled.

He gestured to the cell. "If you're not careful, one of these days this will be real."

Austin's eyes lit with fear.

"If I wanted to, I could cart you off to a social worker who might decide you're better off in foster care."

Yeah, that was fear in his eyes, all right.

"Next time I catch you with drugs, I'm going to have to charge you. What life dished out to you isn't fair," Cash continued, "but you have to keep moving forward. Don't be tempted by this shit, Austin. By the easy way out. When you don't feel strong enough to face it on your own, you call me. Got it?"

Austin finally looked up and Cash was humbled by the gratitude on his face. "Yeah, I got it."

"You want out?"

"I wanna go home."

Cash nodded. "Okay."

He unlocked the cell door and Austin walked past him.

"Give me your jacket," Cash said.

Austin recoiled. "You're gonna make me walk home without my coat?"

He frowned. "'Course not. I bought you a new one."

"Why?"

"Because the one you're wearing is falling apart. Besides, it's not a winter jacket." Looking at Austin, Cash realized he'd misinterpreted the question. As far as he could tell, Austin had meant either "what do I have to do for it?" or "why do you care?"

"Because," he said as he handed Austin the new one, "I'm your Big Brother. It's my responsibility to watch out for you."

Austin took off his old jacket and handled the new one with reverence. He should. It had set Cash back a bit.

Austin's reaction was off. He should have been excited, kid-happy about getting new stuff, but instead he remained subdued and wary as though he expected Cash to take it away. Or as though he couldn't believe he deserved it.

"Those are yours, too." Cash nodded toward a hat and gloves.

"I slipped some granola bars into the pocket

of the jacket. There's a twenty for lunch. Don't lose it."

Austin put on the hat and gloves. He cleared his throat and said, "Thanks," with a small smile. Cash thought he detected a sheen in the boy's eyes before he turned away toward the door.

Cash stopped him. "Does your mom go through your pockets?"

"Yeah," he admitted.

"Best go spend that money at the diner now, maybe buy something for dinner, too, then hide it when you get home."

It didn't feel right warning a boy against his mother, but this was real life, not *Leave it to Beaver*. Austin had to look out for himself.

"I got a place in our shed where I keep things. Mom doesn't know about it."

"Good. Don't think I'm going soft on you just because I'm giving you stuff. Next time I'll have to charge you. Got it?" His stern "cop" voice seemed to make an impression on Austin.

"Yeah, I got it." Cash could tell he did. Finally.

"I'll see you later tonight."

"'Kay," Austin mumbled and left, the tips of his long hair sticking out from under his new hat.

Cash picked up the old jacket and searched the pockets for contraband. Nothing. Not a single thing, not even an empty gum wrapper.

Man, he hated distrusting Austin.

He didn't believe that marijuana led to heavier drug use, but Austin must feel the heavy burden of his life. Any escape from the situation would appeal, no matter the source.

Cash had to find that source. Where had Austin picked up the marijuana?

Just out of curiosity, he emptied his own pockets. Keys. A wallet with enough bills in it to make him feel secure. Change. The remainder of a bag of cinnamon hearts he'd bought the other day.

Austin had so little. Pitiful. Just plain pitiful.

He threw on his jacket and ran out of the office after Austin.

"Hey," he called, and Austin stopped and waited for him.

"Let's go to Sweet Talk. I feel like candy. How about you?"

Austin perked up. "I like candy."

In Janey Wilson's candy store he ordered chocolates and whichever candies Austin indicated he might like. With a mom on welfare, Austin didn't get a lot of treats in his hard life.

By the time they were ready to leave Cash had a replacement bag of cinnamon hearts for himself and Austin's pockets were full to bursting. *Now* Cash felt good, as though he'd completed the job.

They strode to the door, Austin with the slightest of smiles. Man, it would feel amazing to see Austin really smile, or grin, or laugh.

The bell above the door tinkled and Cash looked up. He stopped. So did Austin.

Shannon Wilson entered the shop and, for a minute, Cash couldn't breathe.

Her eyes took in every corner of the shop and everyone in it before she relaxed and concentrated on Cash.

Once out of cop mode, she looked as radiant as the sun rising on a May morning. She wore a short ski jacket and blue jeans tucked into slouchy boots, and that pretty blond hair in a ponytail again. She wasn't a cop now. She was just a woman. All woman.

"Hey," she said, and slid her hands into her jacket pockets. "Do you have a sweet tooth?"

For you. *Stop that!* "Yeah." He put his hand on Austin's shoulder. "So does my Little Brother. This is Austin."

Shannon smiled and Cash could feel Austin hunch his shoulders. "Hey, Austin."

Austin stood on his toes and whispered in Cash's ear, "Can she come tonight?"

No, no, no. Cash didn't want that, but Austin did.

"You want to invite her? Really?"

Austin nodded.

"Okay." If that was what Austin wanted, he'd take the chance and ask. "Friday nights I take Austin to the movie theater over in Monroe. You want to come with us?"

He held his breath. *Don't disappoint the boy.*
"I'm sorry, I can't."

Cash glanced at Austin. He'd put on what Cash called his shuttered look.

She must have noticed it, too, because she said, "Can I take a rain check? I'm probably still going to be here next Friday. I could come then?"

Austin nodded, fast and hard.

When they left the shop, Austin was smiling, first time Cash had seen that in a long, long time.

CHAPTER FOUR

MARY LOU MCCLOSKEY ran her errands about ninety miles west of Ordinary where people didn't know her.

Last week, she'd gone shopping one hundred miles east instead.

She picked up a couple of packages of a cold medication containing ephedrine at the local drugstore, showing a fake ID to make the purchase. She'd bought the ID from a biker. Since she was making meth for them to sell, they'd been accommodating.

Before heading home today she'd pick up more cold medication in a town ten miles west, also. She shopped different towns every week, miles and miles apart so no one could ever connect the dots.

That, along with what she ordered through her husband's pharmacy and what she'd ordered online to be delivered to her parents' old farmhouse, put her in good shape.

WHEN SHE FINISHED with her purchases, she didn't head straight home. Instead, she drove to her parents' farm. They were dead now, killed in a car accident two years ago.

They'd left the property to Brad in the will. Why? This wasn't the 1900s. They should have trusted her to take care of this place just fine on her own. But no, they'd left it to her husband as though she were too dim-witted, too gently-bred, too female to be of much use. She would have loved having a piece of land in her own name.

She was the one with the brains. *She* was the one who'd excelled in school, who'd adored math, science, everything. But she was the one who stayed home to care for the children while Brad had a career, while the town looked up to him, while he made money and she went to him every week for handouts.

They'd raised her to be sweet, to be demure and supportive of her husband, but she was smarter than Brad.

Her parents had never seen that.

She stepped into the RV parked a dozen yards away from the house and turned on a light. A sense of satisfaction ran through her. She was a businesswoman. A clever one.

In the small narrow space, she'd made the sweetest little chemistry lab.

She'd seen photos of meth labs, had done a lot of research before building her own. In every photo the labs had been a mess. Not hers. Hers was clean and tidy and perfect, everything lined up exactly as it should be. Three large plastic jars with lids sat beside an eyedropper, coffee filters, glass dish and funnel.

Her ingredients were precisely lined up in a row along one wall. Iodine. Red phosphorous. Ether. Hydrochloric Acid. Sodium Hydroxide. Methanol. On hooks in the wall, she stored her clean tubing.

She placed her purchases on the end of the table and opened the windows. She dressed in protective clothing and secured a mask around her mouth and nose before starting on her next batch of meth.

First she washed her cold medication tablets in ether to get rid of the red dye covering them and to break the pills down to pure ephedrine.

Then she crushed them into powder and put it into a jar with methanol. Before she started shaking the jar, she checked her watch.

Too bad so many parts of this process were slow and tedious.

She wouldn't have time to clean up after herself today. Her days were a bit longer on Fridays because the boys stayed after school for sports, and she picked up fried chicken and chips for dinner, so no cooking. Even so, she was cutting it real close today.

She'd have to come back on Sunday to clean

up. Time to start coming up with an excuse for not attending church services.

SHANNON PULLED ON a red leather skirt that showed too much leg and too little modesty. Ditto for the black tank top that displayed too much cleavage. She covered it with a fake fur jacket and checked herself in Janey's full-length mirror.

Her legs looked long and sleek thanks to her six-inch stilettos.

Ruby lipstick made her lips look full.

Dressed and ready for the biker bar in Monroe, she still had to press her hand to her stomach to settle the butterflies roiling there.

She knew men. She knew bars. She knew alcohol. The three could be a deadly combination. She'd had plenty of experience dealing with all three in her career. That experience, and her training, would get her through tonight.

Sheriff Kavenagh wanted her to leave this alone, to let him take care of it, but that wasn't in her nature. Tom was her brother. She was going to Monroe.

Not ideal going alone.

It is what it is, she told herself.

She'd been in—and handled—tough situations before and had survived.

Not without backup.

True, so she had to be smart. She stuffed her gun into her purse before heading to the bar.

Meth wasn't called Biker's Coffee by accident. It made sense for her to look at the biker gang first, but she couldn't exactly walk out to the farm where they crashed and ask to see where they were cooking the stuff.

She drove to the bar in the next county wishing she'd rented something sexier to drive than the Fiesta she owned. It didn't make a ballsy statement, wasn't really in character with the clothes.

She cruised a long square of rural roads around the bar to check out escape routes.

A couple of cop cars were parked off the small highway on a side road just yards away from a flashing neon sign. No doubt waiting for Friday night trouble at the biker bar. Perfect. Backup was close.

When she arrived at the bar, the first thing she noticed was the neon sign flashing red and yellow beside the highway—sASSy's. Great. A strip joint. Not her cup of tea, but so what? She was here to work.

The lot was full to the gills with hogs and pickup trucks. The only available spot was a dark corner around back, which she didn't care for. Nothing about this evening thrilled her except the possibility of catching a lead.

She patted the purse she'd slung across her

chest messenger style and drew confidence from the bulge of her Glock as she walked around the building to the front door.

Cops advised women not to carry guns in their purses. A purse could be taken away from a woman too easily and the gun used against her. But Shannon was no amateur. She knew what she was doing.

A group of bikers wreathed in smoke and wearing enough black leather to keep the ranchers of Montana in business for years blocked the entrance.

She struggled with her nerves. She didn't want just the dealer, she reminded herself. She had no choice, she needed to do this if she wanted to nab the creep who was making the stuff.

When she stepped forward and got the bikers' full attention, the competition and posturing started. She planned to use it to her advantage.

"Hey," she said. "Where can a girl get a drink around here?"

"Right here, babe."

"I got it."

"Hey, lady. I'm buying."

Cologne swirled around her, mingling with a whiff of sweat from one of the bikers.

One man went through the door and the rest parted long enough for her to enter the bar, then closed around her after, blocking her exit. Suddenly she couldn't breathe.

Her heart rate kicked in hard. *Easy. Don't panic. Panic is the worst way to handle this.* Jammed in the middle of too many oversize bodies, she forced herself to wrestle her fear under control. She could do this.

She wiped her upper lip.

She had extensive martial arts training. She had a gun and a cell phone. Two cop cars were a one-minute drive away.

The man in front of her stepped aside and she got a good look at the bar.

A stripper gyrated onstage to the throbbing beat of a rock song so loud the bass echoed in Shannon's pulse.

The place was packed. More than a few glances flicked her way.

Lights flashed onstage while the rest of the bar was dimly lit, no doubt covering up all manner of illegal activity. She glanced at every corner, assessing the situation.

She'd gone through Awareness Training when training to be a cop. There were five levels of Awareness, all color-coded. At the moment she'd bypassed Condition Yellow—attentive, but relaxed, and had shot straight to Condition Orange—focus directed and watching for potential threat.

Any one of these jokers could become a potential threat in a flash.

Perfect. She was exactly where she needed to be. If she couldn't find the answer here, the cause was lost. Determination stilled her panic and her sense of purpose returned. She could do this.

Her biggest challenge would be keeping maximum awareness of her surroundings without looking like a cop.

She chose a seat at the bar with her back to a door she was fairly certain opened to the back parking lot.

She'd done as much as she could to keep herself safe. She knew from experience, though, how things could go from safe to shit in a matter of seconds.

FRIDAY NIGHT IN Ordinary, Montana, was small-town quiet. The shop windows were dark and only a few couples strolled toward Chester's Bar and Grill for dinner.

As he'd done every Friday for the past year, Cash drove to Austin's trailer to pick him up and take him to a movie.

Austin's mother answered on the first knock, ready and waiting for Cash. He hated this part. Connie was about the neediest woman he'd ever met. Her most pitiful aspect was the way she looked at him—as though he were her hero, or savior.

He might be trying to save her son, but he wasn't rescuing her. That was beyond his limited powers.

He'd done his time with Mom until another man had come along and married her. He loved his mom, and he would come running the second she needed him, but his duty with needy women was done.

He wasn't taking on Connie.

"Austin ready?" he asked.

Austin appeared behind Connie, but she raised her arm and leaned on the doorframe so the boy couldn't pass.

"How've you been, Cash?" She smiled, probably thought she looked sexy, but all he sensed was loneliness pouring from her in waves. He wished he could help—he really did—but what she wanted, he wasn't prepared to give. The only thing he could do was try to save her son.

That old claustrophobia he used to feel when his mom needed him too much crept around him, choking him. He needed to get away.

Austin scooted under her arm, thank goodness, and out the door, more than ready for his few hours of freedom.

Connie saw Cash start to turn away and she frowned.

"Austin," she called, "don't forget to stop at the Lucky Seven and pick up food. There's nothing in the fridge."

Cash's anger flared. It was a mother's job to take care of the kid, not the other way around.

He wanted to shake Connie, to yell at her, "For God's sake, woman, develop a backbone and do right by your boy," but he was caught in a familiar bind. If he yelled or criticized, he would hurt a woman too weak to defend herself no matter how mildly he expressed it. He remembered how easily Mom used to cry. His anger and frustration had nowhere to go.

He bit his tongue, holding it all in. He left her standing there and climbed into the truck.

"*Harry Potter* is playing tonight. That okay with you?"

"Yeah," Austin said, his low voice barely audible.

Was the giant step Austin had taken away from his Big Brother normal I'm-almost-a-teenager-stuff? Or was there something more sinister going on?

At the edge of Monroe, on the way to the Five Points Cinema, they passed Sassy's Bar. The transient biker population of the next county hung out there, and the parking lot looked jammed full of chrome and bikes.

When they got to the theater, they settled in with popcorn and pop and watched the movie.

Afterward, Cash waited while Austin went to the washroom.

Five minutes later, Austin came out looking pale, with his shoulders hunched up around his ears, setting off alarms in Cash.

"Everything okay?" he asked.

"Yeah," Austin mumbled while he kept his face averted. Something seemed fishy.

"Hold up," Cash said. "I think I'd better use the washroom, too."

He slipped into the men's room and scouted around. Nothing looked out of place. There was a pair of feet under the closed door of one stall. Did someone just sell Austin something? Marijuana? Drugs? Or had someone said something off-color or insulting? Something about his mom? Cash's cop instincts went into overdrive. Why had Austin come out of here so secretive and embarrassed?

He used the urinal and washed his hands, taking his time so he could find out whose feet those were. The toilet flushed and Brad McCloskey walked out. He nodded when he saw Cash.

"Hey, Cash," he said.

Brad owned the only pharmacy in Ordinary. He was a father of four boys, and his wife, Mary

Lou, volunteered at church. They attended services every Sunday.

Brad was one of the good guys.

So why had Austin come out of here with a bad case of *something* going on, with Brad the only other person here?

Had Austin picked up something that had already been stashed in here? They came to the theater every Friday. Had Austin pre-arranged something? No way could Cash go out and search Austin's pockets, though. It would break the fragile trust he had worked so hard to build.

Besides, he didn't have a shred of proof that Austin was doing drugs other than those few puffs of marijuana this morning. All he had was a healthy suspicion of trouble, and trouble didn't necessarily mean drugs.

He left the washroom no wiser than when he'd entered it, his frustration racing double time.

One thing he would do was put his cop skills to use by taking a closer look at Brad. Was there a wolf hiding inside his mild-mannered sheep's clothing?

Cash pulled into the Lucky Seven parking lot, the only convenience store and gas station in the county open twenty-four hours.

"You have money to get groceries?" he asked.

Austin blushed and shook his head. So, Connie was using Cash for...cash.

That anger flared again. It had nothing to do with being stingy. He enjoyed helping people, but Connie needed to find a way to support herself.

Resigned, he said, "Come on," and stepped out of the truck.

SHANNON HAD BEEN in Sassy's for an hour already, surrounded by more bikers than she could count, and still knew nothing. She had five drinks in front of her and hadn't done more than mime drinking them. She wouldn't put it past one of these jokers to try to slip her a roofie.

She finally asked what needed to be asked, interrupting some guy's story about a battle they'd pitched somewhere with a rival gang.

"Where can I get something to take home with me?"

"Something or someone?"

They all laughed.

"What do you want?" the closest guy asked. He was hulking and ugly and determined to keep her for the night. Not a chance. "Mary Jane?"

"Something stronger. Glass."

"I can get it for you," a biker said.

"Does anyone here have any with them?" No way was she leaving the bar with one of these guys.

"Don't know if there's any here tonight."

"Can you ask around?"

A couple of them left to make inquiries. Shannon watched as they approached table after table. Drugs were brought out of pockets, but obviously not meth.

"I've got some at the farm," another biker said, running his hand up her thigh. She ignored the creep factor. "We can party at my place."

"Yeah? Right now?" She just had to determine where it was.

"Uh-huh. Come on."

"Where to?" A new song blared and she leaned close. She needed to know where the farm was.

"She's not going anywhere with you, Rogers," the ugly biker said, the air suddenly electric. Shannon turned to tell the idiot to butt out.

Even as she did so, the hair on her neck stood on end and she felt for the purse she still wore. The heft of her weapon reassured her.

Before she had a chance to say anything, punches were thrown, the sound of glasses shattering filled the bar and all hell broke loose. Somehow she had to get out of this alive without letting these guys know she could fight. She needed them to see her as a sexy but needy female, not someone who could hold her own.

On the other hand, Tae Kwan Do and kickboxing would only take her so far among so many tough characters. Her pulse rate kicked up.

Someone fisted a hand in her hair. When he

went down, so did she. Her forehead hit the floor hard and she saw Stars and Stripes. After that, nothing.

CASH LEFT THE convenience store carrying a bag crammed with milk, bread and canned goods. He'd forced an apple on Austin. Probably wasn't often the kid got fresh fruit. Cash wondered if Connie had ever cooked a vegetable in the boy's life.

He amended that thought. Connie had been fine while her husband Mel had still been alive. Once Mel died, though, Austin's life had deteriorated.

Just as Cash pulled level with Sassy's, the building emptied out, bikers streaming from the bar and taking off on their hogs in waves.

Police cruisers with flashing lights crowded the lot. Monroe's police chief would be calling any second. Cash pulled onto the shoulder opposite the parking lot and waited.

His phone rang. Bingo.

"Cash? It's Mike Gage from Monroe. We got trouble at Sassy's and need everyone out here."

"I'm outside. Be right in."

Cash turned to Austin. "Don't get out of this truck for any reason, got it?"

Austin nodded, but he wasn't fooled. What were the chances a twelve-year-old boy would do as he was told when there was so much happening around him?

Cash stripped off his coat, jumped out of the truck and ran across the road, his adrenaline spiking.

"Hey," he called when Mike Gage came out of the bar escorting a woman none too gently beside him. "What do you need me for?"

Mike had tied the woman's wrists in front of her with a flexcuff, but she was putting up a good fight. Mike would charge her with resisting as well as whatever else he wanted to throw at her.

She had a killer body that her skimpy clothing did everything to showcase.

"Cash," Mike called, "handle this woman for me so I can clear up the rest of this frigging circus."

Cash took the woman's arm, distracted by the cleavage spilling from her low-cut tank top and plumped up by her hands cuffed in front of her. Her nipples hardened in the cold night air.

"Seen enough yet, Sheriff?"

Sheriff? He wasn't in uniform. How did she know who he was?

He prodded her into the light and got a good look at her face.

No way.

Shannon Wilson? Beneath a mass of teased up hair, a cake of eye-shadow and a half-inch of black eyeliner, Shannon stared at him. She looked like one of the sluttiest women he'd ever come across, showing just about everything she owned. In public. In this hellhole of a strip joint. In front of the raunchiest men in the state.

If she'd had a jacket, it was long gone. She shivered, but he'd be damned if he cared when she had willingly put herself out here, half-naked and straight into danger.

Mike led a rowdy biker out of the bar toward his cruiser. The guy tried to bust away and knocked Shannon into Cash. She cried out. Cash's arms snapped around her and hauled her up against his chest, out of danger. While Mike collared the guy and took him away, Cash's gaze swept to Shannon's face. She watched him wide-eyed. A split second later, he realized why. Those hands cuffed in front of her pressed against him.

Against his groin.

He didn't move, afraid that if he did, he would react like a randy boy.

He stared at her. She stared at him.

Move.

He couldn't.

She stayed unnaturally, still then blinked.

A breath whooshed out of him as one rushed into her and those breasts rose, filled out.

Lord, kill me now.

He wanted to drive to an abandoned hollow

in someone's—anyone's—field and ravage the daylights out of her. He was furious she hadn't left things to him to investigate, and instead had come here on her own looking for the meth dealers. Part of him wanted to leave her to her fate, but he'd be damned if he'd let Janey's sister go to jail.

He all but dragged her to his truck. He opened the passenger door. And swore. Where the hell was Austin?

He didn't need this. His days were twelve hours long, five days a week, and then he was on call on the weekend until the town hired more deputies.

By Friday night Cash was beat and didn't need to deal with either a disobedient kid or a woman he found too attractive.

Immediately after he nudged her to get in, he realized she wasn't going to manage it on her own, not in that skirt, in those shoes, with her hands cuffed.

He put his hands on her waist and lifted her onto the seat. A breast brushed his face and he heard her swift gasp. He felt her against his cheek and just about came on the spot.

He swore again and shoved her into the middle of the seat.

He needed to get out of here. Fast.

"Don't move an inch. Not one inch. Got it?"

She glared but nodded. He slammed the door shut and walked away.

More deputies arrived from Monroe. A minute later, Cash recognized a couple of cops from farther afield.

He stepped into the bar. Looked like Mike and his deputies had everything under control.

Pulling Mike aside, he said, "That woman you hauled out of here?"

"What about her?" Mike's gaze shot around the bar while he talked, making sure none of the fires he'd put out were in danger of re-ignition.

"What are you charging her with?"

"Taking a swing at me."

Cash choked. "What?"

"Good thing she missed or I might have swung back."

"You've got your hands full. Let me take her back to Ordinary."

Mike turned and pierced him with a sharp look. "Why?"

"She's my friend's sister. I'd rather not charge her. I'll read her the riot act and throw her in jail for the night. Teach her a lesson."

"Put some clothes on her while you're at it."

Cash winced. "You've got a lot of help here. I'll head out."

Mike nodded, distracted by a mouthy biker on the far side of the bar.

Cash left and glanced around the parking lot.

He didn't have to look far for Austin. The boy stood beside a bike, his hungry gaze chronicling every detail, every spot of chrome, every inch of leather. He stroked the seat.

Cash softened. Austin had nothing and asked for so little. Must be hard to be poor. Cash's parents had been difficult, each in their own way, but he'd always had food, a roof over his head and enough basic stuff to not be embarrassed in front of his friends.

"Let's go," he said, keeping his tone even. Austin had enough to deal with without him jumping down his throat.

"There's a woman in the truck," he said. "I'm driving her home."

"Why?"

"It's Shannon. You met her today. She's Janey Wilson's sister."

Austin perked up and ran to the truck.

Cash grabbed his coat from his seat and threw it into the bed before climbing in. Austin walked around to the passenger door. When he saw Shannon, his jaw dropped open and his eyes widened.

"Hi," he whispered.

"Austin, right?"

He nodded and climbed in beside her.

She scooted to the middle of the seat, her thigh flush against Cash's.

When he buckled his seat belt he had to squeeze his fingers between his own hip and hers. The drive to Ordinary would be only twenty minutes. Thank God. He hated that he found her hot.

When he pulled his hand out from between them, she shivered. It took him a moment to realize she wasn't reacting to his touch. She was cold. Frozen. Her own fault.

"Where's your jacket?"

"In the bar."

Cash studied the bikers being herded out of Sassy's and decided he'd had enough of the place for one night.

He should have thought to give her his coat before he tossed it into the back. She might be dressed like a slut, but she was still Janey's sister and should be treated with respect. He retrieved his jacket and covered her with it. It engulfed her.

She hesitated and then smiled. "Thanks."

He noticed Austin shivering, too, and turned up the heat as he drove. His hand brushed Shannon's bare thigh. She pulled away.

"You want some of this coat?" she asked Austin.

In the dark cab, despite the bad mood his attraction to her put him into, Cash almost smiled. Like Austin was going to say no. He felt more than saw Austin pull the coat over both of them, making sure she was covered. Treating her like a lady despite her clothes.

When they finally arrived in Ordinary, in silence, Cash pulled up in front of Austin's trailer.

"Don't forget the groceries in the back," he said.

"'Kay," Austin mumbled. "Thanks."

Cash waited until he was safely inside before driving away.

"You've got a good job. Why does your brother live in a rundown trailer?"

"I'm not a relative. I volunteer as his Big Brother."

"Oh." She scooted across the seat and leaned against the passenger door.

She didn't smell like vanilla tonight. Some kind of heavy cheap perfume scented the cab and he hated it. He'd smelled it on his dad too often, transferred from some woman he'd been sleeping with.

Cash remembered walking down O'Farrell Street in San Francisco looking for his dad. Dad used to patrol the Tenderloin before he became Commissioner. Cash was only fourteen. He'd never been in the area. It was Dad's old beat, but Cash knew Dad still came down here on his nights off.

Cash found him in a back alley behind a strip

club with a hooker's legs wrapped around his waist. He was banging her against a brick wall.

"Dad."

His father looked up from the woman and said, "Cash." He'd shaken his head to clear the lust. "What are you doing here?"

"Mom's real sick. You need to take her to the hospital."

He'd dropped the woman like a hot potato. Cash had turned his back while Dad straightened himself. Dad had walked away without paying. Cash knew cops got things for free. Coffee and doughnuts, too.

He hated that Shannon's perfume brought back those memories, raised ugly emotions like disgust and anger.

The air sizzled in the cab of the pickup. Cash tried to hold on to his temper, honest to God he did, but this was going to kill C.J. and Janey.

"What were you thinking going to Sassy's dressed like that?" he barked. "What would Janey think? And C.J.?"

She didn't respond.

"Do you have a death wish?"

"No," she answered.

"You could have been killed. Raped. Drugged and date raped. Gang raped."

"I was careful."

"*Careful?* You call dressing like that being careful?"

He felt her watching him in the dark interior of the truck and turned to her. In the light of the dashboard, with the inch-thick makeup on her face and the heavy black mascara hiding those eyes, he didn't recognize her as the same woman he'd met at C.J.'s house last night or in the candy store this morning.

"My clothes are not your concern," Shannon said, as though there'd been no break in the conversation.

"The hell they're not," he all but shouted as he pulled into the Wright yard. "Janey's my friend. C.J.'s my best pal. They wouldn't want to see you hurt. What kind of woman are you anyway?"

Shannon sighed and it sounded like it came up from her toes. "That's none of your business."

In the Wright yard, Cash slammed on the brakes.

"I'm making you my business."

The woman glared back at him. No regret. No contrition. He unbuckled his seatbelt and heard it hit the window before he jumped out.

He strode around the front of the truck and opened her door. Grabbing her arm, he hauled her out and slammed her door.

He didn't wait for her to gain her balance before tugging her toward the house.

"Stop manhandling me," she yelled.

CHAPTER FIVE

MOONLIGHT FELL across Shannon and she looked like something out of a black-and-white horror movie, defiant and eerily beautiful in her cheap get-up. Cash stopped to pull himself under control. She was right. She was none of his business and he had no right to be physical with her.

He took her elbow, gently, and directed her into the house with a lot less force. He headed straight to the kitchen where he turned on the overhead light and hunted through the drawers until he found a knife sharp enough to cut through plastic. A second later, he'd set Shannon's wrists free.

She rubbed her abraded skin.

He couldn't stand to look at her like this.

"Go get changed. I'll make tea."

She left the room and he could breathe again. His attraction to her in this incarnation was too raw, too insanely sexual on a level deeper and faster than thought and reason, when all he wanted in life was to rise above his father's rotten choices.

He knew he wasn't his dad, but neither was he immune to this woman.

Tonight the recycle box held two more cans of pasta and sauce. Cash had always wondered what parts of the animal the ground beef in those meals came from. The woman had a terrible diet. Good thing she was a jogger.

Ten minutes later, Shannon returned in a pair of gray sweats tucked into thick socks and a white cable-knit turtleneck. The sleeves covered her hands and she tucked her arms across her midriff as though still cold.

"Here. Sit." He put a cup of tea on the table then poured one for himself. When he turned back, she sat at the table cupping her hands around her warm mug.

She'd brushed out whatever product she'd put in her hair to make it trashy, but the remnants of that crap made her hair look darker than this morning's blond silk. She had it pulled back into a ponytail.

She'd stripped her face of every trace of makeup. Her eyelashes and eyebrows were so pale they were almost white. Here was the woman he'd met in the candy shop this morning.

He leaned back against the counter and sipped his tea. "You weren't there to pick up a man. You were investigating, looking for drugs, weren't you?"

"Maybe."

"No 'maybe.' I told you to stay out of it unless you want to come here as a professional."

"I *am* a professional."

"You're not on the clock. What you did was dangerous."

"I had my gun. I checked the area out first and saw that the cops were close." She visibly forced herself to relax. "I sat near the back door so I could escape easily. I didn't drink a thing any of the bikers bought for me."

"Then how did you get caught in the fight?"

"It was over me. More than one of them wanted to take me home. Before I knew it, punches were being thrown. Before I could leave, my hair got caught in someone's fist. I got dragged down with him."

For the first time Cash noticed the red mark on her forehead. Cripes, she was hurt.

She waved her hand. "It's nothing. Just a slight headache."

"You're too pretty to go into bars dressed like a hooker."

"But it almost worked. One of the guys who wanted to take me home was taking me to the farm for meth."

"Really? Meth, for sure?"

"He said he had some at home."

"You don't think he was lying to get you to his place?"

"I'd swear he was telling the truth. None of those bikers were surprised when I asked for glass."

"Good work. So we know it's on the biker farm, we just don't know whether it's being manufactured there."

"If the farm is as remote as I've heard, it would be the perfect spot for it."

"Yeah. I want you staying away from it, though. You should have never gone to that bar alone tonight."

"Cash, you don't know what my job calls for. You've lived in this small town too long. I've had experience with this kind of thing before."

"Going into bars, dressed like that?"

"When I have to."

There was that ambition, that willingness to do whatever it took to get ahead, even if it got her into trouble. It was bad enough when his dad had done it, but a woman?

How could a man live with a woman like that, wait for her to come home every night, wondering whether she would be whole or damaged? Would he be waiting for the call a cop's spouse dreaded?

She was right about one thing. She had more

experience than he did. He didn't deal with this stuff in Ordinary.

He didn't think he was a chauvinist, but was it right for a woman to be doing a job so dangerous?

It turned his stomach to ice.

"Why'd you take a swing at Sheriff Gage?"

"It was part of the act."

"You need to keep out of this," he said.

"I can't. Would you if it were your brother in a coma?"

He thought of his half brother, Jamie. Although the kid was spoiled and sullen, Cash loved him. No way he would leave it alone. He wasn't telling Shannon that, though.

"Don't go back there."

"It's the only lead I have."

Brad came to mind. "I've got a possible lead." He still couldn't believe it, though, even if he was going to investigate. "Well, it's just an idea."

She perked up. "What idea?"

He shot her a quelling glance. "None of your business."

She bristled, but stopped her questioning.

He put his empty mug into the sink, then she walked him to the front door. "I need to get my car from Sassy's."

"I'll drive you out in the morning after I take care of C.J.'s horses."

He stood in the doorway for a long time, staring at her, hesitating to leave. He wanted to do something with this too-capable woman, like curling her into his arms and kissing the recklessness out of her, turning her soft and pliable and ready to listen to him when he told her not to go to bars alone at night dressed as a hooker.

Instead, he strode out into the night, to the predictability of his empty house and his well-defined life.

CASH ARRIVED BACK at the Wright ranch early the following morning. No lights shone in the house.

Was she was still in bed? He shook his head to rid it of images that thought called to mind.

He walked past the corrals to the stable across the backyard. In the early-morning stillness, the door hinges complained when he forced them open.

The air inside the stable smelled of hay and horses. The horses heated their stalls. Their breath fogged in the chill air.

His own horse, Victor, sang out his usual morning refrain of "where's breakfast?"

Cash had had trouble sleeping last night, lying awake trying to figure out how to convince Shannon to stay away from those bikers. She wasn't stupid but the woman was driven. She'd get herself in serious danger.

His work with the horses, this ordered routine, these familiar scents, soothed his jitters.

When the horses finished eating, he brought C.J.'s three out to the corral. They danced in the sunlight, frisky. Then he walked Victor out of the stable to join them.

The mutt he'd awakened in the stable trotted across the yard, mounted the steps of the porch and scratched at the back door.

A minute later, the door opened and Shannon peeked out, her hair a rumpled blond halo.

"Hey, you," she said to the dog. Her morning-husky voice stroked Cash's libido. "Wait here."

The dog waited, either well-trained, or intelligent enough to understand her. He whimpered and shifted on his paws, but stayed put on the top step.

She reappeared with a bowl full of who knew what, which she put on the floor. The dog attacked it ravenously, pushing the bowl against the doorsill so she couldn't close the door.

She nudged the bowl back toward the dog with her bare toes and kept her foot there to hold it still while the animal ate.

She wore nothing but an oversize t-shirt. Her legs were bare. And long. And perfect. The breath streaming from Cash's lungs hissed out of his mouth.

She glanced up, startled, and stared at him.

Victor stamped the semi-frozen ground with one hoof and Cash pushed him into the corral. He closed the gate then approached the house.

"His name's Bandit," he said, referring to the dog. "Don't leave a speck of food around. He'll steal it."

"I didn't know C.J. and Janey owned a dog."

"They don't. He comes over from the neighbor's land. The kids have probably encouraged him by feeding him."

Shannon hopped from one foot to the other. "So that's why I couldn't find dog food in the kitchen. I opened a tin of tuna."

She wrapped her arms across her midriff, cupping her elbows against the cold, and the action plumped her breasts. Cash stared at a point behind her left shoulder.

He gestured toward the stable. "I need to clean out the stalls and then we can head out to get your car."

A pair of high beams strained against her t-shirt. Oh, Lordy.

"Did you already have breakfast?" she asked.

"Yeah." A bowl of cold cereal, but no way was he going into that house, that kitchen, with Shannon this morning.

She shifted to her other foot. Pink nail polish twinkled on her toes. A blush stained her cheeks. "I can be ready in half an hour."

She slipped back into the house and closed the door. Thank God. He couldn't have stood to look at her much longer without touching her. That date with Danielle couldn't come soon enough.

HER EYES WERE gritty. She'd had trouble sleeping. She never slept easily after undercover work. Last night had been worse than usual, though, and it was Cash's fault. For too many dark and restless hours she'd thought about the way he'd looked at her in her slut clothes.

He'd practically scorched her with his eyes. He'd wanted her.

The timing couldn't be any more inconvenient for this attraction. Who was she kidding? There would never be a convenient time. Her career mattered more to her than relationships. Than men.

She knew from experience how men disappointed a woman. How women always saved the day. How much stronger they were than men and how much it took to overcome the violence that men dished out too easily.

Even so, Cash drew her. He'd been rough with her last night, but the second she'd told him to stop manhandling her, he had.

He'd gentled his touch, had made tea, had seemed even tender at moments.

That tenderness was more dangerous to her

than his violence. She knew how to fight violence. Tenderness, though? It left her vulnerable. Uncertain.

Because she knew what she wanted in life, she fought that uncertainty. She couldn't let Cash mean anything to her.

After she'd finished breakfast, showered and dressed, she stepped outside. Cash was still working in the barn so she leaned against his truck and absorbed the sunlight.

She felt dirty this morning, as though she'd somehow taken on the grime the bikers lived in. The sunlight was healing, the cool breeze cleansing. She breathed deeply to clear her lungs of last night's filth.

Cash left the barn and strode to the pickup. A big, capable man, his steps were sure and confident. The sun did interesting things to his dirty-blond hair, sparked it with golden highlights.

When he got closer, the sun turned his blue eyes to brilliant gems.

Hell's bells, the man was too attractive.

CASH DROVE SHANNON to Sassy's. She'd dressed in jeans, a sweater and a jacket, and didn't look anything like the woman he'd driven home last night.

They pulled into the parking lot.

"Sure looks tawdry in the light of day, doesn't it?" she said.

"These places usually do."

"Yeah. It looks harmless enough. How does Mike Gage feel about having this place in his jurisdiction?"

"Hates it. Monroe's not a bad town, a little on the tough side, but nothing Gage and his police force can't handle. But those bikers...they're a whole other breed altogether, and Mike's getting tired of spending his weekends here breaking up fights."

"I don't blame him." She tossed her ponytail over her shoulder and it glistened like spun gold.

His stomach clenched. "Don't go there to-night."

She didn't respond.

"Shannon." His voice turned hard.

She turned away from staring at the front of the bar to look at him, her eyes bright pools of green.

"I can take care of myself, Cash. I've been doing it for a long time."

"You're not that old. You're what? Twenty-six?"

"Twenty-seven, but I started taking care of myself real early."

"Why?"

"My mom died when I was six and Janey raised me, but she got pregnant and had Cheryl and moved out. After that, I raised myself."

"How old were you?"

"Nine."

"Where was your dad?"

"Dad was around. He was just pretty useless at anything outside of bringing home a paycheck. So…" She shrugged her shoulders. "I took care of myself and him and sometimes my older siblings, and I've been doing it ever since."

"I get that you're capable, I really do, but those guys—" he nodded toward Sassy's "—are real bad news."

"I know."

"Don't go back."

She didn't answer him, just watched him coolly, and he might as well have been talking to the dashboard.

"Where's your car?" he asked.

"Around back."

He drove along the side of the bar. One small red Fiesta sat in the far corner of the dirt lot, isolated and forlorn, at least a dozen yards away from the closest light standard.

He raised one recriminating eyebrow.

"The parking lot was packed," she said. "I knew the cops were half a block away."

She got out of the truck.

He waited until she started her car and pulled out of the parking lot, then followed her back to the Wright ranch. She turned in and he kept on until he reached his own place on the other side of Ordinary, the entire time wondering whether he should cancel his date with Danielle to cover Shannon at the bar tonight. But that was a foolish idea.

She wouldn't appreciate his interference. When all was said and done, she was her own person, and he had absolutely no control over her.

SHANNON DECIDED ON a different approach to Sassy's tonight.

Cash had been right. She'd taken too great a chance despite her precautions. She'd do a whole lot more for her brother, but she had to do it smartly.

Dressed more conservatively than usual in jeans, a pink sweater—neither of them tight—and a long black jacket, she got into her car and drove to Monroe. No way was she giving men there the impression she was interested in anything other than her job.

The same cops waited down the road from Sassy's. Good.

She'd never call them, but if things went south too quickly, she could discharge her weapon. That would bring them running.

Shannon carried a notebook and a bunch of pens. Tonight, she was an investigative journalist researching an article about the biker culture. None of the men would recognize her. The light-

ing had been dim and they'd probably looked at
her breasts more than her face. This time she
wore minimal makeup and her hair was up in a
ponytail.

She patted the holster under her loose jacket.
She had her gun on board. She didn't plan to take
off her coat tonight so no one would see it. Con-
trary to what Cash Kavenagh might think of her,
she was neither stupid nor careless.

The same men greeted her at the door. She
was right in her assumption. None of them recognized her.

Inside, the same stripper gyrated onstage.

Her gaze flew around the room, checking everything before finding an empty stool at the bar.
She ordered a bottle of beer then kept it close so
none of the men could tamper with it. She drank
little, preferring her senses to remain on high
alert.

She told them why she was here, and asked
who she should interview.

Shannon was still sitting on that bar stool an
hour later, waiting for the leader of this pack of
bikers to show.

They swore he'd be in tonight and would let
her interview him about being a biker. While
she waited she grilled the bikers as subtly as she
could, but got absolutely nothing about drugs out
of them.

She threw her pen onto the bar and shoved her writing tablet into her pocket. This was taking too long.

"Listen," one of the bikers said. "He isn't coming. Let's go. I'll take you out to the farm. You can interview me."

Not on your life, Shannon thought. The man had a lot more on his mind than "interviewing."

"You know Cole won't like that, Chris," the big biker named Rogers said. "He don't like nobody being interviewed by reporters but him."

"He isn't here, is he?"

"She's not going anywhere with you." Rogers pushed Chris.

"Who says?" Chris shoved Rogers back.

Not again.

"Stop," she shouted. They turned to stare at her. "Can one of you call him? Find out for sure whether he's coming in?"

Chris whipped out a cell and punched in a number. "Man, I can't hear a thing. Come outside."

He headed toward the back door but turned around when she didn't follow.

"Out front," she said, her voice hard-edged. The lighting was better in the front.

He frowned but followed her.

In the parking lot, she had trouble hearing him

speaking into the phone. Too many men crowded her, trying to get her attention.

She'd seen plenty of women in the bar, but guessed there was something to be said for fresh blood.

Chris hung up. "Cole ain't coming tonight. He and his old lady are busy. He'll call you tomorrow afternoon, though."

"I don't give out my number. Give me his."

Chris rattled off a number that Shannon wrote down.

"Tell him I'll call."

She walked off, hating to wait until tomorrow. She knew police investigation inside out, knew how long everything took, despite how quickly things got done on the cop shows on TV. In general she was a patient person, but this was about Tom, not a faceless stranger.

She'd always been compassionate, but understood now why the relatives of victims wanted answers yesterday.

What if someone else overdosed?

That's the woman in you talking, Shannon, she could almost hear her boss say. *When you're on the job, you're a cop. Think like one.*

Okay, forget the personal connection and consider your next step.

Good advice, but even so, as she got into her car, started it up and pulled out onto the small highway to head home, she still wrestled with frustration.

She'd gone only about a mile when she noticed a biker on her tail. Her understanding was that the biker farm was in the opposite direction of Ordinary. So why was he behind her heading toward town?

When she increased her speed, so did he. He was following her.

Damned if she'd lead him to Janey's house. She cursed again. She shouldn't be staying at Janey's. She should have anticipated that something like this could happen.

Freaking fabulous. Adrenaline spiked through her. How was she going to lose him? His hog was powerful and her car average. She couldn't outrun him.

CHAPTER SIX

THROUGHOUT CASH'S DATE with Danielle, despite how much he'd enjoyed her company and Timm and Angel's, he'd worried about Shannon.

At the end of the night, determinedly putting Shannon out of his mind, Cash drove Danielle to her door and turned off the engine. Dinner at Chester's had been fun. Danielle was fun.

Now it was time to call it a night.

"I had a great time, Cash," Danielle said.

Danielle always had a good time, wherever she was, whoever she was with. He knew lots about the townspeople. Most everyone's business in a small town was an open book.

There'd been no missing the appreciative glances she had cast him all night. Or the look she was giving him now, with the unmistakable message of desire in her eyes.

He liked her, liked her laugh, liked the way she looked, but something held him back, something that he didn't want to look at too closely.

His mind flashed to Shannon, but why? She was off-limits. He'd already established that. He'd gone on this date with Danielle to take his mind off Shannon.

And that was the problem. It hadn't been fair to Danielle to date her just to distract him from thoughts of another woman. He should have seen that before he asked her out.

She leaned forward to kiss him, but he pulled back, stopping her with a hand on her shoulder. When push came to shove, he had to be honest with her.

"Danielle," he started, and she stopped. A small sarcastic smile turned up her lips.

"Don't tell me," she said. "It's you, not me."

"Basically, yeah, only I don't want it to sound so lame. I don't know how to say this… You're a fabulous girl and I had a great time tonight…"

"But?"

"Yeah, there is a but."

"Is there another woman?"

"No!" *Maybe. I wish.* No, he wished there wasn't a beautiful woman named Shannon tempting him away from the kinds of women he should be getting to know better. Like Danielle, who'd returned to Ordinary just a few months ago after years away. He should have tried to get to know her weeks ago, before Shannon had shown up. Maybe tonight could have ended differently.

But you didn't. What does that tell you?

That there just wasn't enough attraction there.

He shouldn't have asked her out. She was good-looking, fun and had a smart head on her shoulders. Why wasn't that enough?

She didn't heat his blood like Shannon did.

That was it? He lusted after another woman too much to enjoy the woman here willing to be in his arms, and maybe in his bed?

No, it was about more than just sex, passion. Passion could fade. On the other hand, friendship could grow.

So why wouldn't he give Danielle a chance? He didn't know. At one time, fun sex would have been enough. With age, he'd changed. He wanted more.

There was a spark missing here, a spark that had nothing to do with lust.

"Hmm," Danielle murmured. "Sounds like there might be another woman."

Damn. He'd been too strong in his protest.

"Danielle, I—"

"Don't worry about it, Cash. It happens."

Man, she was a great girl. Too bad he couldn't make himself feel what he just *didn't* feel.

Danielle slid out of her seat, closed the truck door and walked to her house.

He watched until she was safely inside then drove away, heading for home.

Just before he turned into his long driveway,

a car sped down the road toward him with a big Harley hard on its tail. The car zoomed past.

So did the biker.

Cash's cop instincts kicked in. He swore and took the flashing light out of his glove compartment. He stuck it on the roof of the truck, then he pulled a U-turn.

A BLACK PICKUP in the oncoming lane slowed down to turn into a driveway. Shannon shot past.

Seconds later, she saw the pickup do a U-turn.

The truck, with a light flashing on his roof, came roaring up behind the biker.

A cop. Thank God.

Shannon pulled over and the biker shot past. She watched until his red taillight disappeared into the distance.

The truck's headlights flared in her rearview mirror and the pickup stopped behind her. A man stepped out.

Cash!

He walked to her door and she rolled down the window.

"What's happening?" he asked. "Why the speeding?"

"That biker was following me." She tried to catch her breath. "I'm trying to get home in one piece, without leading him to C.J.'s house."

He shook his head. "You went to Sassy's again, didn't you?"

"Yes." If her tone was a little hard, so be it. This was what she did for a living. She probably had more experience in her baby finger than he had in his whole body. She'd worked all kinds of drug cases in all kinds of situations.

She'd looked up Cash Kavenagh on the internet earlier. His entire career had been spent in Ordinary.

She wasn't accountable to him. In fact, because she was on vacation, she was accountable to no one but herself.

"Follow me back to my place," he said. "That bozo could be waiting at the next side road to take up the chase again."

Because she worried about that herself, she agreed.

He strode back to his truck, started it up and pulled a U-turn. Shannon did the same and followed his truck as he turned right into the nearby driveway.

Poplars lined the long drive like sentinels. She pulled into a private clearing and parked behind his truck.

The moon cast a glow over trees running along the side of a stream.

When she got out of the car, she studied his house. The front porch light was on. The house was small and decorated with gingerbread. Why on earth had the man painted everything in shades of mauve and purple? Not very manly, but...nice.

Late yellow asters in clay pots led up the steps to the porch. A Halloween pumpkin sat on a wicker table, its carved face dried out and wrinkling, like an oversize apple doll's head. They were feminine touches and yet, the man waiting for her at the front door was anything but effeminate. His big sheepskin coat emphasized broad shoulders and a black cowboy hat shaded his eyes.

She remembered that last night, when he'd covered her with his coat, it had smelled like him, masculine and soapy. Clean.

Boy, he was a sexy man.

"I've got dogs," he said. "A couple of them. They'll be all over you. You okay or do you want me to take them out back?"

"I love dogs."

He opened the door, reached to turn on a hall light and moved aside.

Two dogs ran out, crazy excited to see Cash, until they noticed Shannon. Then they just about turned themselves inside out for her attention.

One was a tall, tanned greyhound, leggy and narrow-chested. The other was a Heinz 57 mutt with wiry gray-black hair and a snub nose. About half the height of the greyhound, he still managed to get his fair share of attention.

Shannon laughed and asked over their barking, "What are their names?"

"Danny and Paddy. Danny's the greyhound."

"A rescue?"

"Yep. When he grew too old to win races, his owners were going to euthanize him."

"Bastards."

"My sentiments exactly."

"How about Paddy? Where'd he come from?"

"The pound."

"They're great. They're so fun and affectionate."

Done with Shannon, they surrounded Cash. Oh, his hands on those dogs… That affection. He stroked Danny's back and the dog loved it, turned around for more.

Cash sank his fingers into Paddy's fur and massaged. Paddy closed his eyes and growled low in his throat, obviously transported to another plane.

Cash loved his dogs.

"Okay," he ordered. "Scoot. Go have a run."

The dogs leapt from the veranda to the clearing, watered a few bushes then took off into the woods.

"They won't get into trouble on their own out there?"

One side of Cash's mouth kicked up. "They were both skunked once. It hasn't happened since. They're fast learners."

"I heard that scent's hard to clean out of dogs."

"Yeah, I used tomato juice. By the time I finished, the bathroom looked like a remake of Psycho. Come on in."

Crazy curious to see how the sheriff lived, Shannon stepped into the house. The interior was as unlikely for the man as the exterior had been—walls painted in bright but tasteful colors, furniture smaller than she would have expected for a man of his size.

She looked at him with a question.

"It came furnished," he said, hanging his coat on a hook by the door.

"Ah. I see. And the colors outside?"

"It came that way."

"And the flowers? The pumpkin?"

"Mine." His hard countenance dared her to comment, to cast aspersions on his masculinity, but how could she while sexual awareness rolled from him in waves?

"It's odd for a man like you to have a house like this."

"A man like me?"

"Single."

"Single men can't buy houses?"

"Yes, but usually as an investment in the future."

"This is an investment."

She cocked her head and studied him. "Yes. I can see that, but not a financial investment. Not out here in the back of nowhere."

She touched a lamp, ran her finger along a side table. It came away clean.

"It's an emotional investment," he said.

His face grew stony. Her curiosity doubled.

"What does this house represent for you?"

"The future."

He didn't say more and didn't look like he would. So if this wasn't financial, if it was emotional, did that mean he bought it for whatever family he might have in the future? Odd. A man with nesting instincts?

He stood in front of her like an immovable enigma. Whatever this meant to him, it ran deeply.

And countered everything she knew about men, contradicted all of her own experience. The men she knew didn't like responsibility, certainly never sought it out or planned for it. At least, not in their personal lives. Dad had never shirked his duties at work. He'd just been useless at home with his family.

Dave Dunlop had turned out to be a good cop.

His personal life, though? She'd heard he already had one divorce under his belt.

"Can I use your washroom?" she asked.

"It's straight down the hall, last door on the left." He stepped ahead of her and reached into a room to flip a switch. The kitchen lit up. By the bright spill into the hallway, she found the bathroom.

Afterward, she stepped back into the hall, but stopped, arrested by the sight of Cash's massive bed in a small bedroom across the way. A faint glow of moonlight illuminated the room.

Okay, this was more like it—a huge bed for a big man—heavy and dark, carved out of oak or some other worthy wood. A dark burgundy duvet covered it and half a dozen pillows lay scattered against the head.

Images of her and Cash flash-mobbed her mind, images of them naked and embraced in passion, those pillows strategically placed for pleasure, that duvet in a dark heap on the floor, she and Cash covered only by moonlight and each other.

She saw his strong back and muscled arms tremble as he held himself above her, the image so puissant, so real, it unnerved her. She didn't do passion. She did controlled sex. She had fun, but always kept the passion under control. Sex was physical. She left the emotion for others.

She remembered the first time she'd seen Cash at Janey's wedding. She'd been only sixteen, but pretty sure of her own mind. She'd wanted him then.

She wanted him now.

She felt his gaze on her. He leaned against the kitchen doorjamb watching her, arms crossed over his chest, his biceps stretching his white dress shirt.

"Need help with anything?" he asked, as though he knew what she'd been thinking as she stared at his bed.

A gold buckle shone on the black belt that held up his dark jeans. She saw herself unbuckling it.

To prove that she was unmoved by these images, that she could meet this man just as she had every other lover in her past, with the control she needed, she stepped forward and rested her hands on his chest.

She rose on tiptoe to reach his lips, to brush hers across his in the cool measured way she preferred.

She could have fun with this man, yes, for sure, but never more.

She licked his lips. When he opened for her, she slipped her tongue inside his mouth, tasting sweet cinnamon.

He stood still while she played with him. Thank

goodness. If he'd responded with too much heat, she might have lost her precious control.

She pulled away and stared at him. His moisture cooled on her lips.

"What game are you playing?" he asked.

"I've liked you since the first time we met at Janey's wedding. I want to go to bed with you."

"No."

She would be offended if she didn't know in her bones that he fought an attraction to her.

"Why not?"

"I got a strong feeling we want two different things in life."

"Like what?" she asked.

"Believe it or not, I want a relationship."

Odd. A man talking about relationships while a woman propositioned him.

"I've rolled around in the hay with enough women. I want kids and a family now."

"I don't."

"Yeah, I figured."

"We can't just have fun together?"

"We'd have fun together, but I want more."

With his talk of taking on responsibility, he was turning things upside down, making a hash of her assumptions of what men were. She didn't know what to make of it.

Shannon shivered. Her independence had been hard-won.

Now this man was talking about taking on responsibility, but *she* knew better. If she became involved with him, she would end up shouldering the burden if anything went wrong. Men didn't handle adversity well. Women did. Would it be her job to make sure their relationship was successful? To keep Cash happy?

She stepped away, putting valuable distance between them. "That biker is probably long gone by now."

"Probably. It's a cold night for a bike. He's given up by now."

"I should head home."

"Unless you're offering more than just a quick tumble, yeah, you should leave."

He walked her out to her car and opened her door, but before she could get in, he wrapped an arm around her back and pulled her against his chest. He kissed her. It was hot and impassioned and, laden as it was with emotion, too much.

When he released her he nudged her gently and she fell into her car.

He swung her legs in then leaned forward. "Now you know where I live, you come around when you're ready for more."

Just before he closed her door, he said, "Let me call in the dogs before you move the car."

Whistling, he walked back to the house, his

white shirt blue in the moonlight. The dogs came running and Cash took them inside with him.

She turned on the engine, swung around in the yard and headed home. Fast.

She asked the empty car, "What the hell just happened?"

CHAPTER SEVEN

ON SUNDAY MORNING, Cash entered Reverend Wright's church and sat in the back row to catch the end of the service.

The Reverend boomed the Lord's message into the quiet hush of the interior. For a thin man, Walter's voice sure packed a punch.

His wife, Gladys, sat in the front row beside her daughter, Amy, her son-in-law, Hank, and her grandchildren.

Many of the town's citizens were here, including Brad McCloskey in the second row with his four children. No Mary Lou today. Strange.

Cash studied his townspeople. He wasn't sure what he expected to see, especially here in church, but it didn't hurt to watch Brad. To watch everyone, and to listen.

There wasn't much that could be kept secret in a small town.

So why hadn't he heard a whisper about methamphetamines in Ordinary before Shannon came to town?

After the last word was spoken, everyone stood

to leave. He watched their faces as they filed down the center aisle, nodding to those who nodded to him. How could he possibly believe that one of these people was capable of manufacturing a drug as addictive as crystal meth? It boggled his mind.

When he'd chosen to live in a small town, he thought there would be fewer temptations for the citizens, fewer opportunities for crime. That the citizens would pull together to take care of their own.

That wasn't to say that he'd had a Pollyanna view. He'd known there would be crime, but thought it would be...smaller...more contained in a place where everyone knew everyone else's business.

That had turned out to be true for the most part, but now there was evidence that a scary drug like meth was not only in Ordinary, but was being manufactured here.

It shook Cash, played havoc with his assumptions. It also spurred him to make sure he found the culprit and wiped drugs out of his town.

Brad walked by with his children. He glanced at Cash and smiled. There was something about that handsome smile that caught Cash's attention, something that hovered on the edge of his mind. He recognized that smile.

Well, of course he did. He'd known Brad since

he'd moved here to work as Deputy ten years ago. Still, something bothered him. But what?

The crowd thinned and Danielle walked down the aisle. She raised one eyebrow and he nodded.

In the light of a new morning, he couldn't believe he'd turned down two willing women in one night. Two incredibly attractive women. His friends would never let him live it down if they knew.

He couldn't believe he'd kissed Shannon that second time at her car when it had been all he could do to resist that first kiss so close to his bedroom and his bed. He'd wanted to make a point, maybe to emphasize his masculinity after she'd questioned him about owning the house.

Or maybe he'd just wanted to kiss her again.

Why had he tempted fate by telling her to come back if she wanted more than just a roll in bed? When she was ready for a relationship?

He wasn't ready for a relationship with *her*.

She was a cop, an *ambitious* cop, and he didn't want that in his life. He had already lived through that with his dad.

Did he harbor some hope that she would give up her career to stay in Ordinary with him? Not likely.

Against all logic and his better judgment, last night he'd just wanted another kiss.

MARY LOU MCCLOSKEY rushed through cleaning up her mess.

By the time she finished, the place looked neat and tidy again. A place for everything and everything in its place.

She locked up her parents' old RV, trapping the scent of the strong chemicals she'd been messing with inside.

She picked up the empty brake cleaner, ammonia and soda bottles around her feet and carried them to the trash pile she'd started in the woods out back. No one would ever see them there.

She threw them on top of empty cold tablet containers, empty iodine jars and old coffee filters.

Her parents would roll over in their graves to see her dump this kind of thing on their beautiful land, but they hadn't thought her responsible enough to take care of it, had they? So, they were getting what they deserved.

She'd been such a good daughter. She should have got this property free and clear.

At the front door of the farmhouse, she took off the lab coat she wore and tossed it onto a chair, then closed and locked the door. She needed to get home before the family did.

Today was the second time she'd used the "I'm not feeling well enough to go to church, you go on without me" excuse.

She prayed her husband had gone straight to the diner for Sunday dinner with the children as usual and hadn't done anything noble like checking up on her at home first. If so, she would have to be inventive about not being at home in bed where she was supposed to have been.

Maybe she should scoot over to the family drug store and pick up a cold medication or painkillers or something. Which particular ailment had she used today? Oh, yes, a headache. Painkillers it was, then.

She still wore the foundation she'd used this morning to make herself pale. She could get away with it. After all, her husband wasn't exactly swift, was he?

This was all his fault anyway. Why did he have to be unfaithful? If he hadn't been, she wouldn't have started down this road.

She planned to divorce him, but not until she had money of her own. Lots of it. She checked her hair in her compact mirror and straightened her skirt and blouse before getting into her car.

No one would guess. She laughed. The poor townsfolk were clueless. They thought she was so sweet. She was. Or had been. She might have remained that way had she not found out about Brad's other child.

In town, she unlocked the pharmacy and took a bottle of painkillers from the shelf. She wrote it up in Brad's book so his records were accurate. There. Alibi covered.

Her driveway was empty when she made it home. Good. Brad hadn't returned. If he had and had found her gone, he would have never gone back out to eat with the children. He would have sat in his armchair and worried about her. She wanted to scream. That worry, his incessant solicitude, smothered her.

She didn't doubt it was real, but how could he have betrayed her and yet remain so seemingly devoted to her? She didn't trust him anymore.

She parked the car with a sigh.

A minute after she stepped into the house and hung up her jacket, someone knocked. Connie Trumball stood on the doorstep.

"You," Mary Lou said, pulling her inside before any of the neighbors saw her. Connie looked like hell. "I was wondering when you'd come sniffing around again. What do you want?"

"I need more stuff," Connie mumbled.

Long before Connie had come around looking for money a month ago, Mary Lou had already guessed there was a potential problem for her in town.

As soon as Connie's son, Austin, became a teenager. How could she not? He had Brad's bright blue eyes, his thatch of straw-colored hair. Brad's mannerisms.

When Connie had come around to blackmail Mary Lou, threatening to tell everyone in town who Austin's father *really* was, Mary Lou had known then that her suspicions had been correct.

Had anyone else noticed? Was it as obvious to them as it had suddenly become to her as the boy grew older and reminded Mary Lou *so* much of Brad as a teenager? Later, when she'd thought about it, she'd realized that she'd spent a good deal of her energy avoiding the boy and her suspicions until she just couldn't anymore, and she'd had to accept that Brad had impregnated Connie while he was engaged to Mary Lou.

A month ago, when Mary Lou had asked, "What do you want?" Connie hadn't been shy in her answer.

"Money."

No way Mary Lou was giving her that. When she left Brad, she would leave as a financially independent woman. She wanted more than half of what Brad had to offer. For the first time in her life, she felt greedy.

Rather than money, Mary Lou had handed Connie something that gave her control over the woman.

"I've got something better than money." Mary Lou had held up a small crystal. "Do you know what this is?"

Connie shook her head.

"Crystal meth." Mary Lou smiled. "Speed."
Connie stared.

"It's yours if you'll go away."

"How do I use it?"

"Smoke it. Shoot it. Stick it up your ass." So vulgar.

She never used to swear. Of course, she'd never before been filled with such rage. "Go look it up on the internet. There are all kinds of things you can do with it." Mary Lou had handed it to her and Connie, being weak, had taken it.

"You won't believe the high," Mary Lou had said.

Mary Lou didn't know from experience. No way would she take a chance on killing brain cells. Her brain was her most valuable asset, even if no one else had figured that out.

And now, today, Connie was back here looking for more.

"Here." Mary Lou handed her a small package. "Next time, don't come to my door."

"You don't want people to see me here," Connie said glumly.

"Of course not," Mary Lou hissed. "We're good people. I don't want the neighbors wondering why I'm socializing with the likes of you."

She glanced through the window beside the door. The street was empty.

"Brad was my boyfriend when you slept with

him," she said with a healthy dose of bitterness. "He was my *fiancé*. Were you trying to steal him from me?"

Connie's bleak gaze slid away and Mary Lou knew it was the truth.

"What on earth did Brad see in you?" she asked.

"I was good at loving him. You never gave him anything."

"I gave him plenty of love."

"Yeah, but no sex."

"I was waiting for marriage. It worked. He didn't marry you, did he, no matter how many times you put out for him?"

"No, he didn't." Connie left the house. A moment later, Austin came out from behind a bush and followed his mom down the street.

How much did the kid know? Was he going to be a problem, too?

Mary Lou hid the rest of her stash and washed her hands.

Her husband was ignorant. Brad didn't know that she'd figured out he'd slept with Connie. With a little luck, if she fed Connie enough meth it would dull her brain so much she'd forget about Brad, and no one in town need ever know that upstanding Brad McCloskey had sired an illegitimate child.

How could the man have slept with that tramp?

So what if it was before they were married? They were dating. Engaged, for God's sake.

The anger that fired her blood felt good. Refreshing.

She walked through her spotless house and sighed—back to her normal life where the most exciting thing that ever happened was a broken nail.

She undressed, climbed into bed and waited for her husband to come home.

Sunday afternoon. By now, he would have dropped the children off to his parents for a couple of hours and he would expect to spend that time here, in bed with her.

She sighed again. He was a nice man, dependable, but so boring. And stupid.

Everyone saw Mary Lou as his sweet little wife, but she was an important person in her own right. These days, she was a businesswoman, and she was making money hand over fist. Even if no one else could ever know, *she* did, and she was the only one who mattered.

When she'd married her husband she had loved him. She'd thought he'd loved her, too, but he'd slept with someone else.

She stared at the ceiling. She'd liked the sex at first, but missionary position became old quickly and Brad was too dull to try anything else.

"I'll bet he did plenty of interesting things with Connie."

What was with Brad? Did he have some kind of Madonna/whore complex? She had certainly played the Madonna well over the years. She was tired of it. Bored senseless. She had a body and mind craving to be used.

Maybe she should have an affair. She closed her eyes and dreamed through local prospects until she'd aroused herself enough to put up with her husband. She heard the front door open and him walking upstairs.

When he appeared in the bedroom doorway, she threw the bedcovers off her naked body and ordered, "Come here."

His eyes widened in his mild-mannered face. She was sick of his tidiness, his gentleness. She wanted more in her life, more stimulation, more money, more control. She meant to take it.

While he approached the bed, he unbuttoned his shirt. She reached for him and unzipped his pants and all but hauled them off of him. When he lay down beside her, he asked, "Feeling better?"

Screw that boring, smothering kindness.

She rose up and straddled him.

"What are you doing?" he asked, and looked almost afraid.

She laughed. "Taking control."

She took him into her body and rode him, setting the pace for her own enjoyment. She'd never known another man. He'd obviously known at least one other woman. *He'd* had experience. *She* wanted more experience from life, to stop settling for what was proper and expected of her. To break out of the role her parents had raised her to take.

This was the twenty-first century, for heaven's sake, not the Dark Ages, when women had no choices, no options available.

Mary Lou thought about her neat, tidy little lab in her parents old RV and smiled. She had options.

Now to take control at home.

She wanted to do naughty, shameful things, starting today. No one else in town need ever know if she turned her husband into the man she wanted him to be—in the bedroom.

In public, he could still be staid. Conservative. Average.

But this room was now hers. If he wanted sex, they were going to do it her way, on her terms.

They did it her way, and then another way, and yet another.

He was late picking up the children.

SHANNON STOOD ON the back porch watching the stable, but nothing moved. She'd gone for her run this morning and had come home to find the horses out and in the corral. Cash had come while she'd been gone.

He'd returned to the ranch an hour ago, had gone into the barn and hadn't come out since.

What was he doing in there all that time? Not that she cared.

She spun away from the window. She was kidding herself. Perversely, she *did* care.

Last night's first kiss with Cash had been...interesting. More than interesting. Warm and fun. He had wanted her, she would swear to that, but had had enough self-restraint to deny her. So, having sex with a woman would be more than a knee-jerk response to a woman's advances. She had to admire that in a man.

But then his kiss at the car...hell's bells, it had been hot, positively scorching. She'd never believed all of that romantic crap about going weak in the knees, but he had done that to her. No other man ever had.

She would have to be careful with Cash.

And yet, he drew her.

She wondered what his reaction to her would be this morning. He had to have been as affected by that kiss as she. How could he not have been?

Her curiosity got the better of her. She made a pot of coffee and rummaged in the cupboards until she found a battered travel mug. She rinsed it, filled it, shrugged into a jacket and stepped outside.

Shannon was a city girl, but had to admit Janey lived on a slice of paradise.

Autumn-brown fields stretched away from the outbuildings. Mauve hills defined the horizon.

In the backyard, sunlight played hide and seek with the remaining leaves on a weeping willow.

C.J. kept his land clean, his buildings and fences painted white.

She approached the stable. Dried leaves crunched underfoot, kicking up the scent of autumn decay.

This was all foreign to her.

Her eyes took a moment to adjust as she stepped into the cool shadows inside the barn. Nothing moved.

At the far end of the aisle, she spotted a pair of long, jean-clad legs crossed at the cowboy boots. She walked toward them. Even though she wasn't trying to be quiet, to sneak up on him, the feet didn't move. When she rounded the last stall to a small desk area, she realized why. The guy was nearly comatose.

Sitting on an old wooden kitchen chair and wrapped in his large sheepskin coat, Cash had his arms across his chest and his cowboy hat pulled forward over his face. A soft snore emanated from inside the hat.

He must be beat. Was policing Ordinary really that exhausting? Really? Nothing happened here.

She placed the coffee on the desk beside him. For a long moment, she stared at him.

They wanted different things in life. Too bad. They could have had so much fun together.

Sometimes the job got to her and all she wanted was to walk away and enjoy life, but it was so much more than just a career. It was her calling.

Because she wanted to lift that cowboy hat from his face and do interesting things with his lips to wake him up, and because that definitely wasn't a good idea, she tiptoed away.

Outside, she stopped at the corral to look at the horses. She breathed deeply. The past week had been a tough one. She wanted this investigation done and over with.

She had nothing on her agenda today and that frustrated her.

She'd already researched as many of the town's residents as she could on the internet and hadn't come up with a whole lot.

They were the normal blend of upstanding citizens, rich, poor and everything in between. There were a couple of people who'd been in a little trouble with the law. Nothing serious.

She'd already called Cole at the biker farm. He was going away for a couple of weeks—to some kind of big biker rally in Wyoming. Yet again her frustration grew. The wheels were turning too slowly.

The good news was that he'd agreed to let her interview him when he got back.

When she realized she was gnawing on her lip and her shoulders were tense, she forced herself to accept the situation.

Relax, girl. As Sam Morgans had said every time he'd tried to convince her to take a vacation, sometimes cops needed to get away and rest. She couldn't remember the last time she'd rested.

Today's rest was enforced.

A big beige horse approached her.

"Hey, girl," Shannon cooed. She patted the horse's nose. Her very, very big nose. What a huge head. Was this girl unusually big, or were all horses so intimidating?

Shannon didn't have a clue.

The horse seemed to like the attention, so Shannon kept it up, talking in a singsong voice that the horse responded to by head-butting Shannon on the shoulder whenever she stopped.

She didn't know what to do with horses, but in the movies she'd seen people brushing them. She went into the stable, found a brush, brought it back out and started on the horse's mane.

"Such a pretty girl," she said. The mane was thick and long and flopped onto one side. Shannon brushed until her arm grew tired, reaching over the fence to groom the entire mane.

After a while, she realized that her shoulders had relaxed, and so had she. This was therapeutic, so she kept it up.

She wanted to go into the enclosure to brush the horse all over, but hesitated. This horse might be friendly, but Shannon wasn't sure what the other horses were like.

"Be right back." She turned to head to the house only to stop short when something pulled her hair.

The horse had her ponytail between his teeth. She giggled. "Okay," she said, "I'll stay."

When the horse relaxed and let go, Shannon jumped away and ran to the house, smiling. Who knew horses were playful?

She gathered a bunch of her hair ribbons and elastics and ran back out to the corral. The horse liked the fussing, so Shannon would fuss to the horse's content.

While she gathered the mane into evenly spaced sections, the animal whickered softly and hummed in her throat. Shannon had no idea whether that was normal.

She wrapped ribbons around the elastics and tied them into bows then tucked the leftover elastics into her jacket pocket.

"Hey!"

The voice startled Shannon and she jumped. The horse neighed.

Cash strode from the stable, his hat firmly on his head and the travel mug in his hand. Even though he'd only just awakened, he looked good enough to eat.

Last night, when she'd kissed him, his body had felt fabulous against to hers, solid and hard. *Get your mind away from that, Shannon.*

"You should step away from my horse," Cash said. "He isn't friendly."

He?

"You shouldn't approach animals you aren't familiar with. You might get hurt."

She was still stuck on the *he* part of Cash's first statement. Oh, no. Oh, wait until he saw what she'd done. She tried not to smile. Tried *really* hard not to laugh.

Despite his flowers and the carved pumpkin, she was fairly certain he wouldn't want his male horse decorated with ribbons.

Glancing at the horse, she noticed that the mane was on the side of the neck facing away from Cash.

"He's plenty friendly with me," she said. "Watch." She made as if to walk away and the horse caught her ponytail in his teeth, not hard enough to hurt but firmly enough to stake a claim.

She grinned. "See? He doesn't want me to stop paying him attention."

"Victor, drop her hair." The horse held on. Cash took one step toward the horse and he let go.

"Thanks for the coffee," Cash said.

"No problem. You shouldn't have been sleeping out in the cold. Why didn't you just go home to nap?"

"I want to take Victor out for a run. He needs exercise."

She turned to leave and Victor grabbed her hair.

"Victor," Cash said in a repressive tone. The horse dropped her ponytail.

As Shannon walked away, he whinnied. She held her breath, waiting for the explosion she was fairly certain was only a minute away.

"Come on, Victor," she heard Cash say, "let's go get you saddled."

A second later, he roared, "What the— *What did you do to my horse?*"

Shannon giggled until her sides hurt as she ran into the house for a jelly donut. She hummed while she bit into it. There was something to be said for taking a day off.

WHILE HE SADDLED Victor, Cash tried to reason with his horse.

"C'mon, buddy, I won't touch the elastics, but let me at least take off the ribbons."

Victor bugled and pulled away.

"Okay. Fine. Have it your way."

Cash walked him out of the stable, mounted and rode across C.J.'s fields while those pretty colored ribbons on his horse mocked his virility.

"Victor," he muttered. "Have you no manly pride?"

Cash couldn't really blame his horse, though. Shannon had looked cute as hell this morning with her hair gathered into a pert ponytail. Her bomber jacket left her bum and hips showcased by skinny jeans tucked into a pair of flat-soled suede boots.

And Cash was a little bit in love with her.

One thing wreaking havoc with his peace of mind was that he wanted Shannon's hands to stay away from his horse…and to reach for him instead. But she didn't want him in the way he wanted her, and anyway, he shouldn't want her the way he did. There was no future there.

Damn!

"Heeyah!" he yelled and Victor set off at a gallop while Cash hoped the speed of the ride and the rushing wind would cool his careless libido.

CHAPTER EIGHT

KNOWING THAT THE Wrights were coming home this evening, Cash returned to the ranch early to put the horses to bed so C.J. wouldn't have to when he got home tired.

He had just finished when he heard a footfall behind him.

"What do you think?" C.J. stood in the doorway of the stable.

Cash laughed and approached. "Hey, buddy, how was your holiday?"

They man-hugged, slapping each other on the back, then separated.

Cash had heard the noisy lot of Wrights return home about ten minutes ago.

"Great vacation," C.J. said, "but I'm glad to be home."

He took turns at each stall saying hello to the horses. It was obvious he'd missed them, even Victor.

"Shannon's been here a few days," C.J. said. "What do you think?"

"Of what?"

C.J. picked up a broom, sweeping up bits of straw in the centre aisle. "Of my pretty sister-in-law?"

Cash clammed up. C.J. was his best friend, but his feelings for Shannon ran too deeply, too quickly. They unnerved him—already—and he barely knew her.

When he didn't respond, C.J. said, "That bad, huh? I always thought the two of you would get something going if you ever spent time together."

"There's nothing going on."

"Ri-i-ight."

"What makes you think there is?"

"Shannon blushed when Janey asked if she'd seen you around the ranch or town."

"She did?" *Really?*

"In the eleven years I've known her, I've never seen her blush. She's fearless. Barely has any use for men outside of working with a bunch of them at the DEA." One of C.J.'s horses nudged his shoulder and he turned to scratch her neck. "Then I come out here and ask you what you think of her and don't get an answer. It's pretty fishy to me."

C.J. grinned. "The girls sent me out to bring you back inside. Shannon made a welcome home dinner and you're invited."

"Yeah? Is she a good cook?"

C.J. blew a raspberry. "In your dreams. She's

even worse than Janey is. Our grand homecoming dinner is canned tomato soup and grilled cheese sandwiches."

Cash followed him to the house and squeezed into a kitchen full of Wrights, including kids who were tired but all keyed-up from traveling. Joyful noise bounced off the walls and ceiling.

Janey barely controlled the bedlam and distributed sandwiches and soup.

And there in the middle of it all was Shannon with a broad smile on her face. Each of the twins had her arms wrapped around Shannon's waist while Ben begged to be picked up.

Seven-year-old Sierra stood watching quietly. Of the whole noisy bunch of Wrights, she was the shy one, and a special favorite of his. She took his hand when he entered the room and held it. She had her father's blond looks and her mother's sharp chin, but with a delicacy that left her looking sweet and vulnerable.

"Hi, Uncle Cash."

"Hey, Sierra. How was Disneyland?"

"Really good. I won a whole bag full of stuff."

"What kind of stuff?"

"Books and dolls and pencil crayons. I gave the baby books to Ben and kept the chapter books for me. The bag has flowers on it and it's reusable."

"No fooling. Sit beside me for supper and tell me about your trip."

Shannon directed the children to the table. "It's time for dinner."

Sarah and Hannah, both jet-haired, ten-year-old versions of their beautiful mother, sat on either side of her.

Sixteen-year-old Liam sat across from her. He was C.J.'s son from a relationship that pre-dated Janey. Janey had been instrumental, though, in helping C.J. get full custody of his son from the boy's drug-addicted mother. Janey loved Liam and treated him every bit as well as she did her own.

Ben cried. "I wanna sit with Shannon."

Shannon laughed. "Come here." She lifted him onto her lap, took a spoonful of soup and blew on it. "We'll share dinner, okay?" She spooned the soup into Ben's mouth.

The woman who Cash thought cared little about having a family sure looked good surrounded by one. In fact, he'd say she was in her element.

She engaged Liam in conversation. Liam seemed like maybe he was infatuated with Shannon.

I know how you feel, buddy.

Cash watched the byplay between Shannon and the children while he ate a grilled cheese sandwich that was barely toasted on one side and burned on the other. The soup was good, though.

Sierra caught him checking out his half-raw, half-burned sandwich and they shared a secret smile. Shannon obviously hadn't really cared much about the cooking once the children had arrived.

So what had happened in her life that had turned her away from having serious relationships with men, that had turned her away from the thought of having children of her own? Just because her mother had died when she was young and her father hadn't really been there for her?

There had to be more to the tale.

He knew only the bare bones of Janey's story—that she'd been raped and impregnated when only fourteen, that she'd kept and adored the child, Cheryl, who'd got cancer when she was five. Cheryl had gone into remission but had then had been struck by a car and killed when she was six—more heartache than one woman should bear.

Whatever went on in Janey's childhood before the rape, though… What had her family been like? Cash didn't really know.

Did he want to know all of Shannon's history? Yeah, despite himself, he did. He was fascinated by her.

That tidbit she'd shared the other day explained a certain amount, but there was more. He was sure of it.

Her laugh caught his attention. For a woman who prided herself on a fierce independence, who could probably arm wrestle a lot of men, and certainly most women, she had a sweet, high-pitched giggle. He'd expected something husky and sexy, not a girlish giggle.

She giggled now and he smiled, couldn't help himself. Her laugh was contagious.

Then she caught him watching her and the ambience shifted, heated up, became serious. He didn't remember another woman affecting him so quickly or so profoundly. Ever.

And the attraction was wrong on so many levels.

He fought it.

After the adults had washed the dinner dishes, Janey and C.J. left to put the children to bed. Liam walked outside to say his own hello to the animals.

"Shannon come upstairs, too!" the twins sang together. Cash watched her leave the kitchen.

He wandered to the living room and listened to the sounds of the children upstairs.

It sounded like Ben was overtired and becoming fractious.

Despite the closed bathroom door, Cash heard one of the kids let loose an echoing fart in the bathtub, which started a serious case of the giggles in a couple of them.

He heard the bathroom door open and close and Sierra say, "Pee-ew. Hannah farted in the bathroom. It's stinky. I can't wash my face in there."

That got those girls giggling even harder and Cash couldn't help but smile.

"Did you brush your teeth, honey?" That was Janey's voice, coming from one of the bedrooms.

"Yes," Sierra replied.

"Good. Don't worry about washing your face tonight. Just get into your pajamas."

He heard dresser drawers opening and closing. "Sierra, take these pajamas in to the twins."

"No way, mom. I can't go back in there. It's probably still smelly from Hannah's fart."

He heard Janey open the bathroom door. "Here are your pj's, girls." She closed the door and laughed. "You're right, Sierra, it is stinky."

So much normal, blissfully happy family activity. It made Cash's heart hurt. He wanted this warmth and noise and mess and camaraderie in his own home.

He'd wanted it desperately while growing up.

He stared through the front window at the fields and hills in the distance. The evening's broody gloaming, with bare tree branches stark against a fading sky, reflected his unsettled emotions. He wanted to be upstairs and he wanted those children to be his.

Impatient with his morose mood, he turned on the room's lamps. They cast wide arcs of warm yellow light.

He stared back at the window, but could no longer see outside. Rather, he saw his own face, full of self-pity, and thought that was even worse.

Ben cried full bore now. Cash wanted to run upstairs and comfort him, to hold him until the child fell asleep on his shoulder.

If he had a family his home would be warm and welcoming, his children would be happy and well-cared for, would never be asked to take on responsibility until they were old enough to handle it. No way would his kids have to take on their parents' care.

He would love the daylights out of them and make sure they knew they were loved.

He jammed his fingers through his hair. Man, he needed to break out of this funk.

So Danielle hadn't worked out, and Shannon was a cop with a successful, big-city career. It wasn't the end of the world. There were still *plenty* of available women out there.

Upstairs, the noise gradually eased to murmured tones. He thought he heard Shannon's rhythmical voice reading a story.

A short while later the adults came back downstairs.

Liam wandered in from the back. He'd grown

tall this summer. The kid was going to be good-looking like his father.

C.J. wrangled a bunch of beers from the fridge and they all sat in the living room.

Without preamble, Janey said, "Tell me about Tom."

"There isn't much to tell," Shannon replied. "I call the hospital every day. He's still in a coma."

She took Janey's hand and squeezed it. "It doesn't look good. I don't think he's going to make it."

Janey grimaced. "I wonder if it's for the better that he's dying. He was half-dead already without his family."

"Maybe," Shannon whispered.

"Tell me about the drugs," C.J. said. "He said he got them here? I can't imagine that."

Cash nodded. "I'm having trouble with that, too."

"When I asked him, he was overdosing," Shannon said, "but he named Ordinary as the source pretty clearly. He knew what he was saying."

She turned to Janey. "Was Tom with you all of the time he visited?"

"No, he couldn't be. I had to run Sweet Talk. He often stayed here with the children and C.J."

"That wasn't easy for him, though." C.J. took a sip of his beer. "He loved the kids, but it pained him to be near them. He asked to borrow the truck one day and was gone for hours. He didn't say where he went."

"What day was that?" Janey asked.

"His last afternoon here."

"Must be when he picked up the drugs." Shannon stood and wandered to the window. "Where did he go, I wonder?"

Cash looked at Liam, who sat quietly on an old piano stool in the corner.

"Have you heard anything around school about crystal meth?" Liam went to high school in Haven. Kids went to elementary and middle school in Ordinary and then had to be bused to Haven for high school.

"Is that what Uncle Tom overdosed on?"

"Yeah."

"I know kids get stuff sometimes. You know, weed. Hash. Even prescription drugs under the table."

"Do you know who they're getting them from?" Shannon asked.

"I think some of it comes from the bikers."

Shannon shot a triumphant glance at Cash, as though to say, *See?*

He shrugged. "I don't know for sure, though," Liam said with a raised hand to forestall Shannon's excitement.

"Do you know whether there's meth at school?" Cash leaned forward in the armchair. If someone was selling the stuff to high school kids, he'd tear them limb from limb.

"No. Do you want me to ask around?"

"Yeah. Can you do it without getting into trouble or getting mixed up with the wrong crowd?" The last thing Cash wanted was to see harm come to a member of this family.

Liam grinned. "Yeah. I can do that."

Cash looked at C.J. "That okay with you?"

"Sure, if Liam can do it safely."

"I can, Dad."

"I'll drive over to the school tomorrow and talk to the principal."

Cash stood to leave. "Shannon, can you walk me out?"

"Sure." She took a coat from the rack beside the front door, turned on the veranda light and stepped outside.

Cash followed her, saying his goodbyes as he went.

"What's your next move with the bikers?" He settled his cowboy hat onto his head and hooked his collar up to cover his neck.

"I'm going to interview the gang leader, Cole, when he gets back from some trip he's on."

"As a reporter? Where?"

"At the farm."

"Interview him in town. At a coffee shop, or something."

Shannon stared at him as if he had a screw loose. "That would defeat the purpose. I need to get on that land, in their house, to look for the lab."

Cash's hackles rose. "That's too dangerous."

"I can handle it."

"Let me come with you."

"No. How would that help? How likely is a reporter to bring a sheriff along with her on a job?"

It wouldn't work. "You're asking for trouble, Shannon. Those aren't little boys playing around."

"I know. I deal with scumbags like them all the time."

"Why?"

She looked puzzled. "It's part of my job."

"I mean, why did you choose this job?"

She turned away from him and wrapped an arm around a veranda post. "I want to help people. I wanted to become a police officer because the cops in Billings never caught Janey's rapist."

"So how did *police officer* morph into *DEA agent?*"

"One of my friends in high school had a lot of trouble with drugs. She got really messed up, almost died, and I decided I wanted to put away drug dealers."

"What about a family?"

"What about it?"

"Why don't you want one?"

"I don't want the burden. I'm dedicated to my career."

Once again, it felt like she was holding out on him. He'd swear on a stack of bibles that she wasn't telling him the full truth.

Yeah, she was serious about her career. He got that message loud and clear. But he'd seen her with the children. She was born to be a mother. There was no reason why a woman couldn't have both a career and a family.

So that left him to wonder why she didn't want a man in her life, a father for those children.

So, would she never have children because she didn't want a serious relationship with a man and would be too busy in her career rising to the top to care for them?

The breeze blew a strand of Shannon's hair over her shoulder. Cash picked it up and twined it around his index finger. It was soft and pliable, sort of like fleeting glimpses he caught of Shannon when she wasn't in her DEA agent über-capable mode.

"Why do you have to do this? Chase Tom's drug dealer? Why can't you wait for the DEA to take care of it?"

"I can't. There are too many people who get caught up in drugs, like Tom did, or like my friend Ruby did. Any drug is bad enough, but meth is viciously addictive."

He dropped her hair and she turned to face him, leaning back against the post.

"I don't know how many people could get hooked on this drug while we're waiting for the DEA to have a couple of agents available one or two months from now. How many will die of an overdose while we wait and do nothing?"

"Okay. Let me ask you this, then. Why do you have to do it alone?"

"I just do, Cash. It's who I am."

"But what shaped you to be who you are?"

She didn't say anything. Just shook her head no.

Cash sighed. He wasn't getting anything else out of her tonight. Time to change the subject.

"Where's your gun?"

"Unloaded and hidden at the back of the top shelf in the closet in my bedroom." She'd understood the question immediately, despite what he'd left unsaid: *So none of the children can get hold of it.* This wasn't the first time he'd had the impression they were on the same wavelength, that they thought in similar ways—maybe because they were both cops and saw the world differently than others did.

"Is there any way you can use your DEA sources to track someone down for me?"

"Of course. I have my laptop here with me."

"Would you mind coming in to the office tomorrow and using mine?"

"Sure. Who are you looking for?"

Cash took his time answering, buttoned his coat, snugged his Stetson more firmly onto his head. Then he said quietly, "My dad."

SHANNON ENTERED THE house. Liam and C.J. were no longer in the living room, just Janey, who sat alone on the sofa flipping through a magazine.

She looked up. "What was that all about?"

"Cash doesn't want me involved in this investigation."

"Well, you are going rogue, aren't you?"

Shannon sat beside Janey then lay down and put her head in Janey's lap.

"Remember when I used to do this after mummy died?" She'd been only six years old and Janey only eleven.

"What's the matter, Shanny-poo?" Janey asked.

Shannon smiled. "You haven't called me that in years."

Janey smoothed hair away from Shannon's face. "You haven't done this in years. What's up?"

"Tom's overdose, I guess."

"And?"

"What do you mean 'and?'"

"Does this blue funk have anything to do with Cash?"

"Maybe. I don't know."

"It sure feels like it does to me." She combed Shannon's hair with her fingers. "Not all men are bad, you know. Not all of them are weak. Look at C.J. and Liam."

"They're exceptions."

"I know Dad was, and still is, incapable of handling stress, but Tom was perfectly normal before he lost his family. You've got such a screwed vision of men because of Dad and because of what happened with Dave Dunlop."

"I know. He turned out to be as unreliable as Dad was."

"He should have been there for you when you got pregnant, but don't forget how young he was."

"Yeah. These days he trips all over himself trying to make it up to me."

"Cash isn't Dad, you know. And he for sure isn't Dave. Cash is one of the good guys."

"I guess." Shannon patted Janey's knee then sat up. "I'm heading up to bed. I'm glad you're home, sis."

ON MONDAY MORNING, Mary Lou drove out to the biker farm. She remembered the first time she'd come out. She'd been terrified, but also luridly curious.

Now these trips were a normal part of doing business.

She wanted to unload her new product as soon

as possible. She didn't like having it in her purse or hidden in the house for very long.

Rogers answered her knock on the door.

"The place is quiet today," she said.

"Everyone's at a biker's rally in Wyoming."

"Why aren't you there, too?"

"Someone needs to watch the place while it's empty." He looked her up and down, taking his time. He'd never done that before. It gave her the creeps.

He scratched his belly idly and said, "You want to hang out for a while?"

She'd liked the spicier sex with her husband yesterday, but she wasn't so eager to experiment that she would lie with another man.

Certainly not a bike gang member.

Especially not this one.

"Can't. I have to pick up my boys for lunch." She pulled the meth out of her purse. "Here's the latest batch, right on time as usual."

"I'll get the money."

He took the drugs into a back room and returned with cash. She counted it before she left.

"Thanks," she said, and dropped it into her purse. "See you next Monday."

As good as her word, Shannon came to the Sheriff's Office right at ten.

"Good morning," she said, as bright and frisky as a puppy.

Cash was sitting at the desk, getting a head start on the research. "Hey, thanks for coming in. I appreciate it."

"No problem." She hung her coat on the rack he indicated then sat on the other side of the desk. She checked out his office, her face carefully neutral, leaving him to wonder what the big city DEA agent thought of it.

Too small, he guessed. Not enough technology, either. And yet, it suited Cash just fine. There were times when old-fashioned footwork was the best police work.

"Do you mind telling me what the problem is with your dad?" Shannon asked. "Is he lost? In trouble?"

"He's dying. I want to see him before that happens. I need to know that he's okay, that he isn't living somewhere in poverty."

"Okay, let's get to work."

She pulled her chair around to his side of the desk, sat beside him and logged into government databases.

In her line of work, she probably had to deal with this stuff all the time.

She smelled like vanilla again, like down-home goodness. It had him imagining sugar cookies sitting on her erogenous zones and him munching each one. Slowly.

He had an intense image of sprinkling sugar

all over her body and licking it off. The thought shot right to his groin.

Cripes, Kavenagh, get a grip. You're not a teenager.

He knocked a pen off the desk, intentionally so he would have to bend over to pick it up, to give himself a minute to pull himself together.

With a real effort, he concentrated on the information Shannon brought up.

"It seems that your father has no fixed address." She turned to him, her face only inches from his own. This close her eyes were alive with intelligence. "Could he be staying with a friend?"

"Knowing Dad, probably a girlfriend. He used to work in the Tenderloin district of San Francisco, but after he went bankrupt and lost everything, he ended up living there, with all the crooks and prostitutes he used to arrest. It couldn't have been easy for him."

"You said he's dying. Of what?"

"Cirrhosis of the liver."

"So, he's visited a doctor or a hospital. He's been tested and diagnosed. If he went bankrupt and lives in the Tenderloin district, he probably wouldn't have health insurance."

"Probably not. He's called asking for money over the years, so I know he isn't often flush."

"Did you send him money?"

"Of course."

"When was the last time?"

"About a year ago."

"Where did you send it?"

"To a Western Union office in San Francisco."

"Let's begin there and look for a medical trail in San Francisco. If he's that sick, chances are he's going to stick to an area he's comfortable in."

The door burst open and Scotty ran in wearing his hardware store apron.

"You gotta come, Cash." The scent of the cherry cough drops he favored drifted from him. "That kid of yours is causing trouble at the pharmacy."

"My kid?"

"Austin."

Austin? Lord, what was it now? Cash jumped out of his chair. "Gotta go." He ran out the door and down Main to McCloskey's Pharmacy.

He could feel Shannon hot on his heels when he entered the store. Brad had a hand wrapped around one of Austin's biceps and a large bottle of multivitamins in the other. Austin looked like he was fighting tears.

"What's going on, Brad?"

"I caught Austin trying to shoplift."

"I wasn't shoplifting!" Austin cried. His gaze shot to Cash. "I been trying to tell him but he won't listen. My mom told me his wife said she could get stuff here without paying."

When Austin noticed Shannon standing behind Cash, his face turned bright red. and tears threatened. The boy had to be incredibly embarrassed.

"It's a lie." Brad shook the boy. "My wife wouldn't tell your mother she could have things for free. That's ridiculous. I'm having you charged. I need to make a lesson of you. You kids can't come in here and steal."

Austin turned to Cash. "I wasn't stealing! You gotta believe me, Cash."

Cash knew Austin was thinking of those consequences he'd listed on Friday morning when he'd kept Austin out of school and had thrown him into jail to teach him a lesson.

Speaking of school… "Why aren't you in school this morning?"

"My mom's really sick."

"I don't care," Brad said. "She has to pay like everyone else."

"I wasn't st—"

Cash raised a hand. "Stop, both of you."

He looked at Brad. "Call your wife. Ask her whether she's been talking to Connie."

Brad looked like he didn't trust Austin not to run if he let go of him.

"I'll watch him," Cash said.

When Brad left to make his call on the Pharmacy floor, Cash asked Austin, "What's going on? The truth, Austin."

"I'm already telling the truth. Mrs. McCloskey said my mom didn't have to pay for stuff from here if she got sick. She's got a cold."

"That seems unlikely."

When Austin looked like he might yell, Cash said, "I believe your mom told you that. I just think she might have misunderstood something Mary Lou said."

Brad returned. "She's coming right over."

"Do you want me to call Connie and get her here, too?"

"No." Brad looked uncomfortable. Why? Why wouldn't he want Connie here to prove Austin wasn't lying?

"I want my mom," Austin said, obviously needing to prove his innocence.

Cash took out his cell and dialed Connie's number.

When Connie answered, Cash told her what was happening and she said she'd come right over.

Austin shot Brad a triumphant look and it was Brad's turn to go red. What the hell was going on?

A small crowd had gathered at the cash register to watch.

"Let's head over to the office. Brad, Lexie's on cash. I assume you can leave for a few minutes."

Brad nodded and told Lexie to send both Mary

Lou and Connie to the Sheriff's office when they arrived.

They filed out the door and again Shannon shadowed Cash. In his office, she picked up some of the info she'd printed out and said, "I should leave."

"No!" Austin shouted, his pride clearly hurt. "I want you to see I wasn't shoplifting."

Shannon looked at Cash and he nodded. She stayed, moving to stand in a corner.

Connie showed up first. Austin was right. She was sick. She looked bad. Tired. Her face was thin. In fact, when Cash thought about it, in the past month, she'd been looking worse and worse. What was wrong? Last thing Austin needed was to lose his one surviving parent.

"What's going on?" Connie asked.

Cash explained what had happened. "Did Mary Lou McCloskey tell you to pick things up from the pharmacy for free?"

"If I was sick, she said they could help me out."

"When would you have seen my wife to ask her that, Connie?" Given the trivial nature of the crime, Brad seemed too agitated and kept putting distance between himself and Connie.

"I seen her in town one day."

The door opened and Mary Lou stepped in. The difference between her and Connie was astounding. Mary Lou looked fresh while Connie looked haggard.

A pretty frown furrowed her brow. "What's happening?"

Brad explained and Mary Lou shot a quick glance at Connie. For a split second, Cash thought he saw a glint of calculation in Connie's eyes before they deadened to a vacancy that had started recently. Cash worried about depression. It made people do crazy things.

"Ye-e-es," Mary Lou said. "I did say that we could help Connie out if she was ill." She placed her hand on Brad's arm and whispered loudly enough for everyone to hear, "She doesn't have money."

"I know, but we can't afford to—"

Mary Lou cut him off. "Please, Brad, for me. Let's just forget about this and go home."

Brad glanced at his watch. "It's only eleven o'clock in the morning. I can't leave work."

"There's something I need to discuss with you. I'll make us some lunch."

Brad's manner softened and he smiled down at Mary Lou. "Okay, honey."

Shannon stepped forward. "You're cleared, Austin. You were telling the truth. Isn't that great?"

Austin smiled at Shannon, that sweet little smile he'd given her the first time he met her, and Cash felt like he'd been knocked over by a two-by-four.

Austin and Brad stood beside each other, and Austin's smile was a perfect match for the one Brad was giving his wife. A *perfect* match.

CHAPTER NINE

AUSTIN CAUGHT CASH looking from one to the other. As always when he was embarrassed, he hunched his shoulders up to his ears.

Mary Lou led her husband out of the office. As she passed Connie, she said, "The next time you need something from the pharmacy, call me and I'll pick it up for you."

If her voice sounded a little tense, Cash thought he understood why.

He reassured Connie there would be no charges pressed against Austin and herded her out the door.

"I'll drive Austin to school."

He closed the door behind Connie and turned back to Austin, who was talking quietly with Shannon.

"Shannon?" Cash said.

When she looked up, he asked, "Did you see that?"

"Yep. It was pretty obvious."

"I guess I've been too close to the situation for too long."

"Do you want me to leave?"

"I think that would be best."

On her way out, Shannon squeezed Austin's shoulder. The action said so much about her, about her depth of compassion.

She dealt with drug-dealing scumbags regularly, but was managing to hold on to her humanity.

"Austin, sit," Cash said and walked around the desk to his office chair.

He put his elbows on the armrests and tapped his fingers together. "When did you find out?"

Austin wouldn't look at Cash. "Find out what?"

"That Brad McCloskey is your father."

Austin mumbled something.

"What was that?" Cash leaned forward.

"I said, about a month ago."

Just when the trouble started with Austin.

"How did you find out?"

"I found my birth certificate."

"Did you question your mom about it?"

Austin picked at a hole in the knee of his jeans, enlarging it with his index finger. "Yeah. She said it was true. She said Brad wanted to marry Mary Lou instead of her, though, so she had to marry my dad. I mean—"

"I know who you mean. How do you feel about that?"

Man, it was a doozy of a thing to find out that

the man you had thought was your father wasn't. No wonder Austin had been acting out. It had to hurt like hell.

"It doesn't matter," Austin said, but Cash knew that it did. It mattered a lot.

"Did Mary Lou really tell your mom she could get stuff for free?"

"I don't know for sure. I just know that my mom visits her and comes home with medicine."

So Mary Lou was sneaking medication out of the pharmacy and giving it to Connie. Good of her to help her out, considering what she must know. If Cash noticed the similarity and Shannon noticed it, surely Mary Lou had seen it.

So when had she found out? And why was she friendly with Connie? Or was something else going on? Was she really that charitable, or was Connie blackmailing her for prescription drugs?

"Do you know what's wrong with your mom? She doesn't look good."

"She won't tell me. Just said she isn't dying so quit worrying."

Cash stood. "Okay, let's get you over to school. Did you have breakfast this morning?"

"I had some toast."

Probably white bread with cheap margarine. That wouldn't last until dinnertime.

"Let's get a couple of burgers from the diner and I'll take you to school after lunch."

"'Kay."

They stepped out of the cop shop and Cash locked up, all the while wondering exactly what kind of man Brad was.

Cash needed to ask around. How long had the McCloskeys been married? Before or after Brad had slept with Connie? Was Brad really the solid citizen Cash believed him to be? How long had he known that Austin was his son? *Did* he know? Was that why he'd been uncomfortable about getting both Connie and his wife in the same room together? Was there someone driven, someone deeply self-interested, hidden under that mild-mannered exterior?

This new information adjusted his opinion of Brad. Could the man be someone to watch, to suspect of dealing drugs?

Most importantly to Cash, how would knowing that Austin had a father who was alive and well affect Cash's relationship with his Little Brother?

It doesn't, he thought. Doesn't affect it at all.

Just before stepping into the diner, he squeezed Austin's shoulder.

MARY LOU DRAGGED Brad into the house, angry enough to scream. When he'd called her, she'd had to speed back from the bikers' farm.

People were starting to notice the likeness between Brad and that boy. Certainly everyone at the police station had noticed it.

Why had it taken her so long to see it?

Because you hadn't wanted to.

She slammed the door, threw her purse onto the floor and yelled, "How could you do that?"

Brad's eyes widened. He stared at her purse. It had opened and cosmetics and her wallet spilled onto the floor. He bent to pick them up, but she stopped him.

"Leave it," she ordered. This taking-control business felt good. Cleansing.

"Why did you sleep with Connie before we got married?"

Brad opened and closed his mouth, then asked, "How did you know?"

"It's written all over that boy's face."

"What?"

"That boy," Mary Lou screamed. "He's yours, isn't he?"

"I don't know. Connie told me she was pregnant, but I didn't believe I was the father."

"Why not?"

"I didn't think I was the only one she was sleeping with."

"Trust me," she said bitterly. "He's yours."

"Are you sure? I always wondered. Connie tried to get money from me a few years ago, but I told her no because I couldn't be sure he was mine. He is for sure, though?" Wonder filled Brad's voice. "Really?"

"Don't even *think* about bringing him home with you. I couldn't stand the disgrace."

Mary Lou felt tears on her cheeks and swiped them away with the backs of her hands. She hated being vulnerable.

"Why did you sleep with her when you were engaged to me?"

"I didn't know what I was doing."

"Give me a break. You knew full well you were betraying me."

"No, I mean I didn't know what to do in bed. I was a virgin. I was embarrassed about it. I needed to know what to do on our wedding night and Connie was easy. She wanted to sleep with me and I knew I could learn everything from her."

Brad splayed his hands out in from of him, as though beseeching her. "It was only a couple of times and then I stopped. I loved you and wanted to marry you. I still love you, honey. More than anything on this earth."

Mary Lou didn't know what to think of that. She was so angry, she needed to release it somehow. She looked around the living room, not sure what she wanted. And then she thought of it. She knew what would make her feel better, what had been exciting her lately. What pleased her more than it had in a long, long time.

She watched her husband while she slowly lifted her skirt. She slid off her panty hose and panties and stepped out of them.

She saw that flash of interest in Brad, that anticipation he'd begun to show when they went to bed at night.

"The children?"

"Pizza day at school," she said, suddenly breathless. "They won't be home until four."

Mary Lou wanted to try something new, and she needed to do it now, not wait until tonight.

She should tell him to kneel on the floor in front of her and do it right here in the living room. She couldn't, though. Her parents had raised her to be a good girl too well.

If she took Brad to their bedroom, closed the curtains and whispered to him what she wanted, he would do it. She was sure of it.

Mary Lou took his hand and led him upstairs.

They fell onto the bed together, where Mary Lou whispered in his ear, asking for what she wanted.

He pulled back and stared at her, shocked, but a sweet smile spread across his face and he said, "Yes," then did it.

It was sinful.

It was wonderful.

CASH DIDN'T MAKE it out to the high school in Haven until Tuesday afternoon, shortly after two.

All of the students either drove here or took a school bus. They represented a wide portion of the county's population and he hoped that one of them had heard something about meth in the area.

He passed Liam Wright in the hallway just before he ducked into a classroom for his next class.

Cash stepped into the school office. The secretary nodded and told him to go on into the principal's private office.

Harris Newcombe looked up when Cash entered. "Sheriff, it's good to see you."

They shook hands.

"What's up?" Harris asked.

"I've heard a rumor there's meth somewhere in the county. Have you heard or seen anything at the school? Kids are usually the first to find this kind of stuff."

"True. I haven't heard about meth specifically. I can call some students to the office, if you like."

"Who are they?"

"If anyone in this school knows about the drugs it will be one of these three. They've all been caught and charged with possession in the past."

"Any cell time?"

"No. They got off with warnings. There's been nothing since then, but that was only four or five months ago."

He got up to speak to his secretary. "Marjorie,

call Steve Brett, Rod Crew and Tony Bayer to the office."

"Sure."

They arrived five minutes later and none of them looked happy about being called to the office. Nor did they look like drug dealers or addicts, more like ranchers' sons or budding rodeo stars.

"This is Sheriff Kavenagh from Ordinary," Principal Newcombe said. "He needs to talk to you boys about drugs in the area."

Almost as one, they groaned.

"We don't *do* drugs," Steve said, clearly frustrated. "It was only that one party."

"Where did you get the marijuana you were smoking?"

"From a guy we'd never seen before, but he was a friend of one of the bikers over in Monroe."

"Have you heard of anything else coming from the bikers lately?" Cash asked. "Or anywhere else locally?"

"Like what?" Rod asked.

"Like meth?"

"I've heard there's a lot of it in Montana, but I've never seen it here in Haven."

"Have you heard of it anywhere in the county at all?"

They shook their heads. Cash pulled three business cards out his wallet.

"Here's my number. Call if you get the slightest sense that it's here. The stuff's deadly. There's already been one overdose. I don't want to see any of you involved in it."

Cash stopped in to see Mike Gage in Monroe. Same thing there. Yes, Mike had heard about meth in Montana. No, he'd heard nothing about it in their area. Yes, he would keep his eyes and ears open and would instruct his staff to do the same. Somehow, the county had managed to dodge the meth bullet. Until now.

On Wednesday, Cash exited the grocery store with bags piled high. He filled the bed of his truck with the food.

"Hey," he heard behind him.

Janey and Shannon were walking from the candy shop.

"Where are you two off to?" he asked.

"I'm taking Janey out to lunch," Shannon answered.

"Are you stocking up for tomorrow?" Janey peered into the bags in the truck.

"Yep. The grocery store was a madhouse."

"What's tomorrow?" Shannon asked.

Both Janey and Cash looked at her strangely. "Thanksgiving."

"I totally forgot!"

"It's at Cash's place," Janey said.

"Will you come?" Cash made sure to keep his expression neutral, but he wanted her there.

"The whole family is going." Janey brushed strands of black hair away from her face. "You'll be home alone if you don't come."

"Okay." Shannon grinned. "What should I bring?"

He shrugged. "I've got all the food. How about a bottle of wine?"

He had a sudden thought. "How would you feel about stopping in Ordinary to pick up Austin and his mother, Connie?"

Cash knew that unless he invited them to dinner tomorrow, Austin would have no Thanksgiving celebration and that would be wrong.

"Sure," Shannon said. "No problem."

"You remember where he lives?"

She nodded. "Do you need any help with the cooking?"

"No!" both Janey and Cash shouted.

Shannon frowned. "Oh-kay."

Janey took her elbow, grinned at Cash behind her back and steered her toward the diner. He mimed wiping his brow at the close call, then drove home to brine the turkey.

At two o'clock on Thursday afternoon, the Wrights invaded Cash's small home. He'd pushed all of the living room furniture against the walls and had moved everything else he could into the two postage-stamp bedrooms.

He'd set up a long folding table and folding chairs in the middle of the living room and had decorated it with Thanksgiving-themed paper tablecloths and napkins.

When he heard the Wrights drive up, he opened the front door and stepped out onto the veranda, forcing the dogs to stay inside until the cars stopped moving.

The weather had warmed—slightly—and the sun shone. A light breeze blew golden yellow leaves from the big old cottonwood beside the stream and the poplars lining the drive.

The Wrights arrived in Janey's minivan. Behind them Shannon drove up in her Fiesta, with Sierra Wright beside her in the passenger seat, and Connie and Austin in the backseat.

To Connie's credit, she'd tried to spruce up a bit in a dress and cheap high heels, but her skin was still sallow and her face lined.

Shannon looked like a model in a red dress and black heels. She and Sierra walked toward the house with their arms around each other and Cash was struck again by how good she was with children, how natural.

She caught him watching her and smiled. Something passed between them that he couldn't quite name, but that felt like harmony, maybe, or understanding. By the slight frown that appeared on her forehead, she felt it, too. She bent low to talk to Sierra, firmly ending the moment.

When she neared, she handed him a white box from the bakery in Haven. Unless he missed his guess, she'd brought doughnuts.

"Okay, everyone," he said, "sit down while I let the dogs out. I don't want anyone getting knocked down."

The crowd sat on the steps or on the few chairs Cash had on the veranda. Janey put Ben on her lap.

Danny and Paddy ran out of the house, insane with excitement, sniffing everyone and moving from one to the other so frenetically that they didn't get the attention they craved.

Danny stood in front of Janey, sniffed Ben's mouth then licked his face.

"Eeew, Mommy, he made my face wet."

"What did you have for breakfast, Ben?" Cash asked.

"Toast and peanut butter."

"That explains it. That's Danny's favorite food."

Paddy curled up against Austin where he sat on the bottom step. Cash couldn't see the boy's face, but his hand curled over the dog's head and Cash made a pretty good guess that Austin was happy.

Cash took the doughnuts inside and Shannon

followed him in with four bottles of wine in a cotton bag.

"I brought a couple each of white and red."

"Great. Thanks. Would you mind finding out what everyone wants?"

"Sure."

Cash got wine glasses out of a cupboard. He owned only cheap ones he'd picked up a few weeks ago, but they would work.

Shannon came back with a bag of juice and canned pop. "This is from C.J. and Janey."

"There are plastic cups for the children on the table."

Why did this seem so natural, doing these mundane chores with Shannon as though she belonged here with him?

Whoa. Whoa. Whoa. Slow down those insane thoughts. You've got some kind of witchy connection to this woman, but she's not for you and you know it.

Shannon slowed her actions and became quiet. She stopped filling the cups with pop and juice and looked up at him.

"What's wrong?" he asked.

"This." She gestured between the two of them. "It feels too good being together, working together. What's— what's happening between us?"

"I was just trying to figure that out. There sure is something going on"

"It's not right. We're not right for each other."

"Then why are we both having the same thought at the same time?"

She shook her head. "I don't know."

She pulled herself together and made an effort to sound natural. "Do you have any trays for carrying these drinks outside?"

He opened a bottom cupboard and pulled out a couple of cookie sheets. "Only the best for my guests."

Shannon smiled, but it looked sad. She put a bunch of the children's drinks on one cookie sheet and Cash loaded the adults' drinks onto another.

Before they left the kitchen, he said, "Come back inside for a minute after you hand those out."

She frowned. "Okay."

When they both re-entered the kitchen, she said, "There's nothing more to say."

"I know. I want to talk about the meth."

She perked up. "You found out something?"

"No. It's just an update."

Cash opened the oven and checked the turkey.

"How come you know how to cook stuff like this?" she asked.

"When I was a kid, my dad was gone a lot and my mom wasn't real...strong. If I hadn't made an effort on the holidays we would have never celebrated them."

He closed the oven door and leaned back against the counter. "I checked out the high school in Haven yesterday. No one's heard anything about meth. They had three kids arrested a few months ago for possession of marijuana they'd gotten from one of the bikers."

"Doesn't necessarily mean there's meth there just because there's marijuana. This is so frustrating."

"This is police work—investigating until something sparks."

"I know. I'm tired of how slow the process is. I'm tired of waiting for this to be resolved."

"I hear you." He placed a hand on her shoulder and squeezed. There was nothing sexual in the action, only commiseration.

Austin ran into the kitchen. "Hey, there's a football game out front. You guys should come."

Cash smiled. "You're right. Let's go."

The two of them followed Austin outside. Shannon kicked off her high heels on the veranda.

"You're gonna play in that dress?"

"Sure. Why not?"

Cash shrugged. Shannon didn't behave like the females he knew.

"Touch or tackle?" she asked.

C.J. held Ben in one arm and the football in the other. "Touch. The kids are playing and the women are wearing dresses."

He tossed the ball to Cash and a formless, no-rules game followed. Cash wasn't even sure who was on whose team. At one point, when he tried to throw to Austin, Shannon jumped to take the ball from him. He wrapped an arm around her waist and lifted her off her feet.

She threw her head back and giggled, her ponytail streaming over her shoulder.

She looked like heaven on earth, and holding her felt like the thrill of victory.

"You laugh like a girl," he said.

"That's because I am a girl." She panted, still trying to get that ball that was just out of her reach.

"You're so sexy, I thought you'd have this low husky Kathleen Turner laugh."

"You think I'm sexy?" Her eyes were wide and green, framed by lashes darkened with mascara, and for a minute he couldn't breathe.

"Hey, throw the ball, Cash," Austin called, breaking the spell.

Cash tried, but Shannon managed to snag it before it got any real air.

"Put me down," she squealed, gripping the ball. Cash dropped her and instantly missed her warmth against his hip. She nearly toppled over, righted herself and ran to the far end of the front yard for a touchdown.

Her dress was tight and her firm behind did interesting, wonderful things when she ran.

AFTER DINNER, CASH carried a couple of plates to the kitchen and stopped dead on the threshold.

Shannon stood at the counter eating a jelly donut and staring out the window.

He must have made a sound because she looked his way. "It's beautiful here. You have a great piece of land."

He would have answered her if his mouth hadn't gone dry. Powdered sugar coated her upper lip and bright red jam sat at the corner of her mouth.

He carefully set the plates on the counter and approached her. She stared at him, puzzled at first, but then her eyes widened when she realized his intention.

He leaned toward her, slowly, to give her time to pull away. She didn't.

He touched his tongue to her upper lip.

"Sweet," he whispered.

He licked again, cleaning off the rest of the sugar, getting down to her skin, and she sighed. Her breath smelled sweet and warmed his chin.

Moving to the corner of her mouth, he scooped

up jam with the tip of his tongue, swallowed it
and then kissed her.

She parted her lips and Cash slipped inside.
She tasted better than the last time he'd kissed
her, after she'd left the bar and ended up at his
house.

That night she'd smelled of cigarette smoke.
Tonight, she smelled like vanilla and tasted like
sugar cookies, and he remembered thinking
about nibbling cookies from each of her erogenous zones.

This kiss… This was somewhere between that
cool, analytical one she'd given him after staring
at his bed the other night—making some kind of
point he hadn't been able to decipher—and the
passion-laden one he'd given her before sending
her home in her car—that had left him lying in
his big bed alone thinking about her for hours.

This kiss… Was perfection. Pure and simple.

The silk of her mouth cradled his tongue. He
wrapped his arm across her back and pulled her
close, flush with his own body.

His hand slipped to her breast and it filled his
palm perfectly. She moaned, softly, and he swallowed it, thought about taking her to his bed and
sprinkling icing sugar all over her body and licking it off, but that was an X-rated daydream and
this was a G-rated family celebration. He was

pushing his luck. One of the children could walk in at any moment.

He nibbled his way toward her ear and whispered, "You sure you don't want to live here with me and make babies?"

Shannon laughed and stepped away from him. She took a big bite from the leftover half of the donut now mangled in her hand. She shook her head.

"Darn," he joked. "No harm in asking." But his body and psyche weren't laughing. He wanted this woman.

A commotion in the living room caught their attention. Austin yelled, "Mom!" with panic in his voice.

Cash ran out of the kitchen.

In the living room, the crowd was gathered around someone lying on the floor.

"What happened?"

"My mom fell down." Austin sounded on the verge of tears.

Cash squeezed his shoulder. "Don't worry. There are a lot of us here to help her."

C.J. lifted Connie to her feet. "How do you feel?"

"Okay," she replied. "I just got real light-headed when I stood up." C.J. walked her over to an armchair.

"Connie," Cash said, squatting in front of her.

"Have you considered seeing a doctor and having a checkup?"

She waved a hand. "I'm fine. Really. I'll be good in a minute once I catch my breath."

Cash looked over his shoulder. Shannon stood in the hall doorway. "Can you put on the kettle? Make her some tea, okay?"

"You got it." She hurried back to the kitchen.

"Hey," Cash said to Austin to distract him and wipe the worried frown from his face. "Go help Shannon bring in the dessert. Ask her to start a pot of coffee."

Austin hesitated for a second, glanced at his mom to make sure she was okay and only then left the room.

"Make sure she doesn't finish off the doughnuts," Cash called. "I caught her filching one a minute ago."

"What's filching?" one of the twins asked. He thought it might be Hannah. Or was it Sarah?

"Stealing. Sneaking a donut while no one was watching. Go protect them or there won't be any left for the rest of us."

Hannah and Sarah squealed and ran for the kitchen. Ben followed on shorter legs.

Sierra had tucked herself into an armchair in the corner and was reading a chapter book she'd brought with her. Paddy was curled up beside her with his head in her lap.

Nothing would break her concentration now, no matter what happened in the room.

He caught C.J.'s eye and they smiled.

Man, he loved these people. His family.

CHAPTER TEN

THE CALL CAME at 9:17 on Friday morning, while Cash sat at his desk reading the latest updates to the State's Policics and Procedures Manual for Police Officers.

He answered the phone with only half of his attention. "Sheriff Kavenagh."

"Is this *Cash* Kavenagh?" The woman's voice was husky and smoke-ravaged.

Cash's focus immediately sharpened. "Yes."

"Your father is dead."

He didn't understand the words at first. He'd only just seen him two weeks ago. He hadn't found him yet.

He still had to help him get decent medical care, had to keep him alive longer.

On the tail end of that nonsensical thought, the news sank in. He wasn't going to find him. Dad was gone.

"When?" he asked, wondering why this woman had been so blunt, why she couldn't have softened the news.

"This morning at eight. He asked me to notify you when it happened."

Cash noticed what he hadn't at the beginning. Whoever this woman was, she was emotionally affected by his father's passing. She was blunt because she was holding herself in. He wasn't sure how he knew, but he'd swear it was so.

"What did he want in the way of a funeral?"

"He wants to be cremated. There will be two visitations. Tonight and tomorrow afternoon. He wanted you there."

"I'll be there."

She gave him the details.

Cash hung up with the intention of making plane reservations. First, though, he just sat, trying to absorb the implications. He'd had precious little to do with Frank for the past twenty years, but somewhere in the back of his mind, he'd known that his dad was still on earth.

He'd had no idea Dad would be gone so quickly. So crazy fast.

Dad was dead. He knew it was going to really hurt at some point, but at the moment, he felt hollow.

As though watching himself in a movie, he turned on his computer and made plane and hotel reservations online.

He called Wade Hanlon and told him he'd be away until at least Monday. Hanlon would have to come in on days and then be on call in the evenings.

He called Timm Franck next to ask him to keep an eye on Main Street—easy enough to do from his newspaper office—when Wade was called out to Sassy's, as he surely would be.

He called Police Chief Mike Gage to warn him that he wouldn't be available and that Deputy Hanlon might need help if anything happened in Ordinary. Cash had helped out Mike so many Saturday nights at Sassy's, he figured Mike owed him.

He knew he needed to call his mom, but not yet. Not quite yet.

After Wade arrived to take over, Cash went home and packed, then sat on the sofa and stared at the cold fireplace.

He couldn't put it off any longer. He dialed his mother's number.

"Mom," he said when she answered, because he couldn't get out anything else.

"He's gone?" Her voice sounded flat. Probably matched his own.

"Yes."

He heard a small sigh on the other end of the line.

"Are you attending his funeral?" she asked.

"Yes. I have to leave soon."

"That's good, Cash. It's the right thing to do."

"Will you be going? It's in San Francisco."

"No." Her voice cracked, confirming what Cash had suspected all along—that she'd never stopped loving her first husband, despite him being the rat that he was.

You shouldn't speak ill of the dead.

I wasn't. I was just telling the truth.

Before driving out of Ordinary to catch his flight to San Francisco, he stopped at C.J.'s ranch.

The yard was empty. The children were out playing somewhere and C.J. would have Ben in the stable with him, no doubt.

Cash walked along the side of the house toward the back, but a movement in a window caught his attention. Shannon—probably checking to see who had arrived.

They stared at each other and need filled him. A need for her.

She must have seen something in his expression because her smile faded and she left the window. A second later she burst out of the back door.

"What's wrong?" She jumped down the steps and raced toward him. "What's happened?"

"It's my dad."

She knew right away. "Cash, I'm so sorry."

"I—" He had this irrational desire to hold her,

to drink in her vitality. To hold on to life and people with both hands because it could all be gone so quickly.

SHANNON STARED AT Cash, wishing this bad news hadn't come today, that there wasn't this big dark thing suddenly between them. She wanted yesterday's fun carefree ease back.

She wanted to hold on to that illusion of him as a strong man, a man who needed no one. Certainly not her.

Don't fall apart on me, Cash. I'm tired of taking care of men.

When she said no more, he nodded and walked away toward the stable, a wisp of disappointment painting his features.

There was nothing she could do about that.

He needed comfort, but she just wasn't the right woman to give it to him.

He turned back to her. "Can you do me a favor?"

No. She didn't want him to need anything from her. "Sure."

"How would you feel about taking Austin to the movies tonight?"

Yes, that she could do. "No problem. He's a great kid. I can do that."

"Actually, two favors. I was going to ask C.J., but I know he gets busy here."

She stiffened, wary. "What is it?"

"Can you see to my dogs? Go to my house twice a day?"

The dogs. Yes. She could handle them.

"Okay."

She could take care of Austin. She could take care of the dogs. She just didn't want a man depending on her.

"You can stay at the house if you want," he said. "There's food in the freezer. There are leftovers from yesterday. There's milk that will go bad if no one uses it."

She nodded. "I might do that. Janey might like the extra space for a few days. If I don't, I'll at least go out twice a day to mind the dogs."

"Thanks, I appreciate it." He strode toward the barn, no doubt to get the support from his best friend that he hadn't got from her.

CASH DROVE TO Havre and took Gulfstream to Billings where he caught a flight to Denver and from there to San Francisco, all the way on autopilot. His mind was stuck on his father.

They'd had no relationship for years, and then the man had shown up to tell Cash he loved him. Now he was gone. Too suddenly. He hadn't left Cash time to prepare.

Once in San Francisco, he parked his luggage in a hotel room then, after a quiet meal in the hotel's restaurant, went to the funeral home for Dad's visitation.

To Cash's surprise, he recognized a handful of people there—some of the guys Dad used to work with, as well as a couple of women, all in uniform.

James Reading stepped forward with an outstretched hand. "Cash, haven't seen you in years. You've grown up."

"I didn't know you were still in touch with my dad. I recognize others here, too."

"Despite his faults, your dad was a good cop."

He was?

"He had great instincts and a sharp mind."

So Dad had his supporters among his fellow cops.

"He had a good sense of humor, too. Used to keep us all in stitches."

Cash had been so wrapped up in Dad's failings as a husband and father, he'd forgotten about his sense of humor.

He remembered now how popular Dad used to be.

He glanced around the room, realizing that he hadn't done that when he first walked in as he usually did, his cop instincts always strong in a new environment, always observing, assessing. They were obviously dulled by shock and grief. Not an ideal situation, but it was what it was.

There were two camps of people. The cops Dad used to work with stood on one side of the room. On the other stood a motley, unpolished group who looked more than a little downtrodden. They must be the people Dad befriended in his later life in the Tenderloin.

Cash wondered how many of these had been on the opposite side of the law when Dad had been a cop in that district. How many had Dad once arrested?

A woman walked toward him and, because of her determined expression, Cash thought she might be the woman who had called him.

She stuck out a hand, almost defiantly, and Cash wondered why. "I'm Alice Gaither."

"Thank you for calling me, Alice." She gave him a firm handshake.

She'd seen better days. He couldn't guess her age, but considered that she might be as old as Dad, with the same problems—dissipation brought on by the excess use of drugs and alcohol. Her gray eyes were clear, though, and hard. She hadn't been using lately.

He wouldn't call her an attractive woman, but she might have been a long time ago. She dyed her long hair black, too dark for her pale skin, and had applied her cosmetics with a heavy hand. The rest of her was heavy, too. She had a big bosom that Dad would have liked.

"Thank you for coming."

What was that edge in her voice? "Why wouldn't I come? Frank was my father."

"Let me introduce you to his friends." She put an emphasis on the last word and led him across the room while he puzzled over her apparent disapproval of him.

He met all of Dad's friends and found that, on the whole, he liked them. They were poor, unabashedly so. They spoke of his dad in positive terms, not glowing, but realistic. They had respected him.

One man in a wheelchair said, "Frank was never short of a few minutes if you needed someone to talk to, or short of a buck if you needed a coffee."

"Yeah," another man said. "He bought me dinner a few times when I had no money."

Nothing had changed. Dad had still spent freely, even when he no longer had much. What Cash had always thought of as free spending, though, could also have been called generosity.

James Reading caught Cash as he was leaving. "Some of us who worked with your dad are going to raise a few pints in his memory at an old hangout. You're invited, of course." Cash accepted, said he'd meet them there.

He returned to his hotel room to process some of what he'd heard at the visitation. Dad was almost two different people, it seemed. The man his friends remembered had not been the man in Cash's house when he was growing up.

Cash stared at the walls, lost, too alone.

He needed out of here. When he stood to leave, his phone rang.

AT SEVEN, SHANNON drove to the trailer park to pick up Austin for their movie date.

She knocked on the door and Connie answered. Why didn't the woman have any lights on in the house? Was she conserving energy? Or had their power been turned off?

"Hi," Shannon said. "I'm taking Austin to the movies."

Austin scooted around his mom. "See you, Mom."

He caught sight of her car.

"Where's Cash?"

"He won't be coming tonight. It's just you and me. Is that okay?"

Austin nodded and climbed in.

"Where's Cash?" he asked again, once they were driving. "How come you're here instead?"

"His father died this morning. He flew to San Francisco for the funeral."

Austin didn't say anything for a minute, then "I wish I could have talked to him before he left. I know how that feels when your dad dies. Even if he turned out not my real father, when he died, I still thought he was my dad."

"Do you want to call Cash?"

"I don't have a cell phone and Mom wouldn't want me to spend all that money on a long distance call from home."

"I have a cell you can use."

Austin stared at her. "Really? That would be okay with you?"

"Sure."

"But I can't pay you back."

"I know. You don't have to." She rummaged in her purse and handed him the phone. "I can't dial while I'm driving. Do you know his number?"

"Yeah. He made me memorize it in case I ever needed him."

Austin punched in the number and a moment later Shannon heard him say, "Cash? It's me. Austin."

This kid humbled her. How many twelve-year-olds would make a call to comfort an adult? It was hard enough for most adults to do.

He's showing you up, girl.

Yes, he certainly is. He's a brave boy.

And you are a coward.

Yes, I have been, with good reason.

Yeah, but how old are you? Maybe it's time to grow up.

She felt good with Cash. She saw beneath his

surface to something she hadn't recognized in a man before. Depth. Strength of character. Someone she wanted to be closer to. But then what? How was she supposed to just throw out everything she'd learned from life, from her direct *experience,* for a big uncertain *maybe* with a man?

Maybe Cash would work out.

Maybe Cash would be someone she could rely on.

Maybe she would get really, really hurt. Either way, maybe it was time for her to deal with her fear of emotion.

CASH GRIPPED THE phone. Austin was calling him in San Francisco?

"Is something wrong?" he asked, suddenly alert.

"Shannon told me about your dad. I'm sorry, Cash. I know how you feel."

Yes, he would. He'd lived through it himself.

In that moment, Cash knew that whatever happened to Austin in adolescence, he would be okay. He would turn out to be a good man.

This boy was so intrinsically good he amazed Cash. Sympathy calls were tough to make and Austin just sucked it up and did it.

Sympathy calls were hard to take, too, and Cash couldn't handle it, couldn't catch his breath or reel in his emotions.

He concentrated on the mundane, because the issue of his Dad's death was too huge. "Are you calling from home? This will cost you a fortune."

"No. I'm in Shannon's car. We're going to a movie and she's letting me use her phone."

"That's good of her." Focus on the mundane.

"It will be okay in a little while." Sincere, earnest support from such a young voice. Mindblowing. Tears he had been avoiding rose to the surface.

"Thanks, Austin." His voice cracked and he cleared his throat. "I mean it."

"Really. Even before I found out that my dad wasn't my father, I started feeling better and stopped missing him so much. You'll be okay."

"Austin, you'll—" His voice cracked again and he stopped and held his breath.

"You'll be okay, Cash."

God, the sweetness of this was going to kill him. "You'll never know how much this call means to me. Thanks."

"That's okay," Austin said. "That's what friends are for. How long will you be away?"

"Until Monday."

"If you feel bad on the weekend, you can call me. If you want to."

"I will." Cash hung up because a mix of sorrow and pride choked his throat. Sorrow that his father was gone, and pride in a child who wasn't his, but who he wished was.

AT TEN THAT night, Cash stepped out of the pub where he'd spent the evening with Dad's old cohorts.

They'd laughed a lot. Even Cash had laughed with them, because the stories they told about Dad were funny.

Cash had forgotten a lot of his good memories of his father because the bad had affected him so adversely.

He called his mother. "Can I come over?"

"You're here? Yes."

Half an hour later, he stepped out of a cab in front of his mother's house. Her new husband had done well by her. The house was solid middle class on the outside edge of an upper middle class neighborhood.

She answered after one knock, drew him into her warm home then closed the door behind him.

She took him in her arms and held him. He didn't cry, but tears were close.

"Are you okay?"

She drew back to look deeply into his eyes. "I think so. I don't know." She gripped his hands. Her hands felt solid, welcoming, supportive.

"Come. Sit down. We'll talk."

In that moment, their relationship shifted and

he knew it was permanent. He might be a grown man, but she was finally giving him what he'd missed through the years of his childhood.

She was being a mother, and he liked it.

She took him into the living room and spoke to her husband waiting there. "Hugh, put on the kettle." She sat beside Cash on the sofa.

Her husband rose to do his wife's bidding, happily as far as Cash could tell.

Where Dad had been a chippy streetfighter, this huge man Cash's mom had married the second time bulldozed his way through trouble and yet, Cash trusted him to take care of his mother.

The first time around Mom had gone for charm, but her second husband she'd chosen for his dependability and strength.

Hugh returned to the living room and rested his big, ham-fisted hands on her shoulders. When he touched her, he was gentle. "You want me to put out some of that banana bread with the tea?"

"Yes, dear, please."

They sat and talked for hours, remembering the positive. That was new was the first time his mother had ever shared her early memories of Dad, when things were still good and Cash small and happy.

It was the first time he heard his mother speak with any perspective, without the bitterness.

When he left, he thanked his mother for being there.

She had supported him in his grief and that amazing about-face in her character really touched him.

ON SUNDAY AFTERNOON, Cash sat in Alice's tidy, tired living room. Only a few chairs and one overflowing bookshelf furnished the room. What had she and his dad been living on?

Dad used to like spreading cash around. How had poverty felt to him later in life?

Alice wore not a speck of makeup and her imperfections showed—coarse, leathery skin, large pores, sun damage. Her fleshy face looked too old, no doubt due in part to the pack of cigarettes on the arm of her chair. She took one out and lit it.

Sometime between yesterday's visitation and today, she'd had her hair cut almost boyishly short. Without the artifice, Cash could see the bones of who she used to be and, yes, she would have been attractive once.

She caught him staring. "Your dad liked my hair long. I was too old for it, and for the heavy makeup, but he didn't like when I said that. He liked my hair dark, too. I'll be changing that in time, letting it go gray."

So she'd put Frank to rest and would now do things her own way. She'd worn everything he liked to the visitations first, though, quite a sign of respect.

"How long did you know my dad?" he asked.

"Thirty years."

So, during the time Dad and Mom had still been married. Had she slept with him way back then?

"He was a cop. I was a hooker." She said the last part defiantly, as though anticipating Cash's disapproval.

"Did he ever arrest you?"

"All the time." She smiled, those memories obviously filling her with affection. "We had a... contentious relationship."

Contentious? How did a hooker know a word like that?

"Your dad and I liked to read." She pointed to the bookshelf.

Was she a mind reader or was he just so judgmental that it showed on his face?

"You and I met once, you know," she said. "Or rather, I saw you once."

Suddenly, he knew who she was—the prostitute Dad had been screwing against the wall behind the strip joint on O'Farrell.

"You grew up nice-looking, like Francis."

"You probably saw my dad more than my mom or I ever did."

"He was comfortable with me. I accepted his flaws."

"Didn't you know he was married and had a son? You couldn't have left him alone? Left him for us?"

"You're looking for stereotypes. I wasn't a hooker with a heart of gold. I wanted Francis and was damned glad when he ended up in the Tenderloin with the rest of us."

"How long did he live with you?"

"Twenty years."

Dad had gone straight from Cash's home to this woman's.

He couldn't stand the pain that caused, the hunger, and lashed out.

"Did he sleep around when he lived with you?"

She didn't flinch. "Probably. Your mom wanted to change Francis. Wanted him to be better than he was. From the get-go, I saw him for who he really was and I was okay with that. I knew who I was getting when I married him."

"*Married? When?*"

"As soon as he divorced your mom." She stubbed out her cigarette in the overflowing ashtray beside her chair. Three feet tall and silver, with a marble bowl, it was a piece of furniture. Cash hadn't seen one like it in years and never outside of a used furniture or oddities shop.

"Francis didn't leave any money. There's nothing for you and your mom to get your hands on."

"We didn't want money." Cash strained to temper his voice. "We wanted *him*. We wanted him to want us."

He drew a deep breath. It whooshed out of him and he said, more calmly, "I know Dad didn't have money. He asked for some over the years, and I always sent it when he asked."

"So that's where the money was coming from." Alice studied him with an assessing eye, as though changing her assumptions about him.

She stood and left the room.

He realized something he'd never known before—why Dad had been two different people, one man with the outside world and another at home.

With the outside world, he'd been himself.

At home, he'd striven to be the man his wife wanted him to be, dependable, faithful, sober. A family man. But that wasn't who Francis Kavenagh was.

He had always been doomed to failure at home.

The real Frank had been the man the world had known and owned, not the man he tried to force himself to be at home.

Cash and his mother had only been borrowing him for a few hours at a time. Dad must have been living under tremendous strain, trying to maintain his unnatural identity when he was with his family.

He'd lasted seventeen years with Mom and Cash. When all was said and done, that was a long time for Frank.

He wished he'd understood all of this years ago. It would have made his life a lot less painful. He wouldn't have wasted so much hope wanting more from his dad than Frank could give.

If he had understood as a boy, he might have accepted and come through childhood better.

Alice returned a moment later with a jar, and he knew immediately what it was. Dad's ashes.

She held it out to him.

He didn't know if he could touch it, but knew that he wanted to, that he needed some connection to the man who'd stopped by his office.

He reached for it slowly.

When he took the small heft of it into his hand, he marveled that all of Dad was here, that in the end this was all there was and the rest only memories.

One reached him now, invaded out of nowhere.

When only six or seven, when he still adored his dad—before he'd learned not to—Cash would kneel on the floor at the end of Mom and Dad's bed. Dad would lie so his head was at the foot of the bed, slip Cash a five-dollar bill and wait for Cash to start brushing. It was a game they played.

Cash pocketed the money and brushed Dad's thick hair until it shone. Dad always fell asleep. Those were peaceful moments. The marital war hadn't yet started.

"Where did Dad want me to put him?" he asked. "Did he want to be buried somewhere? Or his ashes spread?"

"In Yellowstone Park. He wants you to scatter his ashes there."

"Why there?"

"Francis used to visit there with his parents every summer. Since it was in Wyoming."

"What does Wyoming have to do with anything?"

"It's where your dad was from."

"*Wyoming?*" He'd never known. "Where?"

"A little dinky town with a couple of hundred people. I forget the name. Francis hated it. He loved Yellowstone, though."

Dad was from a small town?

Cash nearly dropped the urn, nearly scattered his ashes on the old floor. He would never have guessed.

How ironic that Dad had started in a small town and had moved to a large city, while Cash had been raised in a city and had moved to a small town as an adult.

Most ironic, though, was the fact that Cash had

chosen to live in a town that was only one state and a few hundred miles away.

After Cash had graduated from the police academy, he'd investigated small towns all over the States. He'd finally settled on Ordinary, Montana, when he'd read an article about it somewhere.

It had sounded charming, community-oriented, large enough to be interesting and need a police presence, but still small enough to feel safe.

He'd found nearly every kind of person there, the bad yes, but plenty of good, and that suited him just fine.

In the vast expanse of a country with so much to choose from, Cash had chosen what his father had left behind.

LATE SUNDAY NIGHT, Shannon was in Cash's bed with the dogs. She'd been here all day.

She had her laptop in front of her, researching his dad.

At one point, he'd let slip that his dad had been a cop.

What popped up on her screen astounded her.

Wow, Shannon thought, sitting back against the headboard and staring at the screen. Just wow.

Cash's father had risen high and fast to Commissioner of San Francisco, but had obviously let the power go to his head. The man screwed up, plain and simple. During his tenure, he'd fooled around with just about anything in a skirt, had accepted gifts outside of protocol. Not kickbacks per se, but certainly gifts that rewarded Frank for special consideration. In general, had used the office to get away with everything short of murder.

He'd cost one young female rookie her job and had damaged a female judge's reputation beyond repair.

No wonder Cash wanted something different for himself. Considering what she'd just learned about his father, she began to see what shaped the man Cash had become.

It was a miracle Cash made such a good cop, that he'd even decided to become one after his father's terrible example. But he had, and had then carved himself a new road in what must have been an emotional wilderness.

He had carved himself a niche as his own man. A damned good one.

On Friday, she'd been humbled by Austin's generous spirit and his courage. Tonight she was humbled by Cash's strength and determination, by his success at rising above the limitations of his childhood.

Shannon stared at her cell phone on the bedside table, struck with an insane urge to talk to him. She understood finally that his need might not be the same as her father's, or Dave Dunlop's.

That it might be nothing more than the natural consequence of losing a parent.

She picked up the phone and then dropped it onto the bed like an adolescent girl afraid that the boy she really wanted to talk to would actually answer. Then what would she do? What would she say?

His bedroom smelled like him and she wondered whether deciding to sleep here tonight had been a mistake. She'd arrived early and taken the dogs for a walk, only to get caught in a chilly rainstorm with them.

She'd stayed to have a hot shower and dry off, had made a fire in the small fireplace in the living room and had eaten leftover turkey and mashed potatoes and gravy.

After that the house had felt like a home and she hadn't left.

Now, in his bed, his scent surrounded her. *He* surrounded her.

Treading dangerous ground—Cash wanted a serious relationship, and she didn't—and despite her experience with men, despite her not wanting involvement with any man who needed her, she wanted to know that Cash was okay.

Such foreign ground for her.

She picked up the phone yet again, but this time forced herself call. He answered on the second ring.

"Cash?"

For a moment he didn't speak, but she heard him breathing and knew he was there. Then "Shannon."

She didn't know what to say. *I'm thinking about you and wondering why I'm reaching out.*

"Why are you calling?" he asked.

I don't know. "I just want to know how you're doing. Are you okay?"

"As well as can be expected."

Danny barked beside her.

"Are you at my place?"

"Yes."

"Are you going to stay there tonight?"

"Yeah. I'm already in bed."

He didn't say anything and the protracted silence unnerved her. "Cash, are you still there?"

"Yeah," he answered quietly, "I'm imagining you in my bed."

Oh, this was *very* dangerous territory. She needed to change the subject.

"How did the funeral go?"

"There wasn't one. Only a visitation. My dad was cremated. I have his ashes."

"What are you going to do with them?"

"He wants them scattered in Yellowstone."

"Really? Are you going there?"

"I'll take my scheduled flight home tomorrow and then head out the next day."

Hmm. Yellowstone. With Cash. Was she really considering…? Before she lost her nerve, she asked, "Do you want company?"

He was silent again and she waited, wondering where that thought had come from, and why it didn't scare her as much as it should have.

"I could use some." He sounded low, subdued.

"I could come with you."

"You could. Do you want to?"

Yes, and I'm shocked by that. "I do."

"Okay."

"Which dog barked?" he asked, in a tone that indicated a subject change.

"Danny."

"Is he close? He isn't on the bed, is he?"

"Yeah. They both are. Why?"

"They're not allowed up there and they know it," he said, his voice hinting at humor.

She matched his tone. "They're sleeping with me tonight. I want them here."

Cash chuckled softly and it warmed her. "I'll see you sometime tomorrow."

"Okay." She hung up and turned off the light.

Almost immediately doubts set in. *Why are you going with him?*

Because she'd made her decision, albeit rapidly and without weighing the consequences. She wasn't a woman to go back on her word.

She was going to Yellowstone with Cash and that was final.

She scrunched down under the big duvet with Danny on one side and Paddy on the other.

Surrounded by warmth and Cash's scent, she fell asleep, but not before wondering as she drifted off what on earth had possessed her to offer to go with him to Yellowstone in the first place.

ON MONDAY AFTERNOON, Mary Lou made it home from Grand Falls about ten minutes before the boys would get home from school. She'd gone to her bank there to deposit a sizable sum from selling her last batch of meth. Afterward she'd treated herself to a mani-pedi.

She'd considered getting a Brazilian wax, but her small-town "good girl" values wouldn't let her.

Brad was going to love the new stuff she'd bought, though. She couldn't wait to show him. Somehow, she would have to get the children into bed early tonight.

She felt like a new woman, a modern woman, taking control of her life, and she wondered why she hadn't done it sooner.

She ran upstairs to unpack the items she'd bought. She'd found a small sex shop and had bought things she'd never thought she would dare to wear.

Mary Lou rearranged panties and bras in her lingerie drawer, clearing a corner for her new items—a pretty pink-and-black-striped bustier and tiny black satin panties with pink bows on them. She'd also bought black stockings with pink lacy garters.

My goodness, it had been like shopping in the best candy store on earth.

She covered the items with her old conservative underwear.

She placed the scented candles she'd purchased around the room artfully then sat on the bed, her mind swirling with awareness of an irony that had been bothering her for the entire weekend.

She finally had money, her *own* money earned through her own labor, to purchase pretty things that she loved, and a husband that pleased her—a husband she was slowly forgiving for a thirteen-year-old indiscretion.

She was making money to leave him and, yet, life without him tempted her less and less.

Even though the hurt of that indiscretion was fresh, she was coming around, slowly, and it all had to do with Brad, with his willingness to embrace her new desires.

If only she'd known all of these years that he

would have been open to this, she wouldn't have started her business.

Had Brad been as bored with their sex life as she'd been and she'd just never known?

"If onlys" were a waste of time. She'd been raised to be practical and she would be.

Giving up her business was not an option. Right now, she had it all—a job that brought in good money, and a loving husband who was pleasing her every night.

Shortly after nine that evening, with the children in bed and sound asleep, Mary Lou took a bath in the new scented oil she'd bought.

When she finished, she donned her pretty new lingerie. She caught herself in the full-length mirror. A beautiful and sexy woman stood there, a brand new Mary Lou.

She lit the candles around the room.

She covered up with a thick white spa robe, cinched the belt around her waist and went downstairs in search of her husband.

The sight in the dining room stopped her dead.

Seated at the table, Brad was looking through the store's books.

Lord, no. What if he saw? What if he noticed the extra merchandise she'd been ordering from different sources, which hadn't shown up in the store? That she'd been having delivered straight to her parents' farm, and some to her grandparents' farm, and even some to the biker farm?

Her blood beat loudly in her ears.

"Brad," she said, too stridently.

He looked up with a smile. "Ready for bed so early?"

"I thought we could both go to bed now." *Please, come. Leave those damn books alone.*

"I can't. I have so much to catch up on with the books."

"I told you I'd do those."

Her tone must have been too strained. This time, he noticed.

"I mean," she rushed on, "you're so busy at work. Why don't you let me do that? Now that the children are in school full-time, I need something to occupy my mind."

"We-e-e-ell, if you're sure."

"Oh, honey, I am so sure. Leave those books there. I'll take care of them tomorrow. Come to bed."

"But it's so early. I can't sleep yet."

Oh, you poor clueless boy.

"Who said anything about sleep?" She opened her robe and placed her hands on her hips. "What do you think? Do you like?"

Brad stared at the bustier that plumped up her breasts. His eyes widened as his gaze followed the curves of the corset down to her cinched waist, down farther to the scrap of satin covering her private parts, then farther still to her silk-clad legs and her new frivolous pink furry mules.

His mouth fell open.

"You're so pretty," he breathed, reaching out with one hand to touch her knee tenderly. She'd noticed lately that he did that a lot, touched her with reverence and respect, even when she was asking him to try new things in the bedroom. Really naughty things.

What she had seen too long as her husband being dull had perhaps been something more—a deeply ingrained respect for her.

Had he not wanted to offend her by asking too much from her in bed? Had he been waiting for her to express her desires?

Oh! The time they'd wasted waiting for the other to make the first move.

She returned her husband's smile and grabbed his hand to take him upstairs.

She closed and locked the bedroom door behind her.

Brad's hands traveled her body, landing on her bare bottom.

She laughed. "It's a thong."

"I love you," he said, fervently, and Mary Lou's heart soared.

"What do you want to try first?" she asked.

He laughed. "Everything."

Her husband was changing.

At last.

They played for hours.

In the morning, Brad crawled out of bed and showered, biting her neck before he got up.

"You stay in bed. I'll get the boys ready for school."

With a chuckle low in his throat, he said, "You worked hard last night."

So had he. Her body hummed.

Mary Lou stretched. Muscles she hadn't known she'd owned ached. They'd had four children, but last night she'd learned more about sex than in the past dozen years altogether.

Brad had been aggressive and fun, but also the sweet boy she'd originally fallen for.

He was changing in ways she liked, but keeping those parts she'd first adored.

Startled by a revelation, she rolled onto her back and stared at the ceiling.

Dear goodness.

She was falling back in love with her husband.

CHAPTER ELEVEN

SHANNON CALLED CASH on Monday evening from her sister's house. He'd made it home safely. They made plans to drive the six hours to Yellowstone tomorrow and find accommodations once they arrived. At this time of year, he said, it should be easy.

Early Tuesday morning, he showed up in the front yard. She'd been watching for him.

Jitters messed with her stomach despite her commitment to this trip as she climbed into Cash's pickup truck.

He looked as good as always, his dirty-blond hair a contrast against his blue denim shirt. His eyes were tired, though, and the skin around them dry and lined.

"You okay?" she asked.

"Good."

He pulled out of the yard in silence and that seemed to set the tone for the drive.

She wasn't usually nervous with men, and hadn't been so far with Cash.

So, what's up today, Shannon?

I don't know.
You reached out to him. That's new for you.
It sure is.
So, why'd you do it?
I don't know. Quit asking.

The silence in the cab continued, lengthened with every mile.

Cash seemed unfazed by her presence while she noticed everything about him, from the light soapy scent of his cologne to the way his hands looked on the steering wheel, capable and square with strong fingers that could probably handle anything needed of him.

He turned on the radio to a country station. He drummed the fingers of his right hand on his thigh. She stared at that hand, couldn't seem to make herself stop.

She studied his strong profile.

Why reach out to him, Shannon?

Because he isn't crazy in his need. He isn't neurotic, like Dad is.

He turned to her and caught her staring. Still, even though embarrassment flared at being caught, even though her chest tightened with feelings she couldn't name, she couldn't look away.

What are you doing to me, Cash?

He smiled, sadly, and she remembered what he carried on the backseat. His father's ashes.

She couldn't imagine what he was feeling but

struggled to relate. She'd spent a lot of years burying feelings so she could take care of everyone else. So…how did she relate to Cash's grief?

Janey had said he hadn't seen his father in twenty years, that they were estranged. How did that feel?

Even though she was fully aware of her own father's faults, of him never having been the strong man she wanted him to be, she would grieve when he died.

He had a sweetness that she used to criticize when she wanted him to be stronger, but that sweetness charmed everyone who knew him. At Easter, the man still brought her chocolate Easter eggs even though she was a grown woman. He knew how much she still loved sweets—as much as she had when she was a little girl.

So, although she was a grown woman and hardened by her job, by the evil ways of man, she ate those Easter eggs he brought to her every year and she enjoyed them. Dad never left his Easter visit without getting a hug from her.

Yes, she would grieve for him. Most definitely.

"I'm sorry," she said, and meant it. At that moment, it was more than a polite expression. It was bone-deep true. She was genuinely deeply sorry that this had happened to him.

"Thanks," he said.

"Tell me about him. If that's not too painful?"

He stared at the road ahead of him for a while and she waited.

"When I was five years old, he used to take me to the station to meet his co-workers. I saw some of them at the visitation. They reminded me of Dad's better qualities. That he was a good cop. I'd forgotten about that."

"I researched him on the internet." Shannon slipped off her shoes and put her sock-clad feet up on the dashboard. She leaned her head against the headrest and relaxed into this new, different version of her old caregiver role, into something that felt natural and compassionate. "I read what happened to your dad. How could he have been a good cop and yet have done what he did?"

"You can be a good cop despite sleeping around a lot."

"What about the kickbacks?"

"That surprised me. I think Dad just liked having money to throw around. He liked to spend. He was a big man with big appetites."

"Janey said you hadn't seen him in twenty years."

"Not true." She watched him hesitate, swallow. "The first night I met you—" he emphasized that as though the moment mattered, had weight "—he came to the office. *That* was the first time I'd seen him in twenty years."

"Why did he come?"

"To tell me he was dying."

"I see. He went quickly in the end. Only last week you were trying to find him."

"Yes. He went faster than I expected."

Cash was silent for a long time after that.

They stopped for gas and coffee once then drove straight through until they reached Yellowstone, still on the Montana side of the border.

They went through the north entrance of the park, under the huge stone Roosevelt Arch.

"We don't have to go as far as Wyoming." Cash broke the silence for the first time in an hour. "Dad didn't specify a spot."

He continued to drive for a while until he parked the pickup in front of a small lodge surrounded by cabins and hundreds of conifers. He enquired about renting a cabin for the night, paid for it and then carried their bags to it and unlocked the door.

It was rustic and the only heat came from a woodstove. The bed had a couple of thick quilts on it. *The* bed. One double bed.

She looked at Cash and found him watching her steadily. What did she think of this arrangement? While running the pros and cons through her mind, he approached and took her chin in his hand.

He gave her plenty of time to stop him before leaning forward and pressing his lips to hers, kissing her gently, persuasively.

When he pulled back, he whispered, "My bed smelled like you last night. Like vanilla."

This close his eyes were dark blue, and intense. "I can rent you a separate cabin, if you want."

Usually, yes, that's exactly what she would want. If she slept with a man, she liked having her own bed to go to, so she wouldn't have to wake up with him in the morning.

It was the sex she wanted. Not the intimacy.

But the other night in Cash's bed, she'd felt an intimacy with him even though he hadn't been there, and it had been glorious.

How would it feel to have him in bed with her when she woke up? She wanted to find out.

"I'm only asking for tonight. Only one night."

She nodded. "One tonight." She could do that without giving away her heart.

He took her hand. "Come on, let's explore before it gets too dark." They left the cabin. With only an hour or so before dusk, they didn't have time to spread the ashes today. Instead they found a hiking trail through the woods, and crunched their way across layers of pine needles. They walked through a forest of lofty lodgepole pines.

The land rose steadily. With Cash every bit as fit as she was, they hiked well together, neither of them flagging or breathing heavily.

They came out on the top of a low hill and the view stunned Shannon.

"Here," he said. "This is where I'll lay Dad to rest."

No wonder. The yellowing scrub on the hill sloped away to a valley that cradled Yellowstone River. Half a dozen elk had gathered at the water's edge. Warm shards of the setting sun sparked off the river.

It took her breath away, and the peace of the spot seeped into her. They shared the silence of a perfect moment.

"We're losing the day's light," Cash finally said, though he sounded reluctant. "Let's head back." They returned to the cabin and unpacked. All the while Shannon simmered with an underground but potent anticipation of the night ahead.

They had supper in the main lodge's small café, a simple meal of beef stew and warm sourdough bread. They lingered over coffee while the room slowly cleared of a handful of fellow tourists.

They left and strolled in the cold moonlight, holding hands.

He was quiet. A number of times, she tried to jumpstart conversation before she realized that quiet was better. That Cash was processing his grief and just needed her close. She didn't have to entertain him. She didn't have to soothe and support and build him up. She just had to *be* and Cash was satisfied.

Her mind wouldn't quit comparing this type of need with what she'd grown up with, with Dad's persistent craving for attention, always pushing for more, always needing more no matter how much Shannon gave.

And her brother. Poor Tom. Judging by his actions, she hadn't given him anywhere near close to enough, but she had always tried. She just couldn't replace the wife and children he loved.

Then she thought of Dave Dunlop.

"What happened?" Cash asked.

She glanced up at him. "What do you mean?"

"Your hand just tightened, fast and hard like a spasm. What were you thinking about?"

She bit her lip. Should she tell him? Maybe. It was a night for sharing.

"When I was seventeen, I had a brief fling with a guy from school. His name was Dave. He was my first lover and I thought I was in love with him."

Cash made an encouraging sound.

"I realized pretty quickly that Dave liked a lot of attention, that he had to be the star, both on the football field and off, and with his new girlfriend."

After a moment, she said, "I got pregnant."

"What happened?"

"Dave decided he didn't want to have anything to do with either me or the baby." Cash squeezed her hand. They hadn't worn their gloves to the lodge and her fingers were cold, but her palm was warm against his large one.

"I didn't have anyone to turn to," she continued. "Janey was already in Ordinary married to C.J. and expecting the twins. My dad is useless in times of stress. He said I'd have to move out, just as he had to Janey. He said he couldn't afford to feed a baby."

Cash unlocked the door to the cabin and flicked a switch. The overhead light was harsh. He found a couple of emergency candles in holders and lit those instead before turning off the light.

He urged her to sit in the only chair in the room, an old armchair beside the woodstove, then he constructed a fire. He added a couple of small logs after the kindling caught and closed the door.

Finished with it, he stood and lifted her out of the armchair, startling a small yelp out of her. He then sat down and settled her on his lap. When he wrapped his arms around her and asked, "What happened?" his voice reverberated in his chest beneath her ear.

She enjoyed being held like this. So many firsts with this man.

"I asked Dave for help a couple of times, but he refused. He just disappeared."

"He was a coward."

She sat up and looked at him. "Yes. Totally."

Cash urged her head back against his chest, gently, and she went willingly. She wasn't used to being pampered, to having someone take care of her, and it felt good.

"Why am I telling you all of this? It's ancient history. I'm supposed to be here for you."

This man who should have been crazy with need was actually soothing her, easing the pain of old memories. It turned everything she knew on its head and tumbled over all of her old assumptions, the old stereotypes she knew existed about men and women. It obliterated her experiences, leaving her new and fresh and waiting to be filled with something unique.

He was taking care of her—and she liked it.

"This should be your time," she said.

"It takes my mind away from my dad." His mouth and breath whispered along her neck. "Besides, I want to know about you. What happened?"

"Janey offered me a room in their house, but I couldn't do it. She'd spent enough time taking care of her brothers and sisters after our mother died. I couldn't ask her to take care of me again."

Cash was easing her out of her sweater—a good thing. The fire was warming her, and the room, nicely.

"What happened then?"

"I lost the baby." A flare of pain stabbed her chest. Oh dear Lord, it hurt. Where was this sorrow coming from? Why was she still so emotional about losing her child ten years ago? Shannon rarely thought about the baby these days and yet here was a fresh burst of grief so strong it might as well have happened yesterday.

In a flash, she understood what was happening. In the past, she'd never had anyone to share it with. She'd felt isolated. So alone. It should have been Dave. He should have been all over her trying to make her feel better, but he'd been a no-show.

She'd held it all in, had sucked it up and had gotten on with her life.

But some things needed to be dwelt on for as long as it took, and dealt with so you didn't carry them underground for years. She dealt with it now in the comforting circle of Cash's arms.

She didn't cry—that wasn't in her nature—but she did grieve, and he held her all the while, silently, waiting for any sign from her to tell him what she needed.

What was it about Cash and his caring, nurturing ways that left her vulnerable? That made her want to curl into the warm circle of his arms and let all of her troubles fade? To let him carry her burdens, even if briefly?

He kissed her. He didn't say a word, but his gentle kiss spoke volumes about his compassion.

He'd unbuttoned her blouse. She hadn't noticed. He slipped his big hand inside and caressed her breast.

She unbuttoned his shirt, kissed the base of his throat and felt his heart beat a strong invincible tempo through his veins.

He set her on her feet and they moved to the bed. On opposite sides, they watched each other undress.

Cash was a strong, muscular man, already partially aroused, beautiful with the candlelight playing over his skin.

They climbed into bed and met in the middle under the heavy quilts. The fire hadn't completely dispelled the chill from the air and Shannon was happy to move into his embrace. She liked his brand of fire, needed it after the emotional moments they'd shared.

Never in her life had there been an emotional prelude to sex. It left her stunned and hungry and happy to move with Cash into whatever came next.

She started her explorations.

She ran her palms over his warm skin, memorizing the contours and the sounds he made when she touched sensitive spots.

Shannon marveled at this time of wonder, of

getting to know his body, of this first burst of lust with him. This was deeper than ever before, but for some reason, with Cash she wasn't afraid, wasn't worried about whether she would be called on to give him too much. She'd never met a more caring man.

Something deep inside of him called to her. Pieces of herself, long dormant and seldom used, responded to him.

She asked out loud what she had only thought in the truck earlier. "What are you doing to me, Cash?"

"Touching. Possessing. Loving."

Loving. She couldn't do that. Shouldn't do that. But she did. She loved this solid, honest man with the sun-thatched hair and brilliant blue eyes, with the caring, family-loving tenderness, with the high morals and ethics she rarely saw anywhere, not even in many of the cops she knew.

His hands roved her body, set tiny fires burning on the skin he touched. Her nipples rose to meet his rough palms. They shot a message to her belly—excitement and passion.

Shannon touched his stomach and he hissed in a breath. She moved lower and took him in hand. Like the rest of his body, he was generous.

She opened her legs and cradled his hips, directing him, wanting to take him into her and love him. Wanting to give herself to a man, really give herself, for the first time in her life. Fully, without restraint. He rested his weight on her and filled her. She sighed. He fit perfectly.

Cash raised himself onto his elbows and looked down at her. "Your skin is like gold in the candlelight."

"So is yours."

She loved men's collarbones, the way they stood in relief from muscled biceps and shoulders. She caressed his.

Cash didn't pound into her as a lot of men would, as though staking a claim. He entered her slowly, dragging out the anticipation, making her crazy with want.

She wrapped her legs around him and squeezed. He took one of her ankles and lifted it to his mouth, her athletic body flexible enough to accommodate him.

He kissed her ankle, her calf. "I love your legs."

She ran her tongue along his collarbone, moved against him so he stroked inside of her.

They set a rhythm and she'd never felt anything so good, or honest, or real.

"Take care of me, Cash." *Don't break the promise of partnership, of equality, that I sense in you. Don't disappoint me and ask for more than I can give. Don't come to need me so much that I lose myself.*

"I've got you, babe."

She believed him and because she did, she gave more of herself to him than to any other man.

There was nothing clinical or detached or cool about their lovemaking. It was passionate, became driven, became hot and hard and fast and explosive. Became a baptism, washing away her doubts when they came together.

Dear God, she'd found her man.

CHAPTER TWELVE

SHE AWAKENED ALONE in the morning, missing Cash's presence in both her heart and her bed.

They'd spent the night exploring, playing, exciting and then soothing. They'd taken turns stoking the fire, both the one in the stove and the ones in their bodies, first Shannon taking the lead and then Cash, in a partnership of passion that was so new it left her stunned.

She wasn't sure, but thought it might have been close to dawn when they fell asleep. She'd looked forward to waking him up. With kisses. Slowly.

He'd started a fire in the woodstove before he left to go who knew where.

She remembered the huge, impossible thought she'd had after they'd first made love—that Cash was her man. She hadn't expected to have a man in her life and was blindsided.

This trip was changing her. She didn't quite know what to think or what to do about it, but she wasn't ready to leave, to quit. After her first awkward steps in a new direction, reaching out to a man, and offering to come here with Cash, she wanted to see where things would take her.

The door opened and Cash stepped in, bringing with him a blast of chilly air.

He carried in a couple of foam containers that smelled sausage-greasy. He also carried a couple of coffees.

When Shannon sat up the quilt fell to her waist.

Cash looked at her and groaned. "I'm hungry, lady, but how am I supposed to resist you when you look like a slice of heaven?"

He set the containers onto the bedside table, whipped a flannel shirt out of his bag and tossed it to her.

"If you stay like that, we'll get nothing done today."

The fun, easy camaraderie that she'd felt between them before Cash's father died was back and she reveled in it.

She slipped on his shirt and buttoned it up. She sipped at the coffee he handed her. "Aaaaah, that's amazing. You got the sugar and cream exactly right."

"I pay attention to details."

"You sure did last night." So many details.

His lips slowly curled into a smile that nearly knocked her out of his shirt. "Yeah?"

"Yeah." She smiled and drank her coffee.

"Here." He opened a container and handed it to

her. Sausages, ham, eggs, toast, sliced tomato. Her appetite huge this morning, her stomach wouldn't wait and she dug in, all but inhaling her breakfast.

Satisfied, she leaned back against the wall behind the bed and sipped the last of her coffee.

"Happy?" Cash asked.

"Insanely so. My boss had to nag me for months to take a holiday, but I wouldn't. Now I'm glad I finally did. This place is wonderful."

Cash unbuttoned his shirt. "You don't mind that it's so rustic?"

"Nope." She tilted her head and enjoyed the intriguing bits of skin Cash was revealing. He pushed the shirt off his shoulders and threw it on the armchair.

Next, he unzipped his jeans and stepped out of them. Shannon had been to strip clubs, had hooted and hollered with all the other drunken women, but *this*... Cash removing his clothes as simply as the sun rises, this was potent. Powerful.

He crawled under the quilt and lay beside her. Her body responded full force when he nibbled her breast.

"What are you doing?" she gasped.

"Having dessert."

THEY HIKED THE trail together, in hats and gloves and heavy coats. The day was colder and darker than yesterday.

Standing at the top of the hill, they looked out across the small valley where today bison crowded an area of the river. while wolves harried them, but there were too many of them, and none that were weak, or too young, or too old, or too vulnerable. Strength in numbers.

The wolves eventually gave up after they spotted a lone male elk. They surrounded the full-grown animal. Rather than run, he stood his ground, kicking out with his deadly hooves when a wolf came too close.

"They'll play this game for hours," Cash said.

"Except that it isn't a game. It's about life and death, isn't it?"

"Yeah. If the elk lets down his guard and they have the chance to attack him en masse, he'll die. They'll kill him and feast on him for days."

"So why doesn't he run?"

"Because he stands a better chance of surviving this way. If he runs, they can attack his flanks and dig their teeth in. What he's saying when he stays to fight, when he stands still when surrounded, is that he's stronger than they are. The wolves fall for it, even while they're trying to find a way to attack."

"Is he stronger than them?"

"No. He's outnumbered, but he'll fake them out. If he has enough stamina to last for a couple of hours, he'll survive. The wolves will try to attack and he'll kick out. The wolves know that one of those hooves can kill them."

"So, eventually the wolves will give up?"

"Yep. They'll go hunting for easier game."

For a while, they watched in silence until Shannon said, "It's like a dance, isn't it?"

"Yep. A deadly one."

Cash wrapped his hand around one of hers. "That elk reminds me of you."

In the day's sullen light, Cash's eyes bordered on a dull gray blue. "How so?"

"I'm imagining you in a biker bar with nothing but your bravado to protect you."

"Don't, Cash. Don't worry about me. I have my defenses. I can fight. I've trained in martial arts and kickboxing and even wrestling."

"I know. I read up on DEA training one day in the office."

"Why?"

"Because I was worried about you."

"See? It's extensive and thorough."

"Look!"

The elk had given up and had started to run. One of the wolves leapt at his haunches and latched on with his teeth, slowing him down and giving the others a chance to latch on as well.

Shannon looked away. She saw enough ugliness in her job.

"Come on," Cash said. "We don't need to watch this. We both know how this story ends."

They walked farther along the top of the hill until the kill was no longer visible.

At that point, Cash stopped and opened the jar containing his father's ashes and checked the wind to make sure it was blowing from behind them.

"Here goes, Dad," he said. "You're back in your favorite place." His voice broke. He was saying goodbye when he'd only just gotten to know the man who'd fathered him. And it was a damn shame.

Perhaps they could have had a relationship these past few years, one in which they appreciated each other for who they were, not for who they wanted them to be.

He waited a minute, cleared his throat and then said, "Goodbye."

He tossed his father's ashes out over the side of the hill. The breeze picked them up in a gray ribbon then dispersed them onto the land.

Cash sighed. He didn't reach out to Shannon no matter how badly he wanted to. He'd sensed that she couldn't stand to be needed so he stood apart from her. She reached for him, wrapped her arms around him and he breathed out heavily. Yes. He put his head on her hair and she held him, offered comfort with her body.

No words were needed.

After a moment, he squeezed her so hard he might have been in danger of cracking a rib, but she was a strong girl and took it.

When he let go, she asked, "When was the last time you took a holiday?"

"Last year. Why?"

"Can you take another day off?"

She wanted to stay with him? Longer? "Yes." Absolutely. He watched her steadily. "What do you want?"

"There's so much waiting for us back in Ordinary, the bikers, the drugs, the meth lab. A whole lot of ugliness."

"That's what you see there. I see a great community polluted by a small handful of people."

"I know. I'm paid to deal with the worst of humanity. I've never told anyone else, but sometimes I get so tired of it, Cash. It can be soul-destroying. Even Janey doesn't know that."

"It's hard to hold on to your humanity."

"Yes."

He touched her hair, smoothed back a strand that had escaped her ponytail.

She looked out across the pristine valley below them.

"What are you thinking?" he asked.

"About last night, and how you helped me to forget the ugliness of my job."

She turned to him. "I want to stay here one more day. With you. My boss was right. Vacations are necessary for cops. It keeps us human."

"And your vacation went south a few days after it started, didn't it, when Tom overdosed?"

She nodded. "Yes. Last night was magical. I need more."

Cash's heart flipped over in his chest. She wanted more time with him. The way she looked out over the pristine beautiful valley below had him believing there were possibilities with her. She was falling in love with the country and, dare he hope, with him?

"Let's stay." He wrapped his arm around her and squeezed. "Let's drive farther into the park, really enjoy ourselves. Ever seen a geyser erupt?"

"Last night." Shannon giggled. "A really big one."

"Are you serious? Did you just make a really lame dirty joke?" He poked her in the ribs.

She doubled over, still giggling.

"I *meant* Old Faithful," Cash said, laughing, too. "Seriously, girl."

"Okay. Seriously. Let's do it." She ran back to the cabin and he followed her.

Inside, while packing, she said, "I can't remember the last time I felt so free."

She was glowing and that said a lot, made him believe that the impossible might come true.

While Cash checked out, Shannon loaded the truck.

They stopped for a quick lunch and then drove on until they reached the Old Faithful Inn where they booked a room. The only thing available at the last minute, even at this time of year, was a room in the Old House with a queen-size bed, a sink and a shared washroom and private shower facilities down the hall.

That bed called to him. Cash wanted to be in it now, inside of Shannon, with her body flushed and warm against his.

But Old Faithful beckoned.

They followed a broad walkway away from the semi-circle of buildings surrounding Old Faithful to wait for it to erupt. They waited only twenty minutes before water spurted more than a hundred feet into the air.

Cash watched Shannon to see her reaction. Her eyes widened and her mouth fell open.

When it ended a minute later, she jumped up and down and clapped her hands.

He wrapped his arms around her from behind.

"What did you think of that, city girl?"

She leaned back against him. "It was amazing. I didn't know it would be so loud."

"The water's under a lot of pressure."

He was under a lot of pressure. Feelings bubbled and burbled inside with a need to explode out of him, but he knew better than to voice them now. It was too early, and she was a skittish mare.

He was already head over heels for her.

Was she falling in love with the country?

Was she falling in love with him?

She'd asked to stay another day, another night, with him. That had to mean something.

He needed to know for sure before he said anything.

The crowd cleared out and they were able to get a seat to wait for the next eruption. This time they waited nearly an hour.

The next eruption was long and high, which meant they would probably have to wait another couple of hours for the next one.

"What did you think of that one?"

"It's amazing. Loud and powerful. I've never been so impressed by nature."

She kissed him. "Thank you for showing this to me."

Cash laughed. "I didn't do anything. Nature put on the show. All I did was drive us here."

He took her hand. "The next one won't be for a long time." He rested his forehead on hers and whispered, "I need to be alone with you."

They had an early dinner and went to their room where they undressed at the speed of light.

Under the covers, Cash pulled her to him, overwhelmed by feelings he'd never thought he would experience. How long had he known her? A week and a half? Two?

"How did this happen so quickly?"

"I don't know," Shannon whispered, "but let's enjoy it while it lasts."

While it lasts?

"But—"

She didn't let him finish. She kissed him hard. He kissed her back just as hard, and entered her the same way.

They came together, powerfully.

Cash got out of bed after midnight and looked outside. "The sky cleared up. There are stars. A moon."

"I know." Shannon giggled. "I can see it from here."

He turned around. She was staring at his bare butt. "Not that one. Get dressed. Warmly."

"What? Why?"

"I want you to see something out of this world."

Dressed in multiple layers, they left the inn and took the path to the seating around Old Faithful. They were alone. No one else wanted to brave these temperatures.

He was happy about that. "We'll have our own private show."

"It must be close to freezing out here," she grumbled.

Cash wrapped his arms around her. "It'll be worth it. You'll see."

And it was.

"Spectacular," she breathed. They watched it once, in the ghostly light of a pale moon.

"I've never seen anything so beautiful." Shannon turned her face up to the stars.

He couldn't pull his eyes away from her.

"That's my way of thanking you for coming here with me. It wasn't an easy decision for you, was it?"

"No," she said. "It wasn't. I'm tired of people leaning on me. Of men asking too much and not giving enough back."

He took her hand and led her back to the inn.

"You give so much, Cash. You never stop giving. It almost makes me feel guilty."

"Don't."

Once in their room, he undressed her.

"What are you doing?" She laughed. "I can undress myself. I'm used to doing for myself."

"I know, but I *like* undressing you." Cash made suggestive Groucho Marx wiggles with his eyebrows.

They tumbled into bed. He fell asleep wrapped around Shannon and woke deliciously tangled with her in the morning.

"We have to go," he said, waking Shannon with kisses along her neck.

"Back to the real world?" she murmured.

"I'm afraid so."

When they were an hour outside of Ordinary, he turned to her.

"You've been quiet for a long time. What's wrong?"

"I'm just thinking about what's waiting for us in the real world."

"Yeah," he said, sobering.

"Cash, I've never had such a good, relaxing time in my life. You are someone really special."

"Was there an implied 'but' at the end of that sentence?"

"No. I've never met a man like you." She rested her hand on his thigh. "Yellowstone was a dream. I wish we could have stayed there longer."

He covered her slim fingers with his and held on. "Me, too."

Cash drove into the Wright's front yard, almost spookily afraid to let Shannon go.

He should have kept her in Yellowstone, should have kept her naked and in bed with him, because she was right. Yellowstone and that interlude were not the real world and he had no idea where they were going next with this affair.

CHAPTER THIRTEEN

LATE ON FRIDAY afternoon, with the clouds low and looking like snow, Shannon drove up the lane of the bikers' farm. She felt the chill of winter settle into the world around her.

She shook her head to clear thoughts of Cash out. Yellowstone and those two days with him had been the trip of a lifetime. When she'd told him she'd never met anyone like him, she'd meant it. She just didn't know what to do with that. He left her off-kilter.

He had a career in Ordinary. She had a career with the DEA. She couldn't possibly work from a town this small. She needed to be in a city, in a DEA hub office.

She'd thought she'd been really dedicated to her work with the DEA, to getting the scumbags who hooked teenagers on drugs off the streets but since Tom's overdose, she'd become even more driven.

She wanted everyone, every single person who made, sold, promoted, pushed, or dealt with drugs in any way brought down, taken off the streets and thrown into a jail cell. And she personally wanted to drop the key down a sewer so these people could never hurt another person with their evil.

How could she live in Ordinary and do what needed to be done, what she had to do to fulfill her role in life?

She would feel like she was withering away, wasting her potential and her skills.

She couldn't do that.

Maybe she and Cash could work out some kind of system of seeing each other regularly if she stayed in Montana…but she knew she wouldn't.

She wanted to work at the Domestic Field Division in Denver. She excelled at her job. She brought bad guys to justice all the time. She couldn't waste her hard-earned talents.

Shannon forced her mind back to the job at hand. *Concentrate, girl. Thoughts of loved ones will only get you killed.*

Cole had come home early and called to ask if she still wanted to come out to the bikers' farm for an interview.

She'd jumped at the chance.

Now here she was, pulling up in front of a large ramshackle farmhouse.

When she parked her car, she snapped to attention, noting every detail around her.

She'd already driven around the county roads

nearby, made sure to note exactly where she was and what her escape route would be.

She hadn't met this Cole. He could be an okay guy. He could be a troublemaker. She was ready for any eventuality.

The land was littered with RVs. RVs? For bikers? The world was a changing place.

RVs were perfect for cooking meth, though. The process tended to build up toxicity in a home, so cooks kept it separate from their living area.

The place was eerily quiet. Where was everyone?

Dressed in her unsexy journalist's clothes, she knocked on the front door.

Rogers answered it.

"Hi," she said. "I'm here to see Cole."

"Cole had to step out for a minute. He'll be back soon. Come on in."

She stepped inside. The living room looked like…a normal living room, with a few newspapers and a couple of jackets littering the chairs, but it wasn't the pigsty she'd expected. It smelled better than Tom's apartment had. There was no garbage scenting the air.

She chronicled every detail.

"Where is everyone? I thought there'd be a lot of people here."

"They're all at the rally in Wyoming."

"They're still there?"

The farm had been sitting empty all this time. She could have come out and snooped during the past week. But illegally.

She would have known whether or not the lab was here, at least. But if it was, she would have screwed her chances of getting warrants, arrests and of making them stick. She might have learned she was wasting her time and could have started looking elsewhere.

But, she'd had a fabulous vacation with Cash and that had been worth the delay.

She'd been invited here today. So, no warrants necessary. Anything she saw she would be allowed to act on.

If this rally was so important and Cole was head of this branch, why had he come back early just to allow her to interview him?

The entire scene reeked of risk.

She needed to get out of here.

She stepped back toward the door, but Rogers took her hand and said, "C'mere."

"You didn't go to the rally?"

"Someone had to stay to watch the place."

"When did Cole get back?"

"What?"

"Cole. When did he come back?"

"This morning."

"This morning? He drove through the night?"

"Huh? Yeah. Sure."

Suspicion ran fingers up her spine.

She tugged her hand, testing his strength. He didn't let go—and he was very strong.

She shouldn't fight him. That might excite him. She had to use her wits.

He led her to a bedroom at the back of the house and closed the door behind them. Okay, this wasn't right.

Thinking fast, she said, "Wait," but before she realized what he had in mind, he backed her against the door and had his tongue down her throat.

She let him kiss her for a minute and then forced him back.

"Hey," she said, sounding more stern and confident than she felt. "That's not why I'm here."

Rogers grinned. "Yeah, it is."

The way he said it...the tone he used...it had been his voice on the phone, not Cole's.

Cole isn't here.

She was alone on this stinking farm, in this too-tidy biker ranch house, with Rogers.

Her adrenaline kicked in. She needed to investigate this place and then hightail it out of here.

"You want something special first?" Rogers stepped away from her, thank God.

"Sure."

"What do you want? His grin showcased rotting teeth. He was definitely on something if he thought she was getting into the situation. "I got all kinds of stuff."

"You have any ice?"

He walked to the bed and she got her first clear glimpse of the room. It was surprisingly tidy.

Rogers took a box out of a drawer in the bedside table.

"Why do you have a room inside while others have to sleep outside?" She sat on a sofa sagging against one wall.

"I'm second to Cole. I'm the boss when he's away." He sat beside her and opened the box. He pulled out a plastic baggie with a crystal inside. He also took out a glass tube with a bulbous end that fit into the palm of his hand. He dropped the crystal into the bowl.

A torch lighter sat on the coffee table between two piles of neatly stacked magazines. One stack had a motorcycle magazine on top and the other a mag about horse care. The guy was a neat freak.

He handed her the lighter and pipe.

"You first," she said, so he held the flame to the meth and inhaled. She waited for a few seconds until his eyes became glassy then said, "I need to use the can. Where is it?"

"Down the hall on the right."

Well aware of every drug's effects, she knew he would be too out of it for a while to come after her, but then he'd be like a lit fuse demanding sex.

She had a narrow window and planned to use it to look for the lab before getting off this land.

She opened every door along the hallway. Nothing but bedrooms. Every room on the floor was normal.

She turned on a light and ran down the stairs to the basement. There was no meth lab down here, but there was a grow-op. A huge one. *Must be thousands of plants down here.*

At least she could get this stuff off the streets.

She'd have to deal with it later, though. Her priority was the meth.

She rushed back upstairs.

Outside, she ran from trailer to trailer and peeked inside every single one. They were normal living facilities. What, were these bikers too tame to cook meth?

Looking out over fields as far as she could see, there were no other structures to investigate.

So where had Rogers got his from? She wasn't going back to ask.

A roar went up from the front door of the house—Rogers yelling, "Where are you?"

Damn. Her heart rate accelerated. She couldn't get back to her car while he was in the front yard.

She ran toward the nearest field and, kept running when she heard him lumber around the house, hot on her heels. The second field had once been a huge crop of weed that had been harvested recently. The DEA had missed this stuff.

When she got home, she'd call the office and tell them to get down here to confiscate what was in the basement.

She heard another roar, heading in her direction. If she made it home tonight.

She ran until she came to the road. A motor heading her way caught her attention and she almost jumped out to hitch a ride, then thought better of it.

If coming out here to meet Cole had been risky, hitching a ride with a stranger would be downright brain dead.

It wasn't smart to circle around and head back to her car. In spite of being stoned, Rogers wasn't a stupid man. Once he couldn't find her he'd park himself there.

She was a good runner, thank God, but she couldn't run all the way back to Ordinary.

Adrenaline had her breathing harder than she did on her morning run. She panted.

Damn. She'd been so sure she could handle the situation, so crazy to find that meth lab for her brother that she hadn't been smart enough. Independence was fine and dandy, but sometimes you just couldn't work alone.

She heard Rogers thrashing through the fields. She was a fast runner and in a hell of a lot better shape than he was, but the guy was gaining on her in an almost superhuman way.

Well, they didn't call meth "speed" for nothing.

Until he came down from his high, Rogers could probably conquer the world.

For the first time she felt like she was being pursued by something she might not be able to outrun.

She whipped her cell phone out of her purse and almost dropped it in her haste. She punched in a number. "Come on, come on," she whispered.

When Cash answered, she said, "I need you."

CHAPTER FOURTEEN

"WHERE ARE YOU?" Cash asked, his voice immediately aware and concerned. He sounded so close, so solid and dependable, she wished she could reach out and touch him. "Are you in trouble?"

"Yes."

"At Sassy's?"

"No." She swallowed before going on. "On Highway 85, just past the turnoff onto Sideroad 36."

He didn't say anything for a minute, then "You're at the biker farm?"

"I'm out by the road at the edge of a field."

"Are you safe?"

"For now, yes."

"Do you have your gun with you?" She didn't like how quiet he sounded.

"Yes."

"Why don't you get the biker who took you out there to drive you home?"

"I drove out here myself. I'll explain later. Just get here. Now."

On the other end of the phone, she heard a

truck door slam and an engine start. "I'm on my way. It'll take me about ten minutes to get there."

The breath gusted out of her. "Thank you," she whispered fervently.

"Stay on the phone," he ordered.

Rogers roared again, closer.

"What was that?" Cash asked.

"It's the biker looking for me. I'm going to run down the ditch to the corner of 89 and 36, okay?"

"When you get there, lie low. Don't move."

She heard him swear.

Thank goodness the past few days had been dry and the ditch was empty. Small comfort, but it was something.

She listened to nothing on the other end of the line, but she knew Cash was there and that filled her with relief and confidence.

She kicked off her half-boots. Damn her for wearing something with a heel.

Then she heard thrashing through the window at the side of the field and hissed in a breath. The bugger was too close.

"Cash," she said into the phone, but he didn't answer. He must have put the phone down so he could drive without killing himself.

"Cash," she whispered furiously.

She needed to be ready to run. Hands fumbling, she took her gun out of her purse and threw the bag beside her boots.

The wind had picked up. She shivered.

Furious rustling sounded in the field. She needed help. Now.

"Cash," she shouted.

"What?" was his immediate response. He'd heard her this time.

"He's coming."

"So am I. How far away is he?"

"About twenty yards."

Rogers ran right toward her. "Get back here."

Cash, hurry.

She looked up at Rogers's large frame blocking what little light there was left of the day.

He jumped into the ditch and landed on top of her, knocking the breath from her lungs. Her fingers convulsed on her gun and it went off. The report echoed in the air.

Rogers restrained her arms easily. Damn meth for making people so crazed.

Her pulse rate quickened.

She only needed to hold him off until Cash got here.

She could do that.

Cash, hurry, please.

While Rogers trapped her wrists with one hand, he unzipped his pants. No *freaking* way.

Her blood roared in her ears.

"Go to hell," she screamed and kicked her legs against him, managing to get her knee up high enough to hit him in the groin, but he was on her so heavily, it was nothing more than a nudge.

"Get off of me, you creep."

He swore and tried to get his hand into her pants. She struggled and wrenched one arm free. She slammed the heel of her palm straight against his nose. He roared, but kept trying to get at her clothes. What? Did meth make a person super-human?

She already knew the answer to that.

His breath smelled sweet, but his body reeked of sweat.

She hit him at the base of his throat with her knuckles as hard as she could. While he gagged she squirmed out from under him and hauled her-self up the embankment just as a truck came to a stone-spewing stop on the shoulder, its head-lights blinding.

Cash leapt out of the truck.

"Where is he?"

"In the ditch. I hit him in the throat. My gun went off. I don't know whether the shot hit him."

"So he's still alive?"

"Yes." Her voice didn't sound like her own. It sounded too loud. "He was trying to rape me."

Cash pushed her behind him and drew his weapon.

"Where's your gun?"

She stared at her empty hands. "Down there.

He must have knocked it out of my hand when he landed on me."

Cash shoved her and she crouched on the far side of the truck. "Keep your head down and stay down."

She didn't take orders well, but sometimes it paid to be smart. He had a gun. She didn't.

Cash stood behind the engine and called, "Come out of the ditch, hands in the air."

To Shannon, he said, "What's his name?"

"Rogers."

"Rogers," he shouted, "come out of there."

Rogers climbed out with Shannon's gun in his hand. Cash aimed as Rogers raised his arm toward Cash.

Shannon's ears rang with the shot.

She jumped up. Rogers was on the ground. Cash kicked her gun away from his right hand.

Blood flowed from Rogers's forearm. Cash must have shot it to get him to drop the gun. He hadn't shot to kill.

Masterful.

She stared at him and said with admiration in her voice, "Nice shooting." Cash was good. Damn good.

As though Rogers weighed about as much as a sack of potatoes, Cash flipped him over and put on a pair of handcuffs. Rogers roared with pain.

Cash called the cops and then an ambulance.

He led her to the truck. She stumbled on the sharp stones and hissed.

He retrieved her boots then helped her to sit on the passenger seat with her legs hanging out of the truck so he could put them on her, his actions gentle. She wasn't fooled. He seemed to have a well of anger that he banked for the moment.

"When Chief Gage gets here, you let me do the talking, got it?"

"That's not necessary. I take responsibility for this."

"Tell me everything that happened. What the hell were you doing here?" He'd finished putting on her boots, but his fingers circled one ankle.

"Rogers pretended he was Cole and invited me over for that interview I wanted."

"I thought we decided that journalist plan was too risky because I couldn't accompany you."

She shook her head. "You decided that, not me."

"How could you come alone? You could have been—" Cash forced out a breath, visibly trying to pull himself under control. "You terrified me. Honestly, Shannon, do you know what could have happened?"

A slight tremor ran through his hands. He'd managed to keep his cool even though he was worried about her. His aim had been true. The man was a good cop.

"You're lucky you were able to get away from the farmhouse," he said, "let alone away from him in the ditch."

"It wasn't luck, Cash. It was skill. I do this for a living and I'm good at my job."

"If you could handle it so well, why did you call me?"

She hesitated. "I felt too alone out here."

"You were." He looked away, but she stopped him with a quiet "Thank you."

He nodded, and she could see the cop in him taking over, assessing the situation now that the danger had passed. "Rogers looks like an angry bull on steroids. Is he high?"

"Yes."

"What did he take?"

"Meth. I looked for the lab, but it isn't here. Except for a marijuana grow-op in the basement, this is a dead end." She slammed her hand against the dashboard. "Damn, where do I look now?"

Frustration overtook her now that the threat had been neutralized. "If the meth isn't here, where is it?"

Cash still had his hand wrapped around her ankle and she tried to take comfort from his touch, but her anger knew no bounds at the moment.

"Damn."

She was pretty sure she would have got away

from Rogers, but there were moments in that cold ditch when she hadn't been sure her martial arts skills were up to dealing with a man so large and so high on meth, so full of artificial energy. She'd managed to claw her way to the road, but could she have outrun him?

A couple of cop cars arrived with lights flashing.

Officer Gage approached and the interview started. Shannon spilled the whole truth about who she was and why she was here.

"They've got a basement full of weed. I'll call Denver and get the DEA out here."

It took a while to get everything sorted out, and it was late before Mike Gage drove onto the farm in his cop car and Cash followed with Shannon in the passenger seat.

She got into her own car and drove off with both Mike and Cash acting as escorts.

She followed Mike to Monroe, where she gave him a full statement of what happened.

Finally, exhausted, she arrived at the Wright house. Cash had stayed with her while she gave her statement and now he followed her inside. The house was quiet and everyone in bed.

Before Shannon could turn on the light, Cash wrapped his arms around her and pulled her into his rough embrace. He kissed her hard, as though he would inhale her if he could.

When he finished, he held her head against his shoulder and whispered, "Don't ever do anything like that again."

"Cash," she replied. "It's okay. I got away from him."

"We both know that if he'd come up out of that ditch when you were trying to run away, he could have shot you."

She bit her bottom lip. "You're right."

"From now on, we work on this together."

"Okay."

She turned on the lights in the living room and fell into an armchair.

Cash pulled her out of it and onto the sofa where he sat down and cradled her on his lap.

"What—?"

"Let me do this," he whispered. He held her for a moment before he started to talk. "I know where to start looking in Ordinary."

She held herself far enough away to look at him. "Where?"

"Can you get access to a pharmacy's orders?"

"Of course. I can get anything." She frowned. "You think the owner of the pharmacy is making the meth?"

"I would have sworn Brad McCloskey wasn't capable of it, but lately I've had suspicions. All small stuff, though. I could be wrong."

Shannon jumped up from his lap. "Small is

fine. It's a place to start." She pointed a finger at him. "I trust your cop instincts."

CASH'S RINGING CELL phone woke him up on Saturday morning. He was in bed alone.

He didn't know where he stood with Shannon or what was going on. He did know he was freaking relieved she'd called him from the biker farm. He'd never been so scared in his life.

When he'd heard the report of the gun, when he'd thought he'd lost her. He never wanted to live through anything like that again.

The insistent humming of his phone had him reaching for it from where he left it on the bedside table.

He cleared his throat. "Hello?"

"Cash?" *Austin!* Damn.

Last night was Friday night. For the first time in a year, he'd forgotten all about his Little. Double damn.

"Man, I'm so sorry, Austin." How could he have forgotten about him? "I should have called last night. I was out on police business."

"That's okay," Austin said, but his voice sounded small.

"No, it isn't okay. I should have called. Don't let me off the hook so easily." How many times had Cash's father missed meetings with his son?

How many baseball games had he missed? Every single incident had hurt.

Cash groaned. He knew what Austin was feeling. Friday night's movie was one of so few treats Austin got. He hated disappointing the boy.

"Listen, do you think your mom would let you go tonight?"

"Sure." Austin perked right up.

"Okay, I'll pick you up at seven. See you then."

Later, as they drove to the theater, Austin was subdued.

"You okay, buddy?" Cash asked.

"Yeah." He didn't sound okay.

"Are you mad at me because I didn't come out last night?"

"No. I know you're a cop and you have to do stuff."

"I want to apologize again. Shannon was in trouble with the bikers in Monroe."

Cash watched the road while he drove but sensed Austin swinging his gaze to him. "Is she okay?"

"Yes. I arrived in time to help her."

"Good." Austin settled back against his seat and stared out the window.

"What's the problem, Austin?"

The boy sighed. "My mom is sick too much."

"Still?"

"Yeah."

Cash had been wondering, ever since Thanksgiving, exactly what the nature of Connie's illness was. Could she be taking drugs? Where would she get them though? There was no way she could drive out to Sassy's or the biker farm to buy them.

"Try to convince her to go to a doctor," he said. "Then you can find out exactly what's wrong with her." *And we can rule out drugs.*

If he found out she was taking drugs, he would have a hell of a time not laying into her with near inhuman rage. There was weakness, and then there was weakness.

So Connie couldn't take care of her son well enough. That was bad. But if she was abusing drugs, there would be nothing, *nothing,* of her left to give to her son and a good boy would be lost.

What a fricking example to set for her kid.

THE DEA MANAGED to learn from Rogers that the gang was expected back on the farm on Sunday.

DEA agents arrived in the afternoon the day after the bikers' return, entering Cash's office around two. Both Cash and Shannon waited for them.

One of the men, Sam Morgans, said, "Shannon, you're back on the clock. Holiday's over."

"Sure." She'd guessed this was coming. It had been fun while it lasted.

That evening, she and Cash, along with other

local officers, took part in the raid the DEA orchestrated at the bikers' farmhouse. Before heading out, they donned protective gear. They handed both Cash and Shannon DEA-issued firearms, CAR-A4 Carbines with holographic sights.

A mile away, they congregated, the shoulder of the road lined with local law enforcement. At the agreed upon time and signal, all of the police drove onto the property—without lights and under the cover of darkness—behind the DEA agents and Cash and Shannon.

Local law enforcement ran around the house silently and stood outside every window. Other cops covered the RVs.

SWAT team members closed in on both doors of the ranch house, big men light-footed and moving like cat burglars.

Shannon stood behind them with Morgans and Parson, both good men, big and physically capable. She'd worked with them before.

SWAT entered first, breaking through the front and back doors, yelling, "Police! Don't move!"

Like crabs on a hot beach, bikers scrambled out of windows only to be picked up by police officers.

A few bikers who weren't in the main house for dinner tried to run from their RVs, but cops apprehended them.

For a while, the scene might have looked like

bedlam, but they moved together like well-oiled machinery.

Once the bikers were under control and being moved from the farm to jails throughout the county, a mass of men and women in white protective gear took control of the farm. They had the run of the place while breaking down the grow-op and bringing the drugs in.

Along with the plants, they hauled out grow-op lights, water-cooled air conditioners and carbon dioxide generators. They also removed an illegal electrical bypass that could have sparked a fire at any time. No wonder so many of the bikers slept in the RVs scattered around the lot.

"How many plants do you think there are?" Cash asked.

"This was huge. The house ranch style has a large basement." Shannon guesstimated. "Between fifteen hundred and two thousand."

Cash whistled.

"The owner of the farm will have to be notified. Any idea who owns this place?"

"Albert Will," Mike Gage answered. He had just walked up beside them and had heard Shannon's last question. "He's in a retirement home somewhere. Bozeman, I think. His son rents the place out long distance."

"One of the hazards of being an absentee landlord," Shannon replied. "It'll cost him a fortune to make this house livable again. He might as well torch it." With that, Shannon walked away, so damn disgusted with growers and dealers.

Cash followed her. "Hey, why so down? We got a lot of weed off the streets."

"Sometimes I get so tired of this, so discouraged. There are too many of these places around. And we still don't have the meth manufacturer."

He squeezed her shoulder. "We'll get him. Don't worry about that right now. Celebrate. We just put a huge grow-op permanently out of commission."

"You're right." Shannon smiled. "It is worth celebrating, isn't it?"

On Tuesday, Cash had just finished a late takeout lunch when the door to his office opened and a young man walked in.

"Jamie?" Cash stared. Jamie was supposed to be in San Francisco. "What are you doing here?"

Cash stared at his brother. Hair fell across his forehead in a rough tumble of straw-streaked blond.

Déjà vu all over again, only this time the surprise visit wasn't from his father. It was his younger half-brother, with a mutinous expression on his face that didn't bode well for Cash.

"I ran away from home," Jamie said, daring Cash to judge him.

Cash did judge—the kid had it easy compared to what he had grown up with—but he recognized the futility in arguing at the moment. All it would get him was a boatload of attitude.

Cash tossed the empty Styrofoam containers into the trash can. "What happened at home?"

"Mom and Dad wouldn't let me go on this great sailing course I wanted to take."

"Why not?"

"They said they couldn't afford it."

"A sailing course shouldn't cost too much. Where is it?"

"Somewhere off the coast of Australia."

Cash whistled. "For how long?"

"From next week until the second week in January."

"Holy cow, Jamie. No wonder they won't let you go. It would cost them a fortune."

"It's worth it. It's great exposure to the world." Jamie's lower lip jutted forward. "Besides, Alex's parents are letting him go."

Ah. His buddy was going so he wanted to.

"What does his dad do for a living?"

"He's a lawyer."

"Bingo. They have the money. Your dad's a longshoreman. He's not made out of gold." Mom had been working as a receptionist in a real estate office for ten years. Not a huge moneymaker, either. "Where do you expect them to get that kind of money?"

"Dad can borrow it."

"In this economy? What if he lost his job? He'd be sunk."

"He can take out a mortgage on the house."

"A second mortgage, you mean. I doubt mom and Hugh have finished paying off the first. Do you have any idea how much that house cost them?" Cash was winding into a head of steam. The kid was spoiled. "Do you have any idea why they moved into an area they can afford only by the skin of their teeth?"

Jamie shook his head.

"So they could send you to that school that your well-off friends go to. It had a good reputation and they wanted to give you a solid education."

Jamie still sulked.

"They've kept a roof over your head your entire life. Have you ever gone hungry?"

That jutting lip threatened to drop right off his face. He crossed his arms. "No."

"They fed you regularly. Did they give you bicycles as you grew up?"

"Yeah, but I always had to wait until Christmas."

"Skateboards?"

"Same thing."

"Clothes?"

"Last year, they wouldn't get me the skateboarding shoes I wanted. They gave me a cheaper pair."

"Christ, Jamie, grow up." So much for trying to hide his judgment of the boy.

"Did your dad spend time with you? Did he teach you how to ride those bikes? Does he still want to spend time with you? I thought Mom said you two went away for a fishing weekend in the summer."

Jamie scuffed a toe of his shoe, so like a little kid Cash wanted to laugh. Except that he couldn't. The envy of his younger brother he'd persistently felt reared its ugly head. Jamie had what Cash had always wanted—a father. A *real* father. One who loved his son.

I know you won't believe me, Cash, but I love you.

Had he? Had Frank loved his son?

Maybe. Cash didn't know anymore. Thinking he should give Jamie perspective, though, he checked his watch and made a flash decision.

As soon as school was out, they were going to visit Austin.

"How did you get here?"

"I took a couple of buses."

"Jesus, Jamie, you've been gone for days. Why haven't I heard from Mom?"

"I left a note telling them I was staying with a friend for a few nights."

So much for rebellion. He hadn't even had the nerve to tell his parents he was running away.

"Wait a minute," Cash said, suspicion blooming. "You didn't come here because you were running away. You came to see if I would give you the money for the trip."

Jamie's face turned the color of ripe beets. Bingo. "You got a good job here. *You* could lend Mom and Dad the money."

"No way."

Just then Jamie's stomach grumbled.

"When was the last time you ate?"

Jamie shrugged. "A while ago."

Jamming his cowboy hat onto his head, Cash said, "Come on. I'll buy you lunch, but I'm not sending you sailing."

Jamie followed him out of the office, albeit reluctantly.

Cash took Jamie to the diner where the kid ate a huge platter of fries and a club sandwich.

Afterward, rather than drive to Austin's trailer park, Cash walked, Jamie beside him with his hands shoved into his jacket pockets.

"Where are we going?" Jamie asked.

"To see how the not-so-lucky half lives."

When they arrived at the trailer, Cash wondered what Jamie though of the place.

Cash had always thought of trailers as tin sardine cans, but he knew they could be nice. Connie's wasn't. None of the ones here were. They were cheap and tired and run-down, much like Connie herself.

He knocked and she answered. She looked bad. Her brows shot up. "Cash?"

"Is Austin home?"

"He's out getting our groceries for the week."

Cash shot a pointed look at Jamie, but Jamie didn't get it. He'd probably never run to the store for even a carton of milk, let alone the week's groceries.

"Do you want to wait inside? He should be here any minute."

"Thanks, Connie. I appreciate it."

They stepped into the too-small trailer. Cash had never been inside before and an immediate claustrophobia hit him.

The place was tidy enough and he wondered whether that was due to Austin's efforts or Connie's.

He sat on a small worn sofa and Jamie sat beside him, his bunched fists resting on his knees, as though he didn't know what to do with his hands.

Good. Cash meant to unsettle him, to shake up his world.

Connie filled a couple of plastic tumblers with

tap water then put them on the cracked coffee table in front of them. Cash thanked her.

He opened his mouth to ask about her health when a commotion at the door caught his attention—Austin wrestling a full bundle buggy through the narrow doorway.

He stopped when he saw Cash. Then he spotted Jamie and stared, particularly at his running shoes. They might have been the cheaper version of the skateboarding shoes that Jamie had originally wanted, but they were a hell of a lot newer and nicer than anything Austin had ever owned.

Ditto for the name-brand jeans.

Connie stood up from the only other chair in the room, an ancient fake leather Barcalounger. "Sit and visit. Cash wants to talk to you."

She maneuvered the buggy into the "kitchen" to unpack it. She pulled three loaves of cheap white bread and a huge package of bargain brand toilet paper out of the buggy.

Next came a large jar of generic peanut butter.

All the while, Jamie stared at the tired woman, at the food, at the buggy, at the inside of the trailer.

"Hey, Austin. I just came by so you could meet my brother," Cash said. "This is Jamie."

"Hey," Jamie said, looking anywhere but at Austin, and Cash knew he'd made his point.

"Jamie, I volunteer as Austin's Big Brother. His dad died a few years ago."

Cash looked at Austin.

"You still good for a movie on Friday night?"

Austin nodded.

"Great. Can you walk us out?"

They left the trailer and Cash told Jamie to wait for him on the sidewalk. At the door, he turned back to Austin.

"I didn't bring my brother here to shame you. He's spoiled and this was the only way I could think of to teach him a lesson. To show him how much more he has than a lot of people."

Austin's cheeks must have been hot. They were bright red.

Cash settled his hand on the boy's shoulder. God, he loved this kid. "You take a hell of a lot better care of your mom than all the teenagers out there. I'm proud of you."

He squeezed Austin's shoulder then stepped away. "See you on Friday. Shannon's coming with us."

Austin brightened and Cash grinned.

When he reached Jamie, he didn't say a word, just left him alone with his thoughts on the walk back to Main Street. Jamie was subdued as they climbed into Cash's truck. Cash drove them home, and the silence lasted until they pulled up at his house.

"You live here?" Jamie asked. "With all these women's colors?"

"This is the way the house came. Eventually, I'll add an addition and paint the whole thing a new color."

The dogs went nuts when they saw Jamie, jumping all over him until Cash pulled them off and put them outside. "Behave yourselves."

"I didn't know you had dogs."

"There are a lot of things we don't know about each other." Cash started a fire in the living room fireplace. "We haven't had a chance to spend time together."

They ate dinner on the floor, talking quietly, Jamie chastened and more real than Cash had seen since his adolescent hormones kicked in.

Cash learned a lot about him that night. Jamie learned a lot about Cash.

The following morning, Cash drove him to Havre and put him on the first flight bound for home. Just before Jamie stepped toward the small airline terminal, Cash pulled him back for a hug.

"Come visit me again, but next time with your parents' approval."

Jamie squeezed him in return and whispered, "Thanks," before turning away.

After Jamie's flight left, Cash called his mom to explain where Jamie had been and why, and to tell her he had sent her baby safely home.

CHAPTER FIFTEEN

"THIS BEATS JUST about anything that's ever happened to me," Cash said. He struggled to keep his voice even. His teeth scraped across his lower lip while he sucked in a deep breath. The paper he'd just finished reading trembled in his hand. He set it on the desk so Paul Hunt wouldn't see the motion.

The Ordinary Junior High principal leaned forward and rested his elbows on his desk. Paul had been principal for twenty years. Other than a few crow's-feet and thinning hair, he looked none the worse for wear. "I thought you'd enjoy reading that," Paul said. "You had no idea Austin entered this in the Career Days writing competition?"

"None. He never mentioned it." Cash glanced at the title of the essay. *Why I Want to Be a Police Officer,* by Austin Trumball. The first couple of sentences floored Cash. Man, they just floored him.

"Cash Kavenagh is the kind of man I want to be when I grow up. He's a great Big Brother and a really good cop."

Lately, he'd worried he'd lost his bond with Austin—a year's worth of friendship down the drain. Not to mention how much he missed the easiness they'd had between them. But this... What Austin was saying here... Did it get any better?

A huge balloon of pride welled in his chest. In spite of the tension between them these days and Austin's tight-lipped recalcitrance, Cash had done something right with his Little Brother.

He returned his attention to the essay.

"If I could choose, I'd make Cash Kavenagh my father."

My father. Blinking hard, he leaned back in his chair, away from the essay that was breaking his heart as much as restoring his faith.

"Did you know you'd made such a strong impression on him?" Paul asked.

Cash shook his head. "I had no idea." He tried to laugh off the intensity of the emotions flooding him. "Who knew a movie every Friday night would inspire this?"

Paul's expression remained serious. And compassionate. "This is no small accomplishment, Cash. That boy would be lost without your influence."

"Does he know you're letting me read this?"

"Oh, yes. I got his permission first."

Cash couldn't take it in. Austin had written this

great, great thing about him, and the boy wanted to be a cop, just like him.

"He's one of three finalists." Paul adjusted his large, spotless blotter, squaring it up with the edge of the desk. Cash didn't realize people still used those things. "We're placing first, second and third at the assembly today. I thought you should have a warning before you hear it read in front of the school."

Someone knocked on the door. When Paul said, "Come in," Shannon entered the room.

"What are you doing here?" Cash blurted.

"Now that everyone in the area knows I'm DEA, I asked if I could address the kids about drugs." She wore a conservative black skirt and a white button-down shirt. Must be the official DEA look. "Paul suggested I do it at the assembly today."

Cash nodded and left the office before he lost control. He felt like he had a bad case of the sniffles at the back of his sinuses. He sniffed hard. He didn't think he could possibly sit in the auditorium to hear Austin read all of that in public. He'd embarrass the shit out of himself by crying. Aw hell, of course he would stay. For sure.

Without warning, kids poured out of classrooms and headed toward the auditorium.

Cash melded into the crowd. He'd wrangled his emotions to a subdued awe by the time he found the seat reserved for him in the front row, next to Shannon.

Ten minutes later, Principal Hunt called the assembly to order. He introduced Shannon and she walked up onto the stage.

"Hi, everyone. My name is Shannon Wilson and I'm a DEA Special Agent."

After applause, she started her message.

"I'm going to address the parents here first."

A lot of parents had turned out for the assembly. Plenty of fathers and lots of mothers in cowboy hats sat with their children. They reflected the broader community of ranchers around Ordinary, where the women were as likely to pull calves and help with the branding as wipe children's noses and do laundry.

"There is a lot of temptation in society these days," Shannon said. "Your children are bombarded by it, here at school, among their peers, and especially on the internet."

She spoke with confidence despite the size of the crowd. Pride swelled in him.

"There's one place, though, that can be very dangerous for teens. It's a place that you can control. Your home."

Murmurs spread through the audience.

"After marijuana, the most abused drugs are prescription drugs, and they are being used by teenagers aged twelve to seventeen. That's right, I said as young as twelve."

More murmurs.

"Check out your medicine cabinet. Is there Vicodin for pain? Valium for panic attacks? Cough syrup for colds and allergies? If you are not actively taking these and they are sitting available in your home, your child might already be sampling them. Once you are finished with a medication, flush any leftovers. Better yet, take them to your local pharmacy. They can dispose of them safely, so they don't harm the environment."

Shannon looked out across the audience. "Aerosol spray cans. Cleaning fluids. Paint cans in the garage. All of these are a potential hazard to any young child. I'm here to tell you they can also be a hazard to your teenager if he decides to experiment with getting high."

Shannon kept the message serious. Cash turned and glimpsed a lot of nodding heads from the parents.

"Principal Hunt should have provided your children with a handout this morning. If you don't receive it this evening when your child comes home from school, contact Mr. Hunt. This handout will help you to identify drug paraphernalia. You'll be surprised that it isn't all stuff picked up from drug dealers. A lot of it is available in a normal home.

"A felt-tip marker can be turned into a drug pipe. A lipstick container can be used as a drug pipe."

"So, what are you saying?" a male voice called out from the fourth row. "We can't use felt markers anymore for our schoolwork?"

"Yeah," a female called out. "And I can't use lipstick or lip gloss?"

"Of course you can use all of those. But there is a difference between how these harmless items look when being used as drug paraphernalia and how they look for their intended purposes."

Cash heard a young voice make a snide remark, but didn't catch the words.

Shannon let it all slide off her back.

"Students, I know you don't like me at this moment for telling your parents to distrust you. For you, I've brought a slide show. Austin, dim the lights and start the show for me, okay?"

She'd enlisted Austin's help? Good for her. A nice way to make him feel special.

The room went dark and a white screen descended from the ceiling to the stage.

For the next ten minutes, no one so much as stirred in their seat. Across the screen flashed photographs, two at a time. Each pair was a before and after photo. Under the first photo was the subject's age before starting drugs. Under the other was the person's current age.

The differences were astounding. In slide after slide, young vibrant men and women became haggard, prematurely old, homely. They looked like they'd given up on life.

The images were stark and effective.

Throughout it all, Shannon didn't say a word. What was there to say? The photos said everything.

When it ended, Austin turned the lights back on.

"Before you think that these images were taken many years apart, I'd like to disabuse you of that idea. For most, this transformation took only a couple of years. In the last pair of slides, it took only one year to turn beautiful young Rachel into a ghost of herself.

"One last thing. My brother is in a hospital in Billings in coma." She cleared her throat. "He suffered an overdose when he took crystal meth. He picked it up here in Ordinary. He isn't expected to live."

Gasps spread through the audience.

"If any of you hear even a whisper about this drug in this area, please contact Sheriff Kavenagh. We need to get this dangerous drug off your streets. Look at the people sitting around you, your parents, your schoolmates, your best friends and siblings. Any one of them could wind up like my brother Tom without your help."

When she left the stage, she received a round of applause.

Cash's heart swelled. She deserved it. She might have saved a young life or two today.

Next, the finalists in the writing contest read their work. Austin wore a pair of brand new dark jeans still creased from the store's hanger and a long-sleeved T-shirt sporting fold marks.

Where had the money for new clothes come from?

Austin read the essay and Cash covered his mouth so he wouldn't blubber like a baby in front of the audience. He should have sat in the back row.

He felt Shannon watching him but refused to look at her.

Austin won the contest—a $100 Barnes & Noble gift card.

The lunch bell rang through the school and the assembly ended.

He and Shannon walked down the aisle together, but before they reached the exit, she was surrounded by parents with questions.

A couple of students hovered nearby and Cash heard one ask, "How do you become a DEA agent?"

He left the auditorium. As he traversed the halls toward the front door and the parking lot, a screaming, crushing swarm surrounded him.

"Hey, Officer Kavenagh, you gonna arrest me? I forgot my homework today." Raucous laughter followed Stephen Brewster's remark.

"No, Steve, not today."

Cash reveled in the attention and the camaraderie. Maybe he should have been a teacher. He shook his head. Naw. He was born to be a cop.

Fourteen-year-old Melody Arthurs brushed past him, too close for comfort, with the sensuality and maturity of a thirty-year-old. That girl was heading down a one-way street with no exit. Any day now, Cash expected her to crash into a brick wall called trouble. If she wasn't pregnant by the time she turned sixteen, he'd be amazed. He'd already had a talk with her mother, but his warnings had fallen on deaf ears. In this case, the precocious apple didn't fall too far from the tree.

Cash spotted Austin at the same moment Melody did. She sidled up to him with her too-short skirt peeking out from under the puffy pink ski jacket.

"Hey, Austin, wanna come to my house tonight?" she asked. When she leaned in close to finish the question, her breast touched Austin's arm. He jerked away and mumbled, "No thanks." Obviously, he hadn't developed an interest in girls yet, but they clearly had an interest in him.

He was a good-looking kid.

"Go get some lunch, Melody," Cash said, "and quit robbing the cradle."

Melody huffed and flounced away. She latched onto tall, muscular Mike Forster, who was two years older than her. He'd failed a couple of grades. He handed her a cigarette, then rested one hand on her rump. Bingo. Melody was about to start her one-way slide. Thank God it wouldn't be with Austin.

"Hey, Forster, you know better," Cash called. "Take it off school property." The cigarettes and the sex.

Forster squinted through a cloud of exhaled smoke, then shrugged and pulled Melody in the direction of Main Street and the diner. Cash caught sight of Austin in the parking lot.

"Come over here a minute," he told Austin.

They walked to Cash's cruiser, Austin silent, Cash still churning with the emotions Austin's essay had stirred.

"Thanks for what you wrote," Cash said, staring off into the distance.

Austin shrugged and looked off into the distance, too.

Cash turned to him. "It was great."

Austin's gaze shot to Cash's face, with a brief flash of puppy adoration he quickly hid. "Yeah?" The boy's tone was neutral, careful. He swallowed. "Did you like it?"

"What you said about me?" Cash said. "Yeah. I liked it. A lot."

A thought occurred to him. "Where's your mom?"

"She said she couldn't come 'cause she wasn't feeling well."

"We need to get your mom to a doctor."

"I know. I'm worried about her. I tried talking to her, but she won't go."

Cash squeezed his shoulder. "I'll help you figure this out."

Austin's frown eased but he shivered in a thin fall coat. "Where's the winter jacket I bought you?"

Austin shrugged and refused to return his look.

A second later, Cash remembered something he had seen earlier. Steve Brewster wearing the same jacket he had bought for Austin. He was pretty sure he'd picked up the only one in town.

"How come Steve has your jacket?"

Austin's brows shot up. He tried to deke around Cash, but Cash gripped his sleeve and dragged him back.

"Answer me, Austin." He shook him, lightly. "Talk to me."

Austin stared at the ground.

"Did you sell it to him?" He watched a guilty flush climb Austin's cheeks. "Cripes, Austin, if you need money so badly, come to me."

Austin shrugged. "I wanted new clothes 'cause I had to stand up onstage today."

"Oh." Cash understood that.

He slipped a ten out of his wallet and slid it into Austin's pocket. "Go get yourself some lunch."

"'Kay. Thanks." Austin hunched his shoulders and trudged away.

Cash waited until Shannon finished running the gauntlet of parents with questions.

Brad and Mary Lou McCloskey stopped to question Shannon. Their oldest boy went to this school.

Mary Lou didn't look happy. Strange. She was usually so perky and sweet, but she wasn't involved in the conversation at all. In fact, it looked like she was surreptitiously tugging Brad's hand so she could leave.

Finally, Shannon joined him outside at the front of the school.

"Do you want to go for lunch?" he asked.

"Sure, then I need to head home to do some research."

"What kind of research?"

She glanced around them then said in a quiet voice, "On Brad's bank accounts. I want to see if there have been large amounts deposited lately."

"Good thinking. He wouldn't be likely to put it in the local bank, would he?"

"No, but I can look farther afield."

"Good idea."

Before heading to the restaurant, Cash searched out Steve Brewster, gave him the forty bucks he'd paid Austin for the jacket and threw it into his truck to give to Austin later.

MARY LOU DUMPED a bunch of containers and garbage onto the drug-making detritus already at the back of her parents' land.

Her hands shook.

How could she have been so stupid that she started a drug manufacturing business? In her greed and her desire to get away from Brad with a sizable nest egg, she'd completely ignored how dangerous the drug was, what it did to people.

Brad had come home for lunch today and had wanted to have sex afterward, but she'd felt sick with guilt. She'd sent him back to work.

Yesterday's school assembly had sickened her. The tuna salad sandwich she'd had for lunch today tried to come back up. She swallowed hard.

Tears threatened. She had to stop now. She'd already made good money and would be able to leave Brad soon.

She sank onto her knees and covered her face with her hands.

"I don't want to leave Brad," she wailed to the empty woods. She'd fallen back in love with him. She would have liked nothing better than to have gone up to their bedroom after lunch to love the daylights out of him.

She stalked back to the RV.

She had to close down the lab. If she had her way, she would obliterate it. But how? How did one get rid of a meth lab once it was already set up? These chemicals were so toxic.

She'd polluted the RV. Worse, she'd polluted this beautiful piece of land.

Even the fact that her parents had given it to Brad instead of to her no longer mattered.

She wanted her old life back, but with the new relationship with her husband. He would support her in a career. She knew it. Brad wanted what was best for her. She understood that now, felt it in her soul. He would encourage her while she went back to school to learn new skills. Maybe she could become a science teacher. That would be good and positive, not shameful like…like… drug manufacturing.

What had she been thinking? She'd been so insanely angry with Brad she'd done what she thought had to be done, but there had been alternatives. She just hadn't seen them.

And now she had this awful mess to clean up.

For pity's sake, when she'd figured out about Brad and Connie, when she'd been poisonously angry with her husband, why hadn't she just had an affair with someone in the county rather than starting on this stupid, stupid caper of making drugs?

Yes, she'd made amazing money. Yes, she'd enjoyed having money. Yes, she could have independence if she wanted it.

She didn't.

She wanted her home life and her new deeper relationship with her husband and a legitimate career.

She wanted this business to be done and gone.

People would take anything for a high and the stuff had sold so fast she'd made a fortune. The danger, the money, it had all been seductive.

But someone had nearly died, had overdosed, might still die. On her stuff, and so close to home. Janey Wilson's brother The guilt was killing her.

She'd never meant for anyone to get hurt, let alone die. She'd just wanted money of her own. And she'd thought she was being so clever.

She needed to go home to Brad and her sweet boys, and find a way to atone for what she'd done that was so, so wrong.

Disgusted with herself, she swiped her arm across the table, sending drugs and beakers and jars flying.

As she stepped through the door to drive home to her husband and children, the RV exploded.

CHAPTER SIXTEEN

"CASH, YOU gotta come over." Austin sounded terrified.

Cash jumped out of his office chair and grabbed his coat. Whatever was going on with Austin, he needed help. "What's wrong? Where are you?"

"I'm at home. I can't get my mom to wake up. I don't know what's wrong with her."

"I'll be right there."

On the way to his truck, he called an ambulance and directed them to Connie's trailer.

Austin waited for him at the trailer's front door.

"She's on the sofa." The kid was barely holding himself together, and Cash cursed the fates yet again that Austin had so much responsibility so early in life.

Cash knelt on the floor in front of Austin's mother.

"Damn it, Connie," he whispered, shaking her. Now that he was here and could see she was tripping really badly, his anger dissolved, replaced by pity.

She opened her eyes.

"Cash?" Austin stood behind him. "What's wrong with her?"

Connie's eyes were dilated and she was crying. "She isn't sick, Austin. She's stoned."

She scratched at her skin, picked at her arms. "Get them out," she slurred.

"What, Connie?"

"The bugs under my skin." She scratched at skin that was already bleeding and Cash caught her hands to stop her. She whimpered, "They crawled inside me and I can't get them out."

The smell of sweat flowing from her was acrid. Her hair was dry. Her lips were dry.

"What did you take, Connie?" Cash asked.

"Nothing," she yelled.

"Connie, come on. I can't help you if you don't tell me."

She cried again and whimpered, "Don't hate me."

Her mood changes… Worse than dealing with an alcoholic.

"I won't, Connie." He struggled to moderate his tone when all he felt was frustration with her. "Just tell me the truth."

"Meth."

His heart rate spiked. Yes! A solid lead. He'd make sure she got the help she needed, but damn if he wasn't celebrating a bit at the information.

"Where did you get it?"

"Don't want to tell you."

"You have to." He heard a commotion at the door and knew it was the paramedics.

She sniffled. "McCloskey."

"Brad?" Against all reasonable hope that it wasn't true, he finally had to admit that his suspicions had been correct.

"No, no, no," Connie mumbled.

He stood to let the paramedics get close to Connie…and to go arrest Brad McCloskey.

One of the men said, "Busy morning. There's a big fire out on Sideroad 90. A neighbor called it in. Reported an explosion."

"Okay, I'll head out there."

"No!" Connie said.

Cash spun back around. "Let them help you."

"Is my mom overdosing?" Austin asked.

"No. She's just really high."

"Cash," Connie called while the emergency personnel strapped her onto the gurney.

"Yeah?" he asked.

"Not Brad."

"What? But you said it was McCloskey."

"Mary Lou. Not Brad."

She might as well have slapped him. Sweet Mary Lou?

"Mary Lou," she emphatically, like a drunk

overemphasizing a point. "I wanted money. She said no. Take drugs."

Connie tried to blackmail Mary Lou about Austin's relationship to Brad and Mary Lou had given her meth instead of money?

Human nature and the strange directions it could take never ceased to amaze him.

They wheeled Connie out to the ambulance.

Cash drove Austin to the hospital.

"Austin, I hate to do this to you, but I have to leave for a while."

Austin looked close to panic.

"I'll be back to pick you up and then you'll stay with me. Got it?"

The boy's shoulders relaxed and he nodded.

Cash squeezed one his thin arms. "I'm with you, Austin. You won't have to handle this alone."

SHANNON SAT AT Janey's dining room table with her laptop in front of her, scanning the Controlled Substance databases to see who'd been buying the ingredients to make meth.

No one here in Ordinary, as far as she could tell. There were ways around any law, any source of information the DEA came up with, and any criminal might find a way to cheat it.

She transferred to a database that allowed her access to the local pharmacies' purchase orders.

An hour later, she sat up straight, her heart racing. Bingo! Thank freaking goodness, bingo.

Cash had been right all along. The meth cook was Brad McCloskey.

Shannon's phone rang.

"Shannon?" Cash was on the other end of the line.

"Cash, we got him. Brad McCloskey." Her voice hummed with excitement. "You should see what I uncovered."

"Fill me in when you get here."

"Get where?"

"I'm at a farmhouse on Sideroad 90." Compared to her, Cash sounded subdued. "You need to get out here. Now."

After giving her directions, he hung up. She scooted out to her car and lost no time getting there.

The grounds were covered with fire trucks and cop cars and an ambulance.

And a burned-out RV.

Hallelujah.

The meth lab.

She parked on the driveway and walked to the site. Cash saw her and approached.

"Who's farm is this?" she asked.

"It belonged to Brad McCloskey's parents-in-law. They're both dead now."

Excitement roared through her. They'd caught

the culprit. She grasped his arm. "You were right. He's been ordering through the pharmacy and cooking it out here."

"No."

"No?"

"We were close, but so wrong, too."

"What do you mean?"

"It wasn't Brad. It was his wife, Mary Lou."

"The sweet, conservative, church-going wife?" Oh my God. She'd totally missed that, had not even suspected.

Cash led her to the clearing between the old farmhouse and the still-smoldering RV.

Paramedics were lifting a woman onto a stretcher, facedown, her back badly burned. Her scalp was an angry red where the hair had been singed away.

A car spun crazily into the driveway and side-swiped her car.

"Hey," she yelled and stepped forward to give the idiot a piece of her mind. Cash stopped her with a hand on her arm.

"It's Brad."

"Do you think he was part of this?"

"Mary Lou already said no."

Brad ran to his wife, close to the edge of control. He was clearly terrified and bewildered. The guy didn't have a clue what his wife had been up to.

"What happened?" He reached a hand to touch her then pulled it back, realizing how badly hurt she was.

Mary Lou opened her eyes and whispered something.

Brad bent forward to hear her better. One side of her face was mashed onto the stretcher but she managed to speak again.

"So sorry." Her voice was raw, gritty, her throat no doubt seared by the heat of the fire.

Brad looked from his wife to a paramedic to a firefighter. To the burned RV. "I don't understand. What happened?"

Cash stepped forward. "There was an explosion in the RV and Mary Lou got caught in it."

"What was she even doing out here? We don't use this place. We were going to put it up for sale in the spring."

"We can discuss it later in my office."

"Your office? Why?"

"It's better if we talk about it there."

"No. I want to know right now. What's going on?"

Cash sighed. "Mary Lou was making methamphetamines while you were at work. She ordered supplies through the pharmacy."

"That's absurd. Mary Lou would never do anything like that. I—"

His face was so struck by a realization that

Shannon leaned forward. "What? What are you remembering?"

"She insisted on keeping the books for the store."

Cash nodded.

"She wouldn't let me touch them. But meth? That's— That's illegal. It's immoral." His voice became strident. "Mary Lou wouldn't do that. She's a good person."

"It appears that she did."

Brad bent over Mary Lou again.

"*Why,* Mary Lou?"

"Mad about Connie. Wanted leave you. Needed money."

The paramedics wheeled her toward the ambulance with Brad running alongside. They hit a rock and Mary Lou gasped.

"Careful!" Brad shouted.

"Needed money," Mary Lou said.

"I would have given you money, even if it was to leave me. I love you, Mary Lou. I would have sold the store." Brad stopped to catch his breath. "I would have given you *anything.*"

As she was loaded into the waiting ambulance, tears streamed from the one eye they could see. Thinking of Tom, and whoever else had got hooked on Mary Lou's meth, Shannon wasn't stirred by her tears.

She leaned close to Cash. "I have trouble feeling sorry for her."

"I know what you mean. She isn't the woman I thought she was."

"I guess there's such a thing as limited compassion. I'll save mine for her victims."

A moment later, she and the paramedics were gone, with nothing left of them but dust churned up into the air then slowly settling back to earth.

Brad turned away and nearly broke down. "What will happen to her?"

"After she's recovered from her injuries," Cash said, "she'll stand trial."

Shannon picked up from there. "She'll be charged with trafficking methamphetamines."

Brad swiped his hands down his face. "It's serious, isn't it?"

"About as serious as it gets." All of the compassion she couldn't feel for Mary Lou came through for Brad. Poor guy hadn't had a thing to do with this. She watched Brad stumble to his car.

"Come on." She pulled on Cash's sleeve. "We have work to do."

They checked the house first. They found only a couple of lab coats for evidence. Nothing else inside the house was used for the lab.

"Looks like she'd done it all in the RV." They went back outside and studied the burned-out vehicle. "At least there won't be any contamination left. Here, at any rate," she amended. "There'll be a dump site somewhere. We need to find it."

They walked the grounds until they did.

"What a damn waste of a pretty piece of land." Surveying empty and soiled containers, Cash shook his head. "Look at this crap. The ground will be contaminated."

"Yes." Shannon turned over an empty container with the toe of her shoe. "We need to get it cleaned out before it leaches into the groundwater."

With a disgusted curse, Cash turned and stomped away.

CASH DECIDED TO pick Austin up from the hospital later that evening. He had a load of paperwork to do. He'd done a bunch until he figured he couldn't let Austin wait for him any longer. He'd have to finish up in the morning.

He left Shannon on the phone with the DEA planning the clean-up operation at the farm and headed to the hospital.

He found Austin sitting in the hospital room with his mother. She was sound asleep.

Austin looked up when he entered and the frown disappeared from his face.

"Hey," Cash said. "Come on. I'll take you home. Are you hungry?"

Austin nodded.

"You must be starving."

"Yeah."

Cash drove him back to Ordinary and parked outside of Chester's Bar and Grill.

Inside, he led Austin to a booth. Seemed that all he was doing these days was feeding hungry boys—Austin and Jamie.

He needed to fatten Austin up but his first priority was to make him healthy. He wanted him eating more than his usual burgers and fries.

Chester's wife, Missy Donovan, came to take their order.

He ordered steak for himself, rare. "You think you could eat a steak, Austin?"

"I've never had one."

"Bring a small one for Austin, medium well," Cash instructed Missy. "What vegetables do you have tonight?"

"Broccoli, cauliflower, carrots, parsnips."

"We'll take all of them. Load his plate up."

"You got it, Cash. What'll you have to drink?"

"I'll have a beer." Only one. He could use a couple, but he was driving. "How about a glass of milk for Austin. Whole, not skim."

When the food arrived, Austin blinked.

"Dig in."

"My mom made parsnips once. I hated them."

"Okay, eat around them."

Cash popped one of his own into his mouth.

It was crunchy on the outside and fragrant with rosemary.

"You have to try one of the parsnips. I don't know what Missy did to them, but they're amazing."

Austin looked dubious, but took a small bite of one, nibbled then nodded. "It's good."

He ate the rest of the parsnip and most of the vegetables and steak, but Cash knew he was preoccupied thinking about his mother.

Cash himself was preoccupied. He wanted to talk to Shannon, itched with the need to find out what would happen to them now. Finding that lab had been bittersweet.

What was next for them? He had to wait to find out. He sensed that Austin needed his undivided attention.

Austin put his fork down and asked, "What's gonna happen to my mom?"

"Keep eating, Austin. I'd say she's addicted to the meth Mary Lou was giving her."

"So, like what Shannon was talking about at school at the assembly yesterday?"

"Yes. She'll need rehab. I phoned around and found an available bed for her in a detoxification program in Billings. While she's there, you'll live with me. That okay with you?"

"Yeah. That's good."

There was a subject that he had to broach even

though he didn't want to. "There is an alternative."

"What? The social worker like you said before?"

"God, no. I'm not going to do that to you. I will have to talk to them, but I'm pretty sure they won't have a problem with you staying with me."

"I'll tell them that's where I want to be and if they make me go someplace else, I'll run away."

He raised a hand to stem Austin's rising anger. "They won't make you go somewhere else. I'm as certain of that as I can be."

"Then what's the other place you were talking about?"

"With your dad. Your real dad."

"I don't want to go with him. I want to go with you." Austin had raised his voice and panic ran through it.

"Okay. If Brad kicks up a fuss, I'll talk to him. I don't think there'll be a problem there. His wife got burned really badly today, so he'll be with her."

He put his utensils down on his empty plate and pushed it away.

"I just didn't know whether you would want to go with him because he's your dad."

"I don't know him and I don't like him. He thought I was shoplifting. I know you and I like you." Austin said it as though his word was final and copied what Cash had done with his utensils and plate.

"Can you eat dessert? A sundae?"

Austin nodded and, a few minutes later, ate a strawberry sundae while Cash drank decaf coffee.

They picked up clothes for Austin from his trailer then drove to the convenience store in Monroe and loaded up on groceries.

By the time they got to Cash's house, Austin was asleep.

Cash left him in the passenger seat and carried the groceries into the house. When he opened the door, Danny and Paddy ran out to greet him.

After depositing the groceries in the kitchen and putting a few things away in the fridge, he walked back outside and headed to the car, whistling for the dogs as he went.

They came running.

"There's someone here for you, boys."

Cash opened the passenger door. Paddy jumped inside onto Austin's lap and licked his face. Not to be outdone, Danny put his long front legs on the seat and licked Austin.

Austin came awake with a jerk. "What?" Then he recognized the dogs and knew where he was. "Hey, guys, what are you doing?" He wiped his mouth and pretended to be grossed out, but Cash knew the truth. The boy was thrilled.

Cash set him up in the small bedroom at the back of the house. Austin fell asleep quickly.

Cash let the dogs out to run some more while he unpacked all of Austin's clothes and threw them into the washing machine—no telling when they'd been washed last. They smelled sweaty. He picked up the clothes he'd had on from the floor of the small bedroom and closed the door so the machine wouldn't wake him. The boy was exhausted.

His socks reeked.

When he had the first load running with extra detergent, he called the dogs back in and gave them dinner.

After they finished, he walked down the hall to Austin's room and opened the door.

Danny and Paddy ran in and jumped onto the bed with the boy. Paddy curled into a ball against his chest and fell asleep in seconds. Danny lay across his legs, all three squished onto a single bed.

When he woke up in the morning, if the dogs were still there, Austin would be thrilled.

After he transferred the laundry to the dryer, he glanced at the clock. Eleven-thirty. He walked into the living room and called Shannon. Since they'd found the lab this afternoon, he'd had one underlying question scooting around in his brain. Now that the day was over, he needed an answer.

"Were you asleep?"

"Cash, hi. No. I was getting ready for bed, though. What's up?"

He brought her up to speed on what was happening with Austin and his mother.

"It's good of you to take him in."

"Thanks. Listen, Shannon, I've been thinking. What happens now that the meth lab is gone? You'll be here for a few more days to clean it up. What then? What happens to us?"

"I don't know."

"I gotta be honest. I've fallen for you hard. I want to live with you."

"Where, Cash? Here in Ordinary?"

"Yes. What's wrong with that?"

"It wouldn't work for me."

He picked at a piece of lint on the armchair. "So your career is more important to you than I am." He wasn't surprised, but he was disappointed. Devastated.

"Don't put it like that." Shannon sounded so close, he felt like he could reach out and touch her. He wanted to.

"How should I put it?"

"My job is important, not just to me, but also to the people I protect from scumbags."

"Can't someone else do that job?"

"Of course they can, but I have skills. I have drive and a passion for the job. I was born to do it."

"So, there's no way we can work this out? You don't want to even try?"

"I do. As hard as you've fallen for me, I've got it bad for you. But I don't think you'll like my solution any better than I liked yours."

"What do you mean? That I should leave Ordinary?"

"That would be one way to work it out."

"You would make a commitment to me if I left Ordinary and followed you and your job around?"

"Yes. I never thought I would say that to a man, but yes, I would commit to you, Cash. I love you."

"But you love your career more—"

"Don't say that. It's so unfair and simplistic. I could say that you love your life here more than you love me."

Did he? His life here was important to him. He'd built something solid and so unlike his childhood, he couldn't give it up. What about his friends? What about C.J. and his family who he thought of as his own family?

He'd built here what he hadn't had in his own childhood.

How could he leave that to move to a big city, when he'd left the city because he hadn't liked it one bit? What would he do, become a beat cop?

He enjoyed too much respect here to leave it to start at the bottom again in an incarnation of a job he'd never wanted.

"Judging by your silence," she said on the other end of the line, "you won't leave Ordinary."

"Shannon, wait. I didn't say that."

"You didn't have to. You took too long. I know your answer. I— I don't know what to say. I guess just goodbye."

She hung up.

"Wait," Cash shouted, then heard a thump in the back bedroom followed by one of the dogs coming down the hall.

Danny, always sensitive to Cash's moods, rested his head on his arm.

"I'm not sure what I just did. Either something practical, or something incredibly stupid, and I don't know how to tell which is which."

He leaned forward, rested his elbows on his knees and hung his head. Danny licked his face but Cash didn't respond. He stayed that way for a long, long time.

CHAPTER SEVENTEEN

SHANNON LAY AWAKE for hours, a little stunned. No, shell-shocked, if she were going to be truthful.

How had this happened? She'd allowed herself to fall in love. She'd known better, but she'd allowed it to happen anyway, had practically helped it along when she'd taken those few days in Yellowstone with Cash.

What was his attachment to this place? He hadn't been born here. He hadn't grown up here.

She knew his background, knew what his father had been like. So what? That didn't mean he had to hide away in a small town.

Hours later, she still had no answer.

When she heard the house stir and slowly come awake, she went downstairs.

Janey turned from the stove to say good morning, then saw Shannon's face.

She immediately took her by the sleeve and directed her to the living room.

"What happened?"

"I made a mistake. I fell in love with Cash."

"He won't leave here, will he?"

"No."

"And you won't stay."

"No."

"Oh, Shannon, honey. Come here." Janey held her and rocked her until they both smelled something burning. Sierra called out, "Mom! The oatmeal!"

Shannon followed Janey to the kitchen. Janey tossed out the ruined oatmeal and plopped a couple of boxes of cold cereal on the table. The children helped themselves.

Shannon got herself a cup of coffee then sat at the table with them. Sierra climbed onto her lap. Shannon poured her a bowl of cereal and covered it with milk.

"Eat, honey."

Sierra turned around but remained on Shannon's lap while she ate, and Shannon took comfort from Sierra's warmth and weight.

She looked around the kitchen and, for the first time in her life, realized that she wanted this for herself. She wanted a home and a loving family, and she wanted it with only one man.

Cash.

AFTER ANOTHER SLEEPLESS night, Shannon crawled downstairs for coffee.

"I want you eating something this morning," Janey said, "instead of surviving on caffeine."

She put a bowl of oatmeal on the table in front of Shannon, who added brown sugar and ate it listlessly.

The children ran upstairs to get dressed for school.

"Auntie Shannon, you're phone is ringing," Sierra called. "Do you want me to bring it downstairs?"

Cash!

"Yes."

She ran to the bottom of the stairs and took the phone when Sierra brought it to her.

She answered, but it wasn't Cash on the other end.

Her heart plummeted with her mood, but she said yes when the woman asked if this was Shannon Wilson.

A minute later, she ended the call with a whoop.

Janey and a couple of the children came running.

"Shannon? What is it?"

"He's awake." Shannon's voice trembled, afraid to believe it was true. Afraid that it might be a cruel joke. "Tom is alive and well."

Janey pulled her into a hug, the older sister who had raised Shannon now four inches shorter than her as an adult.

She scrubbed the top of Janey's hair, then returned her embrace.

Janey laughed against Shannon's chest. "Can't breathe."

Shannon laughed, too, and let her go, wiping her eyes and cheeks as she did. Janey did the same to her own face.

"I'm going to see him," Shannon said. "Do you want to come?"

"Sure, I'll call in one of my part-time employees and get her to open today and tomorrow. I'll go tell C.J."

She ran out of the house, followed by the children.

Alone in the quiet kitchen, Shannon called Cash.

"Hey," he said when he answered, his voice full of banked emotion. He obviously had call display and knew it was her.

Her heart reacted to that emotion.

"I'm leaving town today, Cash."

He didn't respond.

"It's Tom. He woke up." Her initial excitement had turned quiet, had become subdued with gratitude and prayers to the Powers-That-Be, whoever they were, for giving her back her brother.

"I'm happy for you, Shannon," Cash finally said. "I really am. I had my fingers crossed. I didn't want to see another death."

He was thinking of his father.

"Yeah, there's been enough bad news going around. How's Austin?"

"Good."

They were silent for a while, then "When are you—?"

"Janey and I—"

"Go ahead," he said. "Janey and you...?"

"We're driving into Billings today."

"Are you coming back today, too?"

"Probably not. I want to spend time with Tom. Janey's getting someone to take care of the store today and tomorrow."

"Give him my best, okay?"

"I will. Thanks for understanding how much this means to me."

"No problem, Shanny-poo."

She giggled. "How did you know that name?"

Cash laughed. "Janey told me."

"I'm going to kill her. Why did she tell you?"

"So you wouldn't have too much leverage over me while I had nothing."

"What kind of leverage do I have over you?"

A long silence. "You haven't figured that out yet?" he asked quietly.

She might have, but was afraid to hope. And why would she hope when it was inconvenient, when it wouldn't fit into her life?

"I love you, Shannon."

Joy filled her. His love might be inconvenient, but it mattered to her.

"I love you, too, Cash."

She heard a long sigh on the other end.

"I'll be returning to work after I see Tom."

"No. Come back. One more time. For one more night."

He hung up, giving her no time to argue. He must have known she would say no.

She kissed and hugged the kids before C.J. drove them to school so Janey could pack.

Shannon threw her clothes into a bag and retrieved her gun from the top shelf of the closet. Once outside, she tossed it into the trunk of her car.

A vehicle came roaring into the driveway behind her. C.J. must have rushed home to say goodbye to Janey before she left.

Shannon turned around to make some kind of joke—Janey would be gone only a couple of days—but it wasn't C.J.

Cash stood beside the open door of his pickup staring at her, looking as handsome as could be in his pressed uniform shirt and black cowboy hat.

He rushed to her, took her in his arms and kissed her.

Don't!

She struggled, but he kissed her anyway, trying to convince her of his passion.

She pulled away, roughly, because she didn't want to end this any more than he did.

"Don't make this any harder, Cash." Something tickled her cheek. She swiped a hand across it. Her fingers came away wet. "I love you. You love me. But we live different lives and there doesn't seem to be any middle ground where we can meet."

His lips thinned. "There must be something we can do."

"What? Meet in a motel room somewhere between my big city and your small town?"

Judging by the look on his face, Cash understood she hadn't meant the offer, that the distance between them was about more than just miles.

They had different jobs to do, different lifestyles to live.

"Cash, go." Her voice sounded shaky. "There's nothing left to say." He took his hat off and banged it against his thigh. He cursed, then spun away from her and left without another word.

Shannon turned her back, determinedly. Time to get back to her old life.

LATER THAT DAY, Shannon walked into Tom's hospital room with Janey.

He lay with his eyes closed, but opened them when he heard her footfall.

"Shannon. Janey." His trembling voice sounded clear, unlike the last time she'd heard it.

He was painfully thin, but his pallor good.

She took his hand and squeezed. Janey walked to his other side to take his left hand.

"How do you feel?" Shannon asked.

"Weak."

"You look well-rested," Janey said.

Tom's answering laugh was subdued, but somehow peaceful. "I guess I should. I've slept for a couple of weeks."

"Something's changed about you," Shannon observed. "I mean, besides not being on drugs. You look serene."

"I am."

"Why?"

"I saw them."

"Saw who?" Janey asked, but Shannon thought she might already know.

"Cathy, Casey and Stevie." He looked first at Janey and then at Shannon, squeezing their hands. "I died for a while. The doctor confirmed it. While I was gone, I saw them. They're happy where they are. When the doctors brought me back, Cathy said they would watch over me."

Shannon's vision misted. She wasn't a woo-woo superstitious type of person. She had her feet planted firmly on the ground, but she believed

Tom. At least, *she* believed that he believed what he saw and that was all that mattered.

"I need to get back to work," he said.

"Work?"

"Yeah, I need to see whether my boss will give me a second chance. Then I have to do something I'll need your help with, Shannon."

"Me? Sure. What is it?"

"I want to talk to high school kids, to tell them how bad drugs are. How they destroy people."

Something inside of her warmed. "I can help you set that up."

"It would be foolish, selfish, to wallow in my grief for Cathy and the boys when I could be doing something good with the rest of my life."

"So...you think you've kicked the drugs?"

"My body has been off them for a couple of weeks and I feel good. It's a fine place to start the rest of my life."

A place to start the rest of my life.

Where was the rest of Shannon's life? Working with the DEA, certainly. But what about her private life? It stretched out in front of her, looking emptier than she could have imagined.

She didn't return to Ordinary.

She went straight to work. That day.

Over the next few weeks, she threw herself into it body and soul. Her boss told her to slow down. The partners she worked with told her to slow down.

She couldn't. She had to save every last addict. She had to bust every creep and criminal out there selling drugs to innocents.

She had to stop thinking about Cash.

She avoided her apartment because being alone, being independent, was no longer a happy option. Without Cash, it was torture.

IT TOOK CASH a few weeks to realize that people were avoiding him. Everyone but Austin.

Austin can't avoid you, can he? He lives with you until his mom recovers.

Austin and he had driven his mum to the detox facility in Billings.

They celebrated Christmas with the Wrights. Cash was miserable there, too, even with C.J.'s great kids crawling all over him and Austin ecstatic about the Christmas present Cash had bought him. New clothes, skateboarding shoes and a skateboard.

Austin called his mother on Christmas Day then went to his room. Cash suspected that he'd maybe cried a little.

If Cash wasn't careful, he would spoil the kid.

Other than that highlight, though, he was in a lousy mood. For an easy-going guy, it was rotten to feel so bad all of the time. Non-stop. As though a piece of him had been ripped alive from his body.

On the Friday night after Christmas, Cash got ready to take Austin to the movies.

He finished changing after work and walked out of his bedroom to the living room.

Austin sat on the sofa. For the first time, Cash noticed the changes in him.

He no longer wore the perpetual frown. That constant look of fear had been banished from his eyes. He'd filled out, because he ate three meals a day every day, and Cash made sure they were all healthy.

His skin looked better. He was happier, more like a normal kid rather than that serious boy who carried too much responsibility, who'd been called on to grow up too early.

Cash also noticed that he wasn't ready to go to the movie.

"Why aren't you ready?"

"I don't want to go."

"We go every Friday night. Why don't you want to go tonight?"

"I want to stay here with you and talk."

"About what?"

"About Shannon."

"*What?* What about her?"

"Sit down, Cash." Austin patted the sofa beside him and that gesture made him look so much like a miniature mature man, or someone's wise old mother, Cash nearly laughed. Except that Austin wanted to talk about Shannon.

Perversely, Cash refused to sit on the sofa. He sat in the armchair across from Austin.

"What do you want?" He sounded like a recalcitrant child and didn't care.

He'd been miserable, *aching,* without Shannon.

He'd known better than to fall in love with her. He was angry with the world and everyone in it.

"What?" he prodded Austin.

"Why don't you see Shannon or talk to her? I never hear you talk to her on the phone. You never say you want to visit her. I could find somewhere to stay when you're gone."

Just the fact that Austin was willing to let Cash out of his sight was amazing considering that in the first few days he'd followed Cash around like a puppy.

"I thought you liked Shannon," he said.

Cash shrugged. "She's okay."

Austin frowned. "I thought you *really* liked her."

He couldn't lie to Austin. "I do," he said quietly. "I love her."

"Then why aren't you with her?"

"Because she won't live here with me in Ordinary."

Austin was silent for a minute then said, "Why don't you live where she is?"

"I don't want to live in the city."

"Why not?"

Should Cash tell him? "Do you really want to know?"

Austin nodded and hair flopped forward onto his forehead, reminding Cash that he was due for a haircut.

"Let's go into Haven for pizza."

Cash had forgotten to pick up groceries—a bad sign. He was usually pretty good in that way, but his mind had been slipping since Shannon left. Everything had been slipping. He was miserable.

He could take Austin into Chester's in Ordinary, but it would be busy on a Friday night and he didn't want anyone to overhear his life's story.

Why not? I thought you'd come to terms with who your father was?

I did.

Well, then, what's your problem?

Be quiet.

They drove into Haven and found the last booth in the pizza restaurant.

After they ordered, he told Austin how things had been when he was growing up, about the kind of man his father had been, ambitious, crazy to get ahead and have it all.

When he finished, Austin was silent for a long

time. Cash could practically see that serious mind of his working.

"So how come you won't see Shannon?"

"Don't you get it? She's ambitious just like my old man was."

"No way. Not even close. She doesn't sound like you said your dad was. Didn't you get to know her at all?"

Yes, he did. That was the problem. He'd gotten to know her too well. He knew how talented and smart she was. And how driven. "She'll do anything to get ahead."

"She didn't help everyone here to get ahead. She was doing it to catch the bad guys. That's not the problem, Cash." He took a bite of his pizza, chewed it thoughtfully. "What's the real problem?"

"Nothing," Cash answered quickly.

"You remind me of a big turkey with his feathers ruffled. I've been paying attention to you lately. You're afraid of something. It feels real big."

"You're a kid, Austin. What do you know?" He had to reel himself in. He shouldn't let his own unhappiness make him mean to his Little.

Austin shrugged. "I don't think there's anything wrong with Shannon. She's pretty."

She's drop-dead gorgeous.

"She's really smart."

She's brilliant. Intelligent. Clever.

"She wants to put the bad guys away."

She wants to annihilate them.

"She wants everyone to be good and be happy."

She wants to save the world.

"So how come you don't want to be with her?"

I don't know.

On the drive home, just as they turned down the long driveway to his house, Austin said, "I think you're scared, Cash."

"What?"

"I think you're scared to be with Shannon. Why?"

He parked the car, the question speeding his pulse. "Scared? Forget it. Why would I be scared?"

"I don't know."

"Well, I'm not," he spat out on his way to the house. Austin followed him inside.

He tossed his coat onto the back of the sofa.

"You want me to hang that up for you?"

"No," Cash yelled. "I'm not scared, got it?"

Austin spread his hands. "Okay."

"It's not okay. Why would you even say that?"

He stomped into the bathroom and slammed the door. When he finished, he washed and dried his hands and strode back to the living room, the question nagging at him.

"Why did you say that?"

Austin looked up from the comic he was reading. "Like I said, I've been watching you, Cash. You just seem scared and I wanted to know why."

The kid was right. Cash fell back into the armchair. What Austin said rang with the force of truth, flooring him. He really was afraid.

He hunched forward and put his head into his hands. Why?

His childhood ran through his mind, all of it, everything that he'd explained to Austin over pizza flashed through him and took shape.

He sat up and stared at Austin, the answer almost blinding in its simplicity.

Oh Lord, out of the mouths of babes. The simplicity of the truth stunned him.

At the end of his life, Francis Kavenagh had come to a place of peace. In the middle of her life, Cash's mother had done the same. But Cash hadn't. Oh, maybe on the surface. Maybe in some superficial sense. But he had only come to a pseudo-peace because he had never challenged himself, had never challenged his life. He'd found himself a safe corner of the world to hide out in and had burrowed in, had stuck his head in the sand like an overgrown ostrich.

All along he'd been afraid that if he started a true, deep relationship with a woman, not a facsimile of what he thought a good marriage looked like, he stood the chance of failing by repeating the mistakes his parents had made.

He couldn't have handled that. He couldn't have stood to go through his childhood again.

But he wouldn't have.

His dad had wanted to be the big man, the charming popular guy, the one at the top who everyone had to look up to.

Shannon just wanted to catch the bad guys. Her ambitions hadn't really been a problem for him, he'd used them as an excuse to hide behind.

Cash just wanted her, but was afraid to take that one big step.

Shannon wasn't his dad. *Cash* wasn't his dad. They were two strong, healthy people who could rise above their backgrounds to forge a healthy relationship.

But they could only do that if they lived in the same place.

He loved Ordinary, he loved his family here, but when all was said and done, he'd been hiding. He smiled at Austin, at this quietly caring boy. "When did you get so smart?"

CASH WAS NOT his father and never had been. He was highly moral, ethical, responsible. He was, and had been since Dad left when he was sixteen, his own man.

"Come on," he said, jumping back up from the

sofa. "Let's go to bed. First thing after breakfast, pack a bag. Okay?"

"Why?"

"You're going to stay on a ranch for a few days."

"Really?"

"Yeah. Let's go see whether C.J. Wright will put you up on a horse."

Austin punched the air and ran to his bedroom.

When Cash got up in the morning, Austin was already sitting in the living room waiting with his knapsack beside him.

"What time did you get up?" Cash asked in a sleep-roughened voice. "The crack of dawn?"

Austin smiled and nodded so hard a lock of hair fell onto his forehead.

"Did you eat?"

Austin nodded again.

"Okay. Give me a couple of minutes to get ready and we'll head over."

Half an hour later, Austin climbed into the front seat of the pickup and Paddy jumped onto his lap. Danny climbed into the backseat. Cash put a huge bag of dry dog food into the bed along with leashes and anything else C.J. might need.

Cash drove to the Wright ranch, screeching into their front yard. Now that he'd made his decision to leave, he couldn't seem to do anything slowly.

Liam answered the door. "Hey, Cash. Hey, Austin. What's up?"

"Are your parents still in bed?"

"Nope. Everyone's in the kitchen having breakfast."

"Can you go get them?"

Liam looked puzzled. "Why don't you come in?"

Cash didn't have time. He wanted to *go,* but he also knew there were things he had to take care of first.

He and Austin entered the kitchen behind Liam.

"You okay, Cash?" C.J. asked when he saw Cash's face.

"Yeah. Great. Finally."

C.J. looked worried. "You want to tell me what's going on?"

"I need to ask you a big favor. Can you keep Austin with you for a few days?"

"Sure. Of course. Where are you going?"

Janey grinned at him and Cash grinned back. She knew. "I'm going to Billings to see Shannon."

"No, Cash," Janey said, but he stopped her.

"Yes. I have to see her."

"I know. Just don't go to Billings. She got a promotion. She's working out of the Denver office. She took an apartment there."

"A promotion?" Considering how much he

used to hate ambition, he thought it would anger him, but no. It filled him with pride. Shannon was good at her job and she deserved it.

Janey took out an address book and a sticky notepad from a kitchen drawer.

She scribbled quickly, tore off one sheet and handed it to him.

"Thanks." Cash took the note. "Can I ask you another favor, C.J.?"

"Sure."

"Can you teach Austin to ride while I'm gone?"

"Be glad to." He smiled at Austin. "I've got a great little lady in the stable who'd love to take you riding."

"I'm sorry to ask, but can you also take care of Paddy and Danny?"

Sierra and the twins perked up.

"Where are they?" Sierra asked.

"Out in the truck. You want to let them out?"

"Yeah." The kids ran out front and a few seconds later the sound of joyous barking rang out.

"I'm sorry to do this to you, C.J."

"Don't worry about it, Cash."

"I'll help take care of them," Austin said, so damn eager to please anyone who gave him anything.

"I'll call and let you know how things go with Shannon."

"Good luck, Cash. I'll keep my fingers crossed."

Liam said, "Come on, Austin. I'll show you to my room. That's where the spare bed is."

"Cool."

Cash snagged Austin before he followed Liam up the stairs and pulled him into a rough hug. "Thanks, kid," he whispered against his hair. "I'll never forget this."

"Say hi to Shannon for me."

"You bet."

Austin followed Liam upstairs.

The children and the dogs ran into the house. The noise level escalated.

"So, you're finally going to take the plunge?" C.J. asked.

Cash grinned. "Yup."

C.J. slapped him on the back.

Janey hugged him.

The children gathered round and hugged him.

Little Ben squeezed in between two of his sisters and wrapped his arms around Cash's knees. "Are you going swimming, Uncle Cash?"

Cash reached down and touched Ben's hair. "Swimming?"

"Yeah, Dad said you're going plunging."

Cash threw his head back and laughed. He was swimming all right, in great huge waves of love, in a flood of happiness that felt so right.

He drove into Ordinary and parked in front of the *Ordinary Citizen's* office.

Timm stood up from the computer he'd been working at.

"Hey, Cash? What can I do for you?"

Cash was here to talk to Timm as a friend, but also as Mayor of Ordinary.

"I'm leaving."

"Leaving? On vacation?"

He shook his head. "For good. You need to hire a new sheriff."

"What? But why?"

"I'm going to Denver to convince Shannon Wilson to marry me."

Timm slapped his hand on the counter. "It's about time you found someone. So, you've fallen for her, have you?"

"So damn hard it hurts."

Timm laughed. "I'm happy for you, Cash. Love looks good on you. I hope she says yes."

"Me, too."

"Think she will?"

Cash rubbed his chest with one hand. "I hope so." She'd said she loved him. That implied forever, right?

"It will be hard to find a sheriff," Timm said. "It's been hard enough just getting another cop here to work as deputy."

"I know." Getting, and keeping cops, in small-town Montana was a real problem.

"We've got a deputy starting tomorrow."

"You finally found one?"

"Yes. Can you stay until then?"

No.

"Sure."

"Good. In the meantime, bring Wade up to speed on your duties until the new guy arrives. Give him a quick rundown on the job and then you'll be good to go."

Cash left Timm's office to walk down to his own. He found Hanlon inside.

"Wade, I've got good news and bad news. Which do you want first?"

"Let's get the bad news out of the way."

"I'm leaving. I've got two days max to fill you in on the Sheriff's position."

"*Sheriff's* position?"

"That's the good news. If you do a good job, you'll likely be elected to that position. Mayor Franck just informed me that we have a new deputy starting tomorrow. He's going to try to hire a sheriff from elsewhere, but I don't think it'll work. I think you'll get another deputy instead, in which case, you can run for Sheriff."

Wade looked dazed, but sat down beside Cash at the computer.

Cash spent the day filling him in, all while he just wanted to be gone.

At six, Timm called and invited him to Chester's for a beer. Why not? He sent Wade home to sleep.

Cash decided to sleep in the office tonight. If there were any problems in town, he could take care of them.

He sure as hell didn't want to go home to his empty house. He'd dreamed of filling it with children. Now, someone else would have to. He hoped like crazy he'd be starting a family in Denver with Shannon. Funny how leaving that little house and piece of land didn't hurt as much as he'd thought it would.

On the way to Chester's, he noticed a light still on in the real estate office and stopped in to put the house on the market.

After that was done, he went to the restaurant. When he stepped inside, his jaw dropped. Most of the town was there.

Timm approached.

"What's going on?" Cash asked. "Why is the place so busy tonight?"

"For you, Cash. They're all here to say goodbye. You didn't give us much time to plan a party."

"My God, this is for *me?*"

He walked through the crowd of smiling

friends, shaking hands and accepting drinks and well-wishes. The generosity of these people overwhelmed him. How was he so deserving of this?

Dad must have been right when he'd said he'd heard that Cash was well-respected as a lawman. *I'm proud of you,* Dad had said.

Yeah, Cash believed that now. Frank had understood his own limitations and would have had no trouble admitting to himself that his son made a better cop than he had.

Cash was respected here as more than just a cop, though, but also as a friend. He'd made friends with just about everyone here.

How could he possibly say goodbye?

Nothing like this had ever happened to him before. When he'd left San Francisco, he'd left a lot of bad memories behind.

But here? In Ordinary? They were all good memories. And would be so hard to leave behind.

He spent the evening among these friends, bathed in more bonhomie and affection than ever before in his life. If he didn't have Shannon to go to, leaving would have been impossible.

At ten, after most of the crowd had gone home, he thanked Timm then walked down Main Street alone to the Sheriff's office.

In the quiet hush of the town, he thought of everything he'd loved about it.

At the office, he took off his jacket then lay

down on the cot in the jail cell. He stayed awake for hours. His life was about to change.

In the stillness of the room, he almost imagined he could feel a thread running between himself and Shannon. They were connected. If he had his way, they would be for the rest of their lives.

No calls came in that night.

The new deputy showed up the next day. Cash welcomed him and put him through his paces. He continued to bring Wade up to speed on the sheriff's duties.

He stayed in the office again that night.

The following morning, he drove out to the house, showered, shaved and packed his bags. Taking one last bittersweet look around, he left the house for good.

Cash drove down Main Street, memories of everything he'd said, touched and done here rambling through his mind.

It had been a great place to live.

Any regrets, buddy?

Not a one.

He drove out of Ordinary to Denver, through Wyoming, with a few stops in Yellowstone park on the way.

CHAPTER EIGHTEEN

SHANNON DROVE HOME to her small apartment, dirty, exhausted, discouraged.

The drug dealer she'd been tailing the past couple of weeks had slipped out of her grasp.

She banged the steering wheel.

To add insult to injury, she had to park a couple of blocks away from her low-rise apartment building.

What, was there a convention in town and everyone just had to park on her street tonight?

She trudged to her place, feeling the cold. She wouldn't call it home. It was a few empty rooms that she slept in then got out of as quickly as possible the next day.

She no longer liked being alone.

Halfway down her street, she spotted a figure sitting on the concrete stairs into her building. Her steps slowed.

Was it? It couldn't be.

He stood and stepped out under the streetlamp.

It was.

Cash.

She stopped.

He walked toward her.

Her eyes drank him in, absorbed every detail they could when he stepped into circles of light from the streetlamps.

She couldn't move, only stare.

Finally, a foot away from her, then an inch, he stopped. He took her into his arms and kissed her with a heat and hunger she'd never experienced, but which matched her own.

She tasted, and tasted, and tasted more.

Then she pulled away. "No. You can't just come to Denver and expect to kiss me as if you have the right to."

"I do." He kissed her again, stealing her breath.

She pulled away again, but more slowly this time.

"What makes you think you have that right?" she asked, her voice trembling.

"I love you."

"You told me that before, but where did it leave us? Living hundreds of miles apart."

"It's different this time."

"How?"

"I want to live with you."

Wary, unwilling to hope, she asked, "Where?"

"Here. In Denver. Or wherever you plan to go next. Wherever you are is where I will be."

"How? What happened?"

"Can we go inside and talk? I'm frozen. I've been sitting on your doorstep for hours."

"Okay."

He wouldn't let her walk alone. He wrapped his arm around her shoulders and squeezed her against his side.

At the apartment building, he picked up several bags.

"Are you expecting to spend the week?" She wasn't counting on anything yet. He had a lot of explaining to do.

"Not expecting to, no." He opened the outer door and she stepped in ahead of him to unlock the inner door. "I'm planning on it."

She looked at him under the foyer light. His nose was bright red. The rest of him was the brawny, strong man she found too attractive in his cowboy hat and sheepskin coat.

"We'll see," she said, with an attempt at coolness, and walked up the stairs to the second floor. The building was ancient. No elevator. She'd rented it for its charm, for its old-fashioned appointments.

He followed her, smiling the whole while. The man had something up his sleeve, but unless he had the right answers to her questions, she was booting him to the curb.

He stepped inside her apartment. She locked the door behind them and hooked the chain.

She turned on a couple of lamps and he looked around at her plain apartment. She knew it was devoid of character, but she hadn't had the heart to unpack the boxes that lined her bedroom wall.

And that was his fault.

She tossed her purse and keys onto the messy dining room table and stepped out of her stilettos.

Cash placed his coat over the back of a dining room chair and took off his hat.

"Love what you've done with the place."

She struggled not to laugh.

He pointed to the fireplace in the living room. "Does this work?"

"Apparently. I haven't tried it."

"Why don't you go shower and get out of that makeup and—"

She'd removed her coat. By his raised brow, he disapproved of her outfit. She'd been in another bar tonight, but not alone. With a fellow agent.

"And that get-up," he continued.

"Why don't we talk first?"

"Why don't you go shower first? Please."

When he looked that earnest and said it that nicely, how could she deny him?

She left the room. She tried to take her time, to make him wait, but she wanted to see him too badly.

After her shower, she brushed her teeth and made sure she'd gotten off all of the makeup.

"What have you done?" she asked the second she returned to the living room.

"I've brought Yellowstone to you."

He had. He'd brought so many pieces of Yellowstone to her.

A fire burning in the fireplace illuminated a white bearskin rug on the floor in front of it.

She gasped. "That isn't real, is it?"

"Nope. Some kind of synthetic something-or-other."

She let out her breath. She might be a meat-eater and she might support Cash in wearing sheepskin to keep warm, but she didn't believe in killing animals so humans could decorate their homes.

"Besides," he said, "there are no white bears in Yellowstone. This here—" he poked the rug with his toe "—is a polar bear coat."

Shannon sniffed. "It smells like pine in here."

"Candles."

They covered every surface in small glass jars with bison on them.

He'd tossed a bunch of pine cones he'd obviously collected in the woods beside the fireplace.

"From Yellowstone?"

"Uh-huh."

He'd stood evergreen boughs in a crockery jug and had decorated them with...she stepped closer...with Christmas tree ornaments. Tiny wooden moose and bison and hugging bears.

A calendar hung from a thumbtack on the wall, open to January, with a stunning photo of Yellowstone in the winter.

On the mantelpiece, wooden bears supported a sign between them that read "Yellowstone."

He held a pair of wineglasses filled with red wine. He handed her one. An image of Old Faithful Inn was etched on one side.

"It's all tacky, I know, but it was the best I could do on short notice."

Tacky, yes, but awesome.

She sipped the wine, trying hard not to be affected, to be bowled right off of her ever-loving, still-aching feet.

"Okay, talk," she said.

"Later." He put his untouched glass on the mantelpiece, took hers from her and set it beside his.

Before she knew what was happening, the world spun and she was on the floor on the fake, but soft, bearskin with Cash on top of her.

She could only stand so much temptation. She kissed him, angling her mouth for the most pleasure, and he responded.

They tore at each other's clothes until they were naked.

Fueled by anger and too much pent up, frustrated need, Shannon gave as much passion as Cash dished out.

He entered her and only moments later they came in an explosive frenzy.

She lay beneath him breathing hard, only partially satisfied. She had weeks' worth of banked desire to assuage, but not before finding out from Cash exactly what was gong on.

He rolled to his side, taking her with him.

"Now, we'll talk," he huffed out, his breathing as erratic as her own.

He held her and told her about the past miserable few weeks, about his conversation with Austin, about his realizations, his new understanding of himself.

While he talked, she relaxed against him, but held a part of herself separate, afraid to believe that happiness might come true for her. For them.

"What now?" she asked, her anger gone, dissipated by his honesty.

"I want to marry you and I want to live with you."

For a woman who had thought she would never have a life partner, it was too much to hope for.

"Where would we live?"

"Wherever your job takes you."

"What would you do? Travel from city to city becoming a cop?"

"I've already made my point by becoming a

cop. I proved to Dad that it could be done well. In the end, it wasn't necessary, but I'm glad I did it. I don't want to be a city cop."

"What would you do instead?"

"How would you feel about a husband who went back to school?"

"Really? For what?"

"To become a teacher. I like teaching kids."

"I can see you doing it."

Cash grabbed one more thing out of the bags he'd brought with him. A box of doughnuts.

He pulled out a jelly donut and took a big bite. Shannon snatched it from him and took her own bite. A big blob of jelly fell out onto her breast.

She looked up at Cash. He did his Groucho Marx waggly eyebrow thing and licked it off.

Oh. Oh.

He started to kiss her and she lost track of what they'd been talking about, other than that it was all good.

This time, they made love slowly, tracing the firelight over each other's bodies with wandering, wondering hands.

CHAPTER NINETEEN

SHANNON DROVE HOME from the bar she'd been in all night, feeling dirty and tired, but buoyed by success. She'd picked up great info tonight that she'd passed along to headquarters. A team was out at this very moment busting a meth lab. Hallelujah.

The sky over Denver glowed with light reflected against the clouds from the city below.

The past two years had been eventful. Perfect. Cash had moved to Denver with her. After they'd married he'd entered college. She knew that leaving his friends in Ordinary had been hard, but they visited regularly. Shannon actually took vacations now and rested after periods of too much stress.

They visited Yellowstone again, too.

They'd bought a house. Four months ago, their son had been born.

Life was perfection.

Shannon had her brother on the line, on speaker phone.

"I haven't seen you since the wedding, Tom. How are you doing?"

"Great, Shannon. I'm speaking regularly and having an impact, I think. How are Cash and my new nephew?"

"Fabulous. I'm just on my way home from work."

"You work the craziest hours."

"You got that right."

"Shannon, there's a reason for the call. I just want to let you know, well…" Tom sounded hesitant, almost shy.

"Yes, Tom?"

"I have a new friend."

"A new *girl*friend?"

He laughed softly. "Yes, a girlfriend." He mimicked her emphasis.

Shannon whooped. "I'm so happy for you. What's she like?"

"She's a high school teacher. I was wondering why she called me back to talk to her class more than once. The last time, she asked me on a date."

"I like her style."

"She is a great woman. She knows how much I loved Cathy. How much I still do. She understands."

"She's perfect, then. Hold on to her, Tom."

"I hope to. I'll let you know if anything comes of it."

Shannon passed along her love and then hung up. Through a break in the clouds stars twinkled in the night sky.

CASH HEARD SHANNON come in the front door. He'd been up walking the floor with Evan on his shoulder for a good hour. Evan fussed and drew his small legs up against his stomach.

Gas. He cried and Cash rocked him.

Shannon entered the living room. "Is Evan okay?"

"Just a boatload of gas that he can't get rid of."

She approached and rubbed his back. "Poor baby."

She wore too much makeup and her slutty clothes.

Not giving himself time to worry about how her night had gone, and whether the bad guys had tried to hurt her, he wrapped his hand around the back of her neck and hauled her close for a deep, grateful, honest-to-God-I'm-so-relieved-you're-home-safe kiss.

She kissed him back hard, happy to be home.

While Evan still fussed, Cash ended the kiss and nuzzled his wife's neck, wanting to put the baby to bed and sink into her on the spot.

Evan let out an enormous fart and filled his diaper.

Both Cash and Shannon laughed.

"Romantic," she said and stepped away from them. "Peee-ew, that's a stinker."

She tickled her son and he giggled, suddenly happy to be clear of what was bothering him.

"I'll go change him and get him into his bed," Cash said. "He should go down okay now." He turned to leave the room but said over his shoulder, "There's a piece of lasagna in the oven."

"Great, I love your lasagna. I'm starving."

"So am I."

"Did you heat enough for both of us?"

"I don't want lasagna."

She stopped walking toward the kitchen, turned around and raised one eyebrow when she realized exactly what he was hungry for.

She grinned. "Okay."

"Good. Eat and then have a shower and remove that sh—" He glanced at his son, who curled onto his shoulder already close to sleep. At four months, Evan was too young to understand cuss words, but it was time for Cash to get out of the habit of using them.

"Remove that junk from your face," he amended. "Let Danny and Paddy in before you go to bed."

He left the room and walked to the baby's bedroom, calling back to her, "Use that cream I like."

He washed Evan and put him into a clean diaper. "Think you can handle a whole day alone with your mom tomorrow? I'll be at school, but she's off for three days."

Evan watched him while he talked.

"Three *whole* days."

Evan smiled. It could have been more gas, but Cash didn't believe that. His kid was an early learner.

"Don't let her start on dinner," he said. "Got it, bud? Don't let Mommy cook. I'll take care of dinner when I get home."

Cash snapped Evan's sleeper into place, kissed his forehead and slipped him into his crib. He patted his back. "So, we're clear. Your job is to make sure you save us both from your mother's cooking."

Evan scrunched his arms and legs under his belly, poked his little bum into the air and fell asleep.

By the time Cash turned off the lights in the house and locked up for the night, the water was running in the shower off their bedroom.

He shooed the dogs off the bed. They never used to sleep with him, but Shannon had ideas of her own.

"She's mine tonight, boys." He put them out of the bedroom and closed the door. They whined until Cash said, "Go to your own beds."

He heard their nails clicking on the floor as

they ran down the hall to their beds in the living room.

He undressed, lit a bunch of candles and slipped into bed to wait for his wife.

Cash didn't know how to hold in all of the great feelings threatening to overflow. His life couldn't possibly get any better.

His career had taken a profound shift. He lived in the city and remained unaffected by temptations that really weren't...temptations.

Shannon still took her career seriously, still worked her butt off to get ahead and to be the best DEA agent she could possibly be. Ambitious, yes, but not his father.

For the next three days she would barely put Evan down. She was besotted and driven to be as good a parent as she was a cop.

They were both good parents.

Shannon stepped out of the bathroom in a big white robe, took one look at the candles and turned off the bathroom light.

"Now *this*," she said, "is romantic."

She approached the bed and let the robe fall from her shoulders to the floor. He loved how direct she was, how uninhibited.

She climbed into bed with him and he pulled her close, wrapping his arms and body around her. She was home safe, and he was happy.

She smelled like vanilla again instead of the

cheap perfume she wore for undercover work and he wanted to nibble on all of those sugar cookies on her erogenous zones.

He licked her from her breast to her navel. "Just a minute."

Reaching to the bedside table behind him, he grasped an object and started shaking it over her.

She gasped. "What are you doing?"

She looked down. He dusted her with powdered sugar from a dispenser. It stuck to the spots where he'd licked.

She smiled. "Are you crazy? It will get all over the bedsheets."

"I'm crazy for you. And I don't care about the sheets."

He licked some of the sugar from her skin. "Yum. Where were we before our son filled his diaper?" he whispered and nuzzled her neck. She giggled. "Oh, yeah, right here."

* * * * *